THE PERFECT PARENTS

J. A. BAKER

Boldwood

First published in Great Britain in 2024 by Boldwood Books Ltd.

Copyright © J. A. Baker, 2024

Cover Design by Head Design

Cover Photography: Shutterstock

Every effort has been made to obtain the necessary permissions with reference to copyright material, both illustrative and quoted. We apologise for any omissions in this respect and will be pleased to make the appropriate acknowledgements in any future edition.

A CIP catalogue record for this book is available from the British Library.

Paperback ISBN 978-1-80415-397-0

Large Print ISBN 978-1-80415-398-7

Hardback ISBN 978-1-80415-396-3

Ebook ISBN 978-1-80415-400-7

Kindle ISBN 978-1-80415-399-4

Audio CD ISBN 978-1-80415-391-8

MP3 CD ISBN 978-1-80415-392-5

Digital audio download ISBN 978-1-80415-395-6

Boldwood Books Ltd
23 Bowerdean Street
London SW6 3TN
www.boldwoodbooks.com

For Ruth P. Such a wonderful lady and philanthropist who enriched the lives of so many local children, including me. Your name and legacy will always live on. You were nothing like the characters in this book which is an absolute blessing.

Children begin by loving their parents; after a time, they judge them; rarely, if ever, do they forgive them.

— OSCAR WILDE

Parents wonder why the streams are bitter, when they themselves have poisoned the fountain.

— JOHN LOCKE

PROLOGUE
BEFORE

Everything was wrong. Messed up and out of kilter. It wasn't meant to turn out like this. She had made a mistake. A bad one. The worst. She had thought that he cared for her, that they had something special, but that had been a grave error of judgement on her part. The worst error she would ever make. And now she was dying. She could tell by the blood – so much of it. A thick, crimson smear on the floor, spreading and pooling as it seeped from her head. The meaty smell of it filling her nostrils. She gagged at the stench, her fingers covering her mouth to stem the rise of vomit that threatened to spill from her, rushing up her gullet and burning her throat like molten lava.

The wound was bad. She didn't have to touch it to feel how damaged she was. How broken she was, both inside and out. The sickness and wooziness told her everything she needed to know. The way her thoughts were fogged up, how the floor tilted and swayed beneath her; that was enough. She visualised a gaping hole at the back of her skull. She was in pieces, a wreck of a thing. And now she was going to bleed to death here on his bedroom floor. All because of that one terrible, terrible mistake. The mistake of thinking that he loved her, that they had a future together and she was more than just a passing fancy. A mere dalliance.

There wasn't any point in trying to move. Her body was leaden, her veins slowly emptying. She didn't have much time left. Thoughts of her family filled her mind: warm, halcyon days, picnics on the lawn, her mother's loving embrace, her father's laughter. And her brother. Her wonderful, caring brother. If she could move, get out of this place, she would be able to see them again, hear their sweet voices, listen to the honeyed sound of her name being called. She would once again be able to smell the sweet scent of the flowers in their garden and stare in wonder at the ivy that slowly snaked its way up the side of the house and the pale-pink peonies that sat in clusters along the wide borders.

Suddenly imbued with a need to escape, a deep longing to see her family once more, she tried to slither along the floor, dragging herself out of the pool of sticky, foul-smelling blood. If she could inch along just a little more, slide under the bed and wait a while, then perhaps she stood a chance, but no matter how much effort she put in, her limbs refused to work as they should, her body inert and wooden. Even breathing was a monumental effort.

So she remained still, storing up what little energy she had left and concentrating only on the next few seconds, on surviving them. That was all it would take to escape this place, to get out of this house and get help. Just a few vital seconds.

Then, as if her prayers had been answered, the pain in her head began to ease. She let out a small gasp, tears threatening to fall. Perhaps she was going to be okay after all. Her arms and legs felt lighter, full of air. She was made of silk, everything fluid and effortless. Except her eyes. Leaden, they drooped, as heavy as stone, gravity forcing them downwards. Sleep, that was the answer. She would take a short nap, restore some strength into her ailing body, gather her thoughts and then rise, and flee this godforsaken place forever.

It only took a second or two for her to fall into the deepest of slumbers. One from which she would never wake...

1

THE PARENTS

He takes off his jacket and shoes and lays them on the floor next to where he is standing. She does the same, watching him, mimicking his movements. He has no idea why they're removing items of clothing. It's a pointless task. Once they take those few steps forward, make that leap into the darkness of the night and sink below the surface of the water, it won't matter what they're wearing. He visited the river earlier in the day before the sun made its sluggish descent below the line of hills, and could see how strong the current was. How perilous it was. It's fast down there. And deep. Weeks of rain has turned the river into a dangerous deluge. Still, leaving items of clothing behind is a sign. It shows everyone they've actually done it, that they have taken that jump and left their troubles far behind them. If their bodies aren't found, their garments will be there as evidence. He doesn't want to think about the aftermath: their bloated carcasses, their grey, distorted feature as their bodies get hauled out of the water. He doesn't want to consider his lack of control after it's all over. That was always his thing – being in charge. But it couldn't last forever. Nothing ever does. Better to end it now while he is ahead.

It's dark out there. He stares ahead, squinting into the night, wishing it hadn't come to this. And yet it has, and no matter how hard he tries, he can't see any other way out of it. They've made the decision. A macabre pact. There's no turning back, no route back to how things used to be. It's just the two of them, locked together for all eternity. Whether that's a comfort or an affliction is up for debate.

The breeze picks up, gathering in strength: a strong squall that pushes at their backs. 'Come on,' he says, his voice just loud enough to be heard above the rush of the river and the howling of the wind that whips at their bodies. 'It's time.'

She doesn't reply. He takes her hand but she snatches it away and turns to look at him, the moon silvering her features, accentuating every contour and crease, her once smooth, unblemished skin now an atlas of laughter and worry lines. Life has done that to her. To them. He didn't want it to end like this but at least it will save everybody from having to endure what would have come next had they not decided to take this unorthodox step. Sometimes, life takes a sharp turn, catching everyone by surprise, and people have to adapt and accept what comes next.

'I'm ready,' he says, watching her closely. She stares at him and nods, her eyes dark, her mouth a thin, tight line. God, he loved her. They loved each other. That was before. Before it all went wrong and their world began to disintegrate, crumbling away to nothing. She blames him, and perhaps she's right to do so. He made mistakes. Many of them. But in the end, it was her mistake, her refusal to do the right thing, that pushed them into the darkest of corners with no way out. This – the cold, raging water – is the only thing left for them. The only escape they have from the brutal truth of their damaged lives. They used to be somebody, the pair of them together, their names spoken with love and reverence. In time, their deaths will be forgotten. People will move on. This time next year, they will be nobody. A pair of forgotten lost souls. Probably better that way. Better to be forgotten than talked about with hostility and bitterness.

She shows no emotion, her eyes narrowed against the howling gusts, her face expressionless as they both climb the metal barrier, their legs dangling over the edge. Is she nervous? He can't tell. She was silent on the journey here, his questions and inane talk met with blank stares. Hardly surprising given what they had been through. What they are about to do. And now they're here, she is still silent. Distant and impassive. Life and their actions and the decisions they made have pushed them apart. At least now, they will do this thing as one. Divided for a period of time, but together at the end. That thought buoys him up, driving away the fears that have begun to niggle at him, small threads of anxiety burrowing beneath his skin. Fear is a hindrance, a thing to be banished. It's an alien experience for him and an unwelcome one at that. Confidence had always come easily to him. It's suddenly vanished when he needs it the most, leaving him feeling lost and bewildered. He clings onto the handrail and closes his eyes.

Behind them, all is quiet. Hardly any traffic. It's the early hours, everybody at home tucked up safe and warm in their beds while they're both out here facing the storm, perched high above a fast-flowing river, ready to do what needs to be done. Brave. That's what they are. That's how he wants them to be remembered: as a brave couple who did this because it was the right thing to do. Not as people who made a terrible mistake. Not as a man who led a debauched existence or a woman who tried to stop him. People don't speak ill of the dead, do they? He hopes not. He hopes that their secrets will be buried with them. As they should be.

'I'm going to count to three. Then we're going to do it, okay?'

He opens his eyes and watches her. She nods, refusing to look at him, still refusing to speak. He gets that. She's upset and angry and probably very frightened. She has every right to be. This is not normal. What they are about to do is absurd and terrifying and utterly abnormal. It isn't how they wanted their future to be. But it's here now. No turning around.

The metal grid of the barrier is cold to the touch, his fingers curled around its icy surface. He stares down and swallows hard, listening to the roar of the dark water beneath. She does the same.

'One, two, three...'

He removes his fingers from the metal and touches her shoulder, slowly pushing the top half of her body forwards, then lowers his hand until his fingers are firmly pressed into the small of her back. She flinches but he doesn't move away. There isn't anywhere for her to go. Besides, they need to do this. She knows it. It's what they agreed. He gives her a firm push before letting himself go, the wind buffeting his body, the feeling of weightlessness a thing to behold. His shuts his eyes. He doesn't need to see the raging river beneath. He doesn't need to see the frothing, foaming current and the endless depths of the freezing water. He knows what comes next, is ready to embrace it, and instead prepares himself, holding his breath, saying a few words to a God he doesn't believe in as he waits for that wave of iciness to swallow him.

It's like a sharp pain, a knife slicing across his abdomen, when he does hit the water, the small rocks tucked into his pockets dragging him lower and lower. And the cold, it's all-encompassing, slowing his movements, muddying his thinking. He takes a sudden gulp, his chest convulsing, and then counts to three, stars bursting behind his eyes as he waits for death to take him.

2

FLO

The church is full. Packed to the rafters. So many people. So many friends and neighbours and hangers-on, and then there are the ghouls who have come along for the ride. I suspect the guy at the back dressed in a white shirt and ill-fitting trousers is from the press. I don't recognise him. He'll be after a story, a snippet of information that he can turn into something newsworthy. My parents were the closest thing this town had to landed gentry. Except they weren't. Landed gentry, that is. We lived in a very big house, which although large, isn't quite as grand as some of the more salubrious stately homes dotted around North Yorkshire. It's a six-bedroomed, Palladian-style structure that was built in 1720 and rumour has it that my great-great-great-grandfather won it in a game of brag. I don't suppose we will ever know the truth of that particular story, especially now that both of my parents are dead. Or presumed dead. My father is in that coffin, that much I do know as I was the one who identified him, the make-up applied by the mortician doing little to disguise his grey pallor, but my mother's body has never been recovered. She's probably halfway out to sea by now, the thought of which makes me feel quite ill. I suppress a shiver, pulling up my collar against the chill of the badly heated church, and stare down at the pamphlet on my lap.

In Loving Memory of Jackson & Lydia Hemsworth

Two young, smiling people stare out at me, their faces full of happiness and hope. When did it disappear, that happiness? I place a kiss on my finger and rest it over my mother's mouth, so much love and need behind the sentiment. I didn't get to say goodbye and miss her so much. I miss that last farewell. It sits inside me like a yawning abyss. A cavity that will never be filled. She ripped a hole in my life that day when I found out. They both did. It will never leave me, the memory of that time. The sight of two police officers standing at my door, asking if they could come inside, ushering me to a chair before breaking it to me: the news that my parents had jumped to their deaths from the Newport Bridge into the freezing water below. Everything after being told that piece of news is a blur. I think I may have screamed. Or let out a guttural roar. One of the officers shuffled off into my kitchen, coming back with a glass of water, handing it to me with trained precision and compassion, that much I do recall. I think perhaps I swore and made a dash to the bathroom to be sick. Even the memory of it stirs up another visceral reaction, my stomach clenching in revulsion, as if a hundred knives are in there, slowly slicing at my innards. I swallow and push the thought away.

Behind me, somebody sniffs and clears their throat. The sound of rustling as they rummage for a handkerchief drags me back to the present, back to a point in my life I never thought possible. Or maybe I did. Maybe my siblings and I blocked it out, the possibility of what could happen once we all left home. Things were never easy. They clearly worsened after we all moved out and got our own houses. I try to not think about it, about how much our mother had to endure in our absence.

We've called it a memorial service rather than a funeral even though the body of my father is lying in his coffin atop a plinth right next to where I am seated. It seemed more fitting. How could we have a funeral for one and not the other? They died together and their lives should be remembered as they were – a couple. Not separate. Even though they had tremendous differences. I shut out that thought as well. My head seems to be full of them – dark, festering memories. Sitting here at their funeral, focusing on how disparate they were, doesn't feel right. The least we can do is to look as if we are trying to bring them together, even though the drama of them ending their lives in such an inexplicably awful way almost tore the rest of us apart.

The noise in the church lowers when the priest approaches the lectern. We should have had a humanist service. I have no idea why we chose this church. I guess it was because it's so close by and many people thought of my parents as pillars of the community, the charitable couple who for many decades, like their parents before them, lived at Armett House, and it was expected that Ezra, Jessica and I would give them a decent send off, the sort of memorable funeral that befits such well thought of people. To some, however. Not all. My parents had a knack of helping and upsetting people in equal measure. Or at least, my father did. It was his defining feature. His forte. All Mother did was try to cancel his squalid ways by always being there, and doling out as much kindness as she could in a bid to counterbalance his challenging behaviour.

The organ begins its thunderous pitch, the notes echoing around us in a swirling, melodic roar. I inhale sharply and listen to the voices nearby as they sing 'Amazing Grace', our mother's favourite hymn. We didn't choose one of Father's favourite hymns. I'm not even sure he had one. Our father danced to his own tune.

Ezra stands to the left of me, his eyes fixed ahead on a point beyond the pulpit. Jessica is on the other side of me. None of us sing. I think we're beyond caring whether people think it odd and disrespectful that we don't join in. Funerals don't come with sets of rules. We can do or say whatever we want. We could have agreed to sing 'Knees Up Mother Brown' if we had wanted and nobody could have stopped us. This is our time to grieve and grieving comes in all shapes and sizes, covering a wide spectrum of emotions. If Ezra and Jessica and I want to shout and scream, then so be it, and if we prefer to stand, shoulders hunched, expressionless, then that's perfectly acceptable as well. I think, given the circumstances, we're all doing remarkably well to have remained upright and not be in a crumpled heap somewhere at the back of the vestry with an exasperated priest stood close by, wringing his hands in desperation as he tries to work out how best to untangle us and lead us back into the church where he can conduct a half-decent service. But I digress.

The music is no more than white noise in my head. As much as I loved my mother, I can't wait for this to be over. My brother, sister and I have work to do: a house to be sorted, rooms to be cleared. I think of my mother's sewing room and my father's study and feel faint and slightly overwhelmed. So much stuff. Fifty years' worth of clutter to work through. But before that, we have a funeral to focus on, people to see, hands to shake. A community to feed. I didn't want a get together afterwards. It feels unbecoming. In fact, the thought of it rather sickened me. Jessica was ambivalent but Ezra insisted, if only out of respect for our mother, the stalwart of our family. The lynchpin that held us all together. Except she didn't, in the end. At some point, the lynchpin buckled and broke under the strain. The idea of eating, drinking and chatting while my mother's body remains undiscovered feels ghoulish and discourteous. At least my father is in his coffin, his remains clean and dry. My mother is currently God knows where, her poor, distended body floating somewhere downstream. Part of me hopes she is never found, that she is left in peace wherever she is, and yet a part of me wants her home, back where she belongs. Back with us, her family.

A silence descends as the music and the singing stop. We wait for the priest to speak, every swish of clothing, every breath, whisper and sigh, a sonic boom in my head. His words provide little or no comfort. We weren't a religious family. Maybe we should have been. Maybe if we had turned to God and listened to the teachings of the Bible then perhaps our problems could have been solved. But then again, the ancient words of an invisible deity would probably have done little to alleviate our issues. They're certainly not helping to locate the body of our mother. I would give everything I have to find her. She deserves that much and more.

I hear our names being spoken: Jessica, Ezra and me. Father McLeod, the parish priest is reading out the eulogy we gave him. Just words on a page. That's all they are. They don't represent who we are now, or who we once were. It's merely a snapshot of the best bits of our childhood. The parts we don't mind everyone hearing about. The most memorable and happiest parts of the marriage of our parents. Because there were some before the rot set in and blighted our everyday lives. Not everybody saw it or recognised it for what it was, even members of my own family. We all have our blind spots, don't we? We see what we want to see in order to make our existences that much more bearable. And we all have our own tipping points, that crucial moment when everything comes crashing down, our lives in freefall. Some of us have been falling for many years now, waiting for the moment when we hit the bottom with a sickening crash. I'm hoping the news of the suicide of my parents is the sickening crash and there isn't any more to come, but you never know. Not with the Hemsworth family. You just never know.

A lull descends once more. A fog swirls in my head. I feel a nudge in my side and turn to see Ezra watching me, gesturing for me to stand up. It's over. It's time to leave. Jessica is standing, staring straight ahead, her face impassive, her cheeks dry, eyes devoid of tears.

I take a deep breath and ready myself for the next part. The burial and then the gathering in the local community centre. I feel tired and dazed before any of it has even begun.

Amber, Ezra's partner smiles at me and leans across to squeeze my hand. I return the gesture because it's the polite thing to do and rise from my seat, my legs feeling weak, then follow as we all file out of the church and walk down the aisle in a silent shuffle, following father's coffin. A sea of faces watch our movements, their eyes lowered when we pass, before they slowly and quietly slide out of the pews and walk behind us, a conga of quiet mourners exiting the church.

It's a family-only burial. Ezra, Amber, Jessica, and I walk to the rear of the churchyard, following the pall bearers with our heads bowed in quiet, respectful reverence. Not that I feel that respectful. I'm just doing what is expected of me. It wouldn't do to make a public fuss, would it? Not when quite a lot of these people think our family were the best thing since sliced bread. So I will do the right thing, act like the dutiful, grieving daughter for the day and then after it's all over, I will go home, curl up in bed and stay there until everything feels better. Less oppressive. Less traumatic. And I will stay there until life feels as if it has returned to normal again. Whatever normal is.

The rain comes down in sheets as we stand at the graveside, the gaping, coffin-sized hole filling with water and sludge. I look away while my father is lowered into his grave, thoughts of his final minutes filling my head – how cold he will have been. How frightened. And yet how he went ahead and did it regardless – how they both did. I think of them taking off their coats and shoes on that wild and stormy night, and jumping into the freezing, fast-flowing river beneath, and for as long as I live, I won't ever be able to erase that image from my mind: the horribly clear picture I have in my head of their frozen features and flailing limbs as they made that leap, the icy water swallowing them and pulling them downwards to their inevitable deaths, leaving me, Jessica and Ezra to pick up the pieces of their fragmented and disturbed lives. I wonder if we crossed their minds? Did they think of us at all when they took that final plunge into the river? Or were they both so wrapped up in their own maelstrom of misery that there wasn't room for anybody else?

Father McLeod says a brief blessing once the coffin is in place. Ezra and Amber throw a single red rose on top of it. Jessica lets out a small sob. I wipe at my face with my sodden, rain-drenched sleeve, then turn and walk away.

3

FLO

This was never going to be easy. The whole thing is shitty and awful but it's just something we have to get through in order to move on with our lives. I watch Amber lean into Ezra, their bodies shivering, the driving, endless rain hindering our route out of the graveyard. It's a quagmire, mud sloshing up the side of Ezra's trousers. My own feet are soaked through. I stop and bang my soles on the pavement to shake off the excess water and grime, and then attempt to wipe down my clothes with freezing fingers that feel as if they're made out of blocks of wood. My shoes are caked and my socks soaked through. I should have worn heels. As it is, I look like I've spent the last few hours ploughing a sodden field with my bare hands, my palms now also smeared with mud and dirt. It's been a long day and it's not over yet. Somehow, after we're done here, I need to plaster a smile on my face and make pleasant conversation with people I barely know and, in many cases, don't even like.

'Come on, let's get back onto the path and get into the car. It's fucking freezing out here.' Ezra's voice is a growl, sharper than his usual manner, the weather and the setting making us all restless and edgy. I say sharper than his usual manner but when I think about it, his usual manner has been askew for some time now. I shrug that thought away and focus on getting out of the wet and into the dry car.

Amber places her small, black clutch bag over her head to shield her carefully coiffured hair from the rain, and breaks into a run, her spindly heels hindering her progress. Ezra takes her hand and pulls her along beside him, doing his best to make sure she doesn't fall, stopping every few seconds to wait for her to get her balance. In the end, they hold one another up as the wind picks up speed and the downpour grows even heavier. I leave the graveyard first, rushing ahead without glancing back. I'm standing next to the car when the other three round the corner, their faces set into a grimace. Jessica is following behind Ezra and Amber, her heels clicking on the concrete paving. It's going to be a tough few weeks, perhaps even months. We've all got lots to do, plenty of paperwork and documents to sort out, although until Mother's body is found, we're limited as to what we can do. And then there's the house. That fucking big rambling old house that none of us want. Darkness grips me, pulling me towards its shadowy corners, awful memories nudging ever closer to the surface. I resist their clutches and manage a tight smile.

'Ready?' I ask.

Ezra and Amber nod, Jess replies 'yes' in a squeaky, childlike voice and the door is opened for us to get in.

'Thank God for leather seats, eh?' Amber says a little too cheerily once we're all safely ensconced inside the sleek, black vehicle. 'Otherwise, we would have soaked through the fabric in no time at all.'

'Stupid fucking weather,' Ezra mutters, his eyes glued to the window.

I also turn away and trace a line of water down the glass with my fingernail. 'Miserable weather for a miserable day,' I reply glumly.

Ezra then turns to look at me as if he's waiting for me to say something else. So I do. 'I'm not staying long. At the community centre, I mean. I'm not really in the mood for idle chatter.'

His eyes have a look that says, *me neither*, but he remains silent, those dark lashes of his hiding his true feelings. He's good at that: disguising his emotions. I guess he's had to be, but then, haven't we all?

Instead, he nods, possibly aware of my own downward spiralling mood. Being the elder sibling has never really sat well with me. I have always felt some sort of stupid need to control everything and take care of my younger brother and sister, even now when they are both adults. I like to think I've always done my best to try and protect them. Sometimes it worked and sometimes it didn't. Even now, after the death of our parents, I feel like the burden of their unconventional and shocking demise is mine and mine alone to manage. I can't seem to let go of the reins, to treat my younger siblings as equals. That's because they're innocent. I'm not sure that they know the half of our father's sordid past, or maybe I'm being naïve and they know more than I care to admit to myself. It shames me to even think of the things he did. Speaking about it isn't something I'm easily able to do.

'I'll stay a while and chat to people, Ez,' Jessica says.

I smile at her suggestion. Poor Jessie. Always the peacemaker. Always keen to smooth things over and paper over any cracks. I almost laugh at the thought of that word – cracks. More like huge craters. Sinkholes that almost swallowed us whole. Not that Ezra and Jess saw all of it. I've never been able to work out whether they chose to not acknowledge what went on or whether I really did manage to protect them from the lion's share of the heartache. I took it on their behalf and am now bitter to the point of being toxic, the residue of my childhood sticking to me like tar, coating every inch of my skin.

The journey to the community centre is quiet, the atmosphere strained. There isn't a lot we can say to one another, not without it descending into chaos. We're not an argumentative family but we are fractured, our damage hidden from the outside world. And we're tired. Or at least I am. Sleep has been erratic since hearing the news of their deaths, but we're managing to hold it together, disguising our desperation and unhappiness. It wouldn't do for the wealthy family to show their seedy underbelly to the local community, would it? They think of us as privileged and above reproach. If only they knew. So instead, we make idle chatter about the terrible weather and the heavy traffic, how busy the roads are and how the new local clutch of houses has put extra pressure on drivers, increasing the flow of vehicles through the town.

When Ezra, Jess and I were growing up, Armett House sat on the edge of a village. But Armett is no longer classed as a village and is now a town, and a growing one at that. Maybe that's a good thing, the newer residents unaware of who we are. Unaware of our family and its strange and often unfathomable ways. Not that any of it matters anymore now they're gone, our parents. The thought of it, how they died, still has the capacity to stop me in my tracks. I run my fingers through my hair and watch Ezra for signs of any distress or anger. He's definitely on edge, his eyes darting around like dark, shiny marbles. Amber must sense his unease. She reaches across and squeezes his hand. He waits a few seconds, then pulls away, anger and displeasure emanating from him. Amber is often overbearing. Sometimes, her mannerisms are welcome and then at other times, Ezra has told me that her affectionate ways make him feel as if he is being smothered. Today is one of those times. She will probably take the huff. They may even have words later. Right now, I doubt he cares. Today is about us and our family. Me and my

sister and brother, and my bohemian mother and her errant
husband, the man who was my father. Was he intentionally bad? It's
hard to tell. He was weak and had a roving eye for sure. That was
his undoing: his penchant for younger females. It was the undoing
of all of us, I think, driving a wedge between our parents, darkening
our memories of Armett House.

My thoughts trail off. No point pondering over it now. It's all in
the past. Time to attempt to put it all to bed. I almost laugh out loud
at my unintended pun.

'I need a drink.' I don't think Ezra meant to say those words out
loud but it's too late; they are already out there, gathering momen-
tum. Attracting unwanted attention.

All eyes turn to him, their collective judgemental gazes
sweeping across his face, studying him like a lab rat. I sigh and look
away. Ezra hasn't had a drink for over two years now. So far, sobriety
has worked for him, or so he says, the months passing by without
any real hitches that I know of, but today's events are on another
level. I know that he was sorely tempted, after hearing the news
about the death of our parents, to grab the nearest whisky bottle
and pour himself a large tumbler, but he didn't. All credit to him, he
managed to resist, but I imagine that sitting here in this car with all
these females and their whispers and austere, frightened expres-
sions, he probably feels like he is drowning and right now a slug of
whisky would help blur the edges of this fucking awful scenario.

Nobody says anything, but I see Amber's spine stiffen. Jessica
stares out of the window and I just lower my gaze, wishing this
damn car would hurry up and get us there.

'But I'm not going to, so don't worry. Needing and doing are two
different things. You don't have to sit there like a load of frightened
bloody rabbits.'

Amber's face flushes pink. Jessica fiddles with the hem of her
coat. I can feel my tolerance levels waning. The car seems to

shrink around me. The sooner we get there, the better. I need to get out of here, to have some space to breathe. I feel like I'm choking.

Jessica rests her head back, turning to me and giving me a tight smile. 'I wonder if there'll be egg and cress sandwiches and stale sausage rolls on offer at the community centre?'

'Oh, I hope so. And if we're lucky, they'll have some of those bloody disgusting vol au vents stuffed with pink mayonnaise and salmonella prawns that should have been thrown out days ago. All served up by Poison Pamela, the same woman who almost wiped out half the village with her undercooked ham and egg pie at the summer fete.'

Our laughter fills the car, loosening the tight atmosphere and elevating the low mood somewhat. Even Ezra manages a quiet chuckle. Amber smiles at me and then takes Ezra's hand. I wonder if he is forgiven for brushing her off earlier. We've got the rest of the day to get through. Better to do it together than make their connection as a couple just another problem that needs to be dealt with. He pats her hand and shuffles closer to her. Poor Amber, being part of such a dysfunctional family. She's anxious and worried that Ezra is about to descend into a whirling vortex of madness, his grief and shock forcing him to look for happiness and resolutions at the bottom of a bottle. I don't think it will happen. Our parents aren't worth it. We'll get through the next few hours and then we can all go home and prepare to spend the next few weeks tackling Armett House and its contents. I reckon that will be enough to drive anybody to drink. If he manages to stay sober while doing that, then Ezra should get a bloody medal.

'We're here.' Jessica sits up and pulls at the door handle.

She is as keen as I am to get out of this car, the sense of claustrophobia and the wildly oscillating atmosphere feeling like a hugely oppressive bulk, making it difficult to think straight.

The driver stands by, fingers resting on the door handle, his head bowed as we all slide out of the vehicle.

'Thank you for everything,' Jessica says, her voice croaky, eyes downcast. She walks towards the open doors of Armett Community Centre and I can almost feel the negativity and dread oozing from her, emanating out of her pores in vast waves.

Trepidation is also swirling at the pit of my stomach, the thought of mingling making me eager for a drink. I won't, though. Not while Ezra is here. I'll be the dutiful daughter and the faithful, supportive sister and stick to tea, coffee or juice, but by God, the need for a wine is all-encompassing. None of us want to do this; it's just something that we need to get through. There are so many memories to deal with – a few good, many dark and unpleasant – but I will hide that from everyone here. I will smile politely, shake a few hands, and quietly slink out to my car before heading back to my house in Church Road on the edge of town. Once there, I will close the blinds and cut myself off from the rest of the world. Just me and my tainted, sleazy, childhood recollections. That's my default position. Alone yet not lonely. Some people operate better on an insular level. It's just how I am. It's what they turned me into, my unpredictable and unorthodox parents. I love and hate them at the same time. Scratch that. I hate *him*. For all he clearly loved me, I in return hated him.

'Max! Lovely to see you,' Ezra says as we head into the small vestibule. 'So glad you could make it.'

Max and Ezra have known each other since they were toddlers and although Max's home life was very different to ours, having been brought up in a tiny, two-bed, terraced house next to the park where druggies hang around waiting for their next fix, he and Ezra have always remained close. Money and privilege don't necessarily define class. My father was testament to that fact. Max is one of the most decent people I have ever met and I have always been happy that he and Ezra stayed as good friends.

'Prepare yourself, fella,' Max says, frowning. 'Half the town is here, some friendly, some not so much. I've tried to hold them off speaking to you, but I can't keep them away from you for much longer.'

'Not so friendly?' Ezra replies, looking genuinely perplexed. 'Why, what's the problem?'

'You'll find out soon enough,' he sighs, taking Ezra's elbow and ushering me, Amber and Jessica into the grubby room where a large throng are standing, waiting for us. 'You'll find out soon enough.'

4

JESSICA

A sea of faces turn towards us, watching our arrival at the community centre. Heat rises up my neck, burning at my cheeks. A hush takes hold as we step over the threshold and into the room. The silence doesn't last long. It starts as a low murmur and is fully broken when Jeff Wolf steps forward, fists clenched at his sides.

'Money,' he says to Ezra, eyes narrowed, spittle flying out of his mouth when he speaks. 'I need my money and I need it now.'

My stomach lurches. This could go either way. I hope Ezra has enough to pay him. I also hope that Ezra keeps the peace and this doesn't descend into chaos. I want time to pass at lightning speed so we can all go home as quickly as possible. I turn to look at Flo, who is wide-eyed and clearly despairing of this situation.

'How much?' Ezra replies, his hand dipping into his jacket pocket.

'£150.'

I inhale sharply. Ezra won't have enough. Who carries £150 with them in this day and age? Everything is bought using debit and credit cards. I have £40 with me, tucked away in a side pocket of my purse. I'm a cautious person. I keep it for emergencies in case I ever lose any of my cards or they refuse to work. I can hand it over if need be. Flo might also have some cash. We could all chip in.

'Here you go. £160 for the inconvenience.' He shoves the money into Jeff's palm and smiles at him. 'Sorry about that, bud. Help yourself to food and drink.'

I watch Ezra saunter away and envy his confidence, the way he is able to handle my father's adversaries with such ease. Our father died without paying the staff who maintain the house and gardens. Jeff Wolf isn't the first person to come to us for money and I'm almost certain he won't be the last. He is the thin end of what could possibly prove to be a very large wedge.

'I brought it with me just in case,' Ezra says, glancing over his shoulder to me with a pat of his top pocket and a gentle wink. 'I had an idea this might happen.' He turns away and his shoulders slump a little, an invisible weight bearing down on him.

I inwardly reprimand myself. I should have helped. Ezra has a clearer idea of how our father operated, having worked with some of the maintenance staff over the summer when he was home from university, whereas I have been sheltered from the brunt of his failings. His financial failings, that is. I know my father for what and who he was in other areas of his life, but that's a story for another time. One I would rather not relate.

My heart starts up, an arrhythmic stutter in my chest, when I think about our family. My thoughts are interrupted by a tap on the shoulder. I spin around to see a familiar face staring at me.

'God, I am so sorry for your loss, Jess. Words fail me. I really don't know what to say.'

Amanda MacDonald, an old schoolfriend is standing only inches away from me, her eyes glistening with faux tears. She reaches out to place a hand on my forearm. I instinctively take a couple of steps back, keen to put some distance between us.

'Thank you. Good of you to come.' My words sound crass. Ill-fitting. I wish there was a handbook for the bereaved that gives a clear-cut idea of how to behave and what to say to well-wishers at the funeral of close family. A family that took the decision to end their lives in such a dreadful and highly publicised way.

'Oh, I couldn't *not* come!'

I bet you couldn't.

Amanda and I haven't seen each other since we left college over a decade ago. Gossip. That's why she is here. Jackson and Lydia Hemsworth were the closest Armett ever got to having celebrities in its midst, albeit damaged ones. People were able to observe their peculiarities from afar without being tainted by them, unlike me and my siblings, who were forced to endure my parents' wild eccentricities on a daily basis. I'm being unfair. Our mother did her best to compensate for our father's failings by being effervescent and bubbly, which was often perceived as giddiness and marginally manic behaviour. She was anything but that. What she was, was hurt and damaged, and trying hard to keep everything and everyone around her on an even keel.

Amanda's clothes belie her true age. She is dressed in a knee-length, tweed skirt, a black shirt and a long, dark, checked cardigan. With her nondescript, mousy hair, she could easily be mistaken for somebody decades older. We weren't enemies, Amanda and I, but neither were we friends. We simply existed in the same social circle, lived in the same town, and attended the same school, and now here she is, acting as if we are long-lost pals and close soul mates.

'Well anyway, thanks for attending. Help yourself to refreshments.' My voice is bland, denoting no emotion. I neither like nor hate Amanda. She is simply another attendee: a person I will make small talk with before moving onto somebody else and then eventually leaving this place and going home, relieved that it's all behind me.

I'm about to walk away when she says it, her timing, unlike her attire, impeccable. 'Pity they left a shadow, isn't it? Everyone is saying they did it for a reason, to cover up for something. I mean, they must have, don't you think?'

My heels click on the floor when I spin around to say something in return, but she is already moving away, undoubtedly satisfied by having the last word. I would love nothing more than to march up behind her, grab her by her arm and demand to know what she meant by that barbed comment, but of course, I'm too cowardly to be so forthright so instead, I do the dignified thing and disappear into the crowd of people standing next to the table of food. It's easier, shying away from confrontation. Life is difficult enough. Why heap more misery on top of what we already have? My earlier feelings of ambivalence for her rapidly change to dislike.

I mingle and chat, doing my best to erase Amanda's comments from my mind, but no matter how hard I try, they refuse to leave, hanging around like unwanted guests. My parents weren't perfect, far from it, and let's face it, whose parents are? But her insinuations rankle me. Florence, Ezra and I have been to hell and back in the last few weeks, trying to work out why they did it and attempting to fathom the machinations of our parents' thoughts: what went through their heads and why they decided to do what they did, leaving us to piece together the shattered fragments of our lives. The last thing we need is locals making up stories and adding fuel to an already simmering fire. Once the flames start to rage, it will be hard to stamp them out.

Deciding to grasp the nettle, I finish my drink and scan the crowd for her, determined to ask what she meant, and am disappointed to see her head out into the car park. Before I can catch her, she opens the door of her vehicle and jumps inside. She is driving out of the gate by the time I reach the parking area, and is oblivious to me waving my arms about to get her to stop. Her gaze is fixed firmly ahead, hands clasped around the steering wheel of her old

Ford. A nondescript woman driving a nondescript car, her mind riddled with toxic thoughts because she is a lonely, pathetic specimen of a being.

Part of me wonders if she deliberately ignored me but then I remember that Amanda MacDonald lives for slanderous titbits of gossip. If she thought there was a chance of gleaning any information out of me, she would have most certainly stopped that car and jumped out, desperate to delve into and rip apart the grimiest parts of my family's lives. God knows there is plenty of dirt to be had, but we don't speak of it, especially to outsiders. And especially to the likes of Amanda MacDonald. She came here to fish for information and left when there was none to be had. That's what we Hemsworths do best. We hide our dirty linen, never putting it out to air, which is why people are guessing at the truth, picking at the tiniest of visible scabs to try to get to the deeper wounds that are festering beneath.

In the distance, I spot Amber's mother. She glances my way and gives me a cursory nod and what seems to be a genuine smile before disappearing into a gathering of people. Amber and I are very different people but her mother has always radiated warmth towards me and my siblings.

I spend another hour in the community centre, watching people scoop up the remaining bits of food and drink, exhaustion beginning to tug at me. Grieving is tiring, but nothing compared to the shock of finding out your parents jumped to their deaths into the freezing river below the Newport Bridge in the north east of England. That sort of news dominates one's life. It's debilitating. For days afterwards, exhaustion wrapped itself around me, dragging me down to the ground. Going to bed was a big ordeal, getting up the following morning even bigger. I'm putting up a good fight against the physical effects it has had on me, however. I may be thought of as quiet and reserved but I'm not soft. We have a lot to do now, me and Flo and Ezra. A huge house to sort, a will to be raked over. The thought of that gives me the shivers. Flo is the reluctant executor of the will, her lip curling in disdain every time the subject is brought up, claiming that nothing can be done until they find Mother's body. It does, however, need to be done at some point. The sooner we get on with it and clear and sell the house, the better. Then we can all move on, get on with the rest of our lives, stop the local gossips – the likes of Amanda MacDonald – from dissecting our family and feasting on the bones of our remains. Except of course, for one thing: our mother, Lydia Hemsworth hasn't been declared dead yet, but I'm guessing it's only a matter of time before her body is found.

'I'm ready to go now but Ezra seems intent on talking to everyone and anyone.' Amber sidles up next to me, a small glass of wine in her hand. Her face is flushed from the alcohol. I had hoped she would abstain today, if only for Ezra's sake, to make things easier for him, but it appears not.

'I think he's trying to win everyone round. Some of these people adored our parents, some were ambivalent, and some hated them. He wants them to go out on a high, not be regarded as the local villains just because Father died owing the maintenance people their wages.'

My reply is met with a protracted silence. On the pretence of readjusting the collar of my jacket, I turn to glance at Amber, trying to see the expression on her face, willing her to say something – anything – to unfreeze us from this awkward moment. Instead, she takes a sip of her wine and turns to smile at me. 'Well, anyway, one more glass of this and I'll be asleep within an hour. Daytime drinking never did suit me.'

'Best stick to the lemonade then,' I murmur, wishing I could climb inside her head and read her thoughts.

Amber and me, although not arch enemies, have never really

bonded. We're polite and cordial towards one another but there is something missing in our relationship. I've never been able to put my finger on what it is that's lacking between us. I guess sometimes we gel with people and sometimes we don't. Overall, we manage to rub along together without any real hitches, but then she says something that sets my senses alight, making the hairs on the back of my neck stand to attention, and at that point, I think that I was right to be wary of her for all these years and not get too close.

'Bit more than a lack of wages causing friction, don't you think? Time to scratch that surface, Jess. Maybe you now need to wake up and take a long, hard look at who you really are. Who your family are. And what they did.'

And with that, she walks away. My face burns, sweat prickling my scalp and forming a damp arc around my hairline. She is the second person in less than an hour who has thrown a hand grenade into the conversation and then chosen to make a hasty exit, leaving me to deal with the damage caused by the shrapnel and debris.

I put down my drink, suddenly acutely aware of why I've never got on that well with her. Has she spent all morning thinking up that caustic remark or is it the drink talking? I watch her head towards my brother, her walk more of an exaggerated swagger. Once she has moved away from him, I'll ask her what she meant by that pointed remark and I won't let her dodge and weave and evade my questions. I won't rest until I get a proper answer, but before I have a chance to do anything, cold hands grip my upper arm, bony fingers pressing into my flesh. I recognise the voice all too well – that sibilant hiss. The air of menace. The accusations.

'They're both gone, your parents. But I'm still here. And I'm not going anywhere until I get some proper answers.'

5

FLO

Coops is pottering about in the stables when I pull up and rummage for my keys to open the door of the house. Damien Cooper, affectionately known as Coops, has worked for my parents at Armett House for as long as I can remember. He's practically part of the family and lives in a cottage on the lane behind Armett House. He appears out of the open door, wiping his hands down the side of his trousers, spots me standing here, then smiles and walks towards me.

'You left the community centre early as well, then?' I say, watching as he shakes his head and gives a wry smile.

'Can't be doing with that lot. All there for the free drink and food. Full of fake sympathy and useless platitudes.'

I laugh and raise my eyebrows at him in agreement. He's right. I stayed for as long as I could, but in the end, I wasn't able to stand it anymore. All those people milling about, helping themselves to the refreshments, gobbling up sandwiches while telling us how sorry they were while smiling and gossiping inanely, so I quietly slipped away. The debacle with Jeff Wolf and the money was more than I could bear. I shouldn't have left Ezra, Amber and Jess to speak to everyone and I shouldn't be here, but as I left the community centre, going back home to my own house didn't appeal to me, so I came to Armett House to hopefully lay a few ghosts to rest.

'Watch out for the mouse traps in the house, Flo. Seems the little buggers are determined to outstay their welcome. I've put the traps and the poison in the kitchen and the old larder so keep an eye out when you're in there. Right,' he says, pulling off his old leather waistcoat that he's worn for so long now, he looks strange without it. Seeing him at the back of the church in a formal jacket forced me to do a double take. 'I'm off home now. Do you need anything doing before I go?'

'No, I'm good thanks. And thank you for attending the funeral and for everything you've done around the house since Mother and Father's death, Coops. I'll keep an eye out for those pesky bloody mice.'

'Aye, well if you see any in the traps, just give me a knock and I'll come and dispose of them. It's a grisly job but somebody's gotta do it.'

We say our goodbyes and he wanders through the wooded area that leads to the back lane behind the house.

I let myself in the front door and stand for a few seconds, looking around the large hallway with its many ornate fixtures and fittings. It's odd. I was convinced after leaving the community centre that I didn't want to go home to my own house and was pulled towards coming back to stay at this old place, but now that I'm here, it feels rather weird. Empty and lonely. They're everywhere and yet they are nowhere, my parents, their trademark eccentricities still permanent fixtures in this rambling, old place. From the wall-mounted stuffed peacocks that grace the walls of the stairway, each one placed in an upward line to appear as if they are moving, to the paintings of my father dressed in military attire even though he wasn't ever in the army or navy or any type of combative unit, everything feels intense and overpowering. Strange how when I lived here, these things blended into the background but since moving out into my own place, which is decorated in muted pastel shades with few accessories cluttering it up, the extravagant décor chosen by my parents now seems garish and lacking in the humour which was intended. Or at least that's how my mother explained it to me.

'Oh, it's just your father's strange ways. You know how he is, Flo. Best to just ignore him and let him get on with it.'

So we did. Perhaps we should have questioned him a little more. Not that it matters now. All of this will soon be a thing of the past. Discarded and thrown away, or sent off for auction. I don't want any of it and can't see Ezra or Jessica rushing to take ownership of any of these ghastly items either. Some are undoubtedly priceless but many are completely worthless, picked up from charity shops or reclamation yards on a whim.

I turn on the lights as I walk from room to room. There are too many dark corners in this place, too many shadows lurking. When I was a child, I was convinced Armett House was haunted. Little did I know the things I should have feared were very much alive. I brush away those thoughts. If I am to spend the night here, I'd like to do it with a clear head and not have any childhood demons perched on my shoulder. As the eldest, I saw more of what went on than Ezra or Jessica ever did. I'm not sure they know the half of it. Better it stays that way. Why share out the worry and misery? I'm the eldest. It's my job to shoulder the burdens and the accompanying anxiety. They certainly had dreadful times with our father but I'm not sure they knew the levels of depravity to which he would stoop. I swallow and run my fingers through my hair, weariness chiselling its way deep into my bones.

By the time I reach the kitchen, every room is flooded with light. I open all the shutters and turn on every switch, banishing any dark, lingering memories. On the wall is a framed picture of my father handing over a cheque to the local hospice, his grin a mile wide. My mother is standing in the background. She is neither smiling nor frowning. I've looked at that photograph a thousand times and wondered what was going through her head when it was taken. I recall asking her once and being given a dismissive answer.

'Oh, I can't really remember, Flo. It was such a busy day. I was probably tired.'

At the time, I think that maybe I believed her but feel sure now that things at that point were already starting to crumble in her life, the carefully constructed façade of normality they had built at Armett House slowly turning to dust.

I heat up the ready-made meal I found in the freezer and pour myself a glass of wine from my father's prized collection. I managed to stick to the soft stuff at the community centre and so feel that I truly deserve this. Drinking in front of Ezra doesn't sit well with me, although it hasn't stopped his girlfriend who happily takes to the bottle at every available opportunity.

The wine is surprisingly bitter given its value. It doesn't stop me drinking it, however. I wrinkle my nose and glance around the kitchen. I'm suddenly aware of an unpleasant smell that is present. I presume it's the dead vermin that have been caught in the traps. I take a long drink and then another until my senses begin to dull and the world is blurred by a soft, welcome haze, its ragged edges smoothed out by my father's expensive wine. I'll give Coops a knock in the morning, tell him about the stink of dead mice in the place. For now, I'm happy to sit here, drink as much alcohol as I can, and ignore it.

My ears are attuned to the heartbeat and low pulse of the house as I sit and eat my food and sip at my Chardonnay. Outside, birds land on the empty feeder, searching for scraps of seeds, their tiny beaks pecking at the mesh of the basket for remnants. I'm savouring both the food and the expensive drink and the near silence when a loud banging sends me into a tailspin, my glass falling to the floor with a crash.

I stand up, ignoring the spillage, and march into the hallway, fury building in me at being disturbed. I pull at the door, the large metal handle hitting the wall as it swings wide open.

'Sorry. Hope I haven't disturbed you?' DI Harvey is standing there, a sympathetic tilt of her head making her look marginally lopsided. 'I know it's the funeral today and I apologise for the bad timing but I also knew you'd want to hear this piece of news straightaway.'

I nod and step aside to let her in, unable to manage a smile, wondering how she knew I was here. She heads towards the living room and stands next to the coffee table, speaking quickly as if she is able to read my thoughts. 'I spoke to Ezra on his phone and he said if you weren't at home then you'd probably be here.' She turns and looks at me. 'He said it was okay to speak with you and that I could communicate with him and Jessica later. Hope that's all right with you?'

I nod and sit down in one of Mother's favourite overstuffed old armchairs and gesture for DI Harvey to do the same.

'So,' I say, bracing myself for news of how they have found my mother's body, every sinew, every muscle in my own body, straining and taut with apprehension. 'I'm presuming you've located her?' My voice cracks a little. I clear my throat and try to compose myself, my hands clasped around my knees.

'No, I'm afraid not, but we have found some items: a piece of jewellery and some spectacles.'

She waits for me to reply. I sit there, mute, any words I would like to say, trapped in my throat. My tongue is glued to the roof of my mouth. I tighten my abdomen to control my breathing and hold onto the arms of the chair to stop myself from falling to the floor.

The room is spinning like a carousel. I thought I was prepared for this. I thought wrong.

'If you could call to the station and take a look at them to see if they belong to your mum?'

'What is the piece of jewellery?' I need to know now. I can't be expected to make my way down there without being given some idea of what it might be. I half expect DI Harvey to tell me that she can't disclose that information but she doesn't, speaking instead in a soft, well-rehearsed manner.

'It's a silver necklace with a heart-shaped pendant on it. The glasses have a gold metal frame. They were found embedded in the mud on the riverside. The necklace was entangled in the weeds close to where your father's body was found.' Her eyes bore into me while she waits for a response. I look away, lowering my gaze to the floor.

They belonged to my mother. They're hers. She's not going to be found. I can sense it. If she does ever wash up, she'll be unrecognisable. I don't want to think about it. I don't want to think about how cold and frightened she will have been as she made that leap and landed in the freezing, deep river. Mother wasn't a particularly strong swimmer. One swift, unforgiving current and she will have been dragged under, her limbs thrashing about as she struggled to breathe.

When I eventually look up, DI Harvey is still watching me, her face soft and full of pity and compassion. I don't know how she does this job, breaking the bad news to relatives of the dead. I often consider my job as a teacher stressful, but DI Harvey's workload is so different to mine, the expectations of what she must do every single day, beyond my capabilities.

'They belong to my mother but I'll go to the station anyway to identify them. Ezra, Jess and I bought her that necklace. She never took it off.' I speak without my voice breaking.

'We're still searching that stretch of river and beyond, but the current has been really strong and with all the rain recently...' She stops and sighs. 'But that doesn't mean we're going to give up. The search is still ongoing. I can assure you, we're doing our absolute best to try and find her.'

I thank her for letting me know and show her to the door, the need to be alone stronger than ever.

'I'll be at the station first thing in the morning.'

She nods and I close the door behind her, leaning back on it to stop the swirling and seesawing of the room around me once she has left. Mother's necklace and glasses. That's one step closer to actually finding her body. Later, I'll call Ezra and Jess, let them know, and then I'll take that wine bottle up to bed with me and drink away my worries and sorrows. But first, I need to sort out the mess in the kitchen.

I grab a damp cloth, get the dustpan and brush from under sink, then drop to my knees and begin to sweep.

6

JESSICA

'Bella, please let go of my arm. You're hurting me.' I all but roll my eyes at her, my voice more of a hiss than a whisper.

The last thing I want is for her to cause a scene. Not here and not now at the funeral of my parents. At least let us have today to be free of any more drama. The Jeff Wolf thing was bad enough, and now I have this to contend with.

'Hurting you? What the hell do you think I've had to go through because of your so-called well-to-do parents?' Flecks of foamy saliva gather at the corners of her mouth. Bella, although only in her mid-fifties, looks old enough to be mistaken for somebody two decades older. That isn't her fault, I understand that, and I'm sorry for what she has been through, but that's no excuse to grab hold of me and start making wild accusations.

Already I can see people watching us, can almost feel the heat of their bodies as they edge closer, eager to hear what's being said. I imagine most of them have already hazarded a guess. It's the scandal they're interested in, seeing the unsightly demise of our family name. Everyone likes to see the mighty fall, don't they? It helps them sleep at night, knowing that purported wealth and status don't always mean grace and dignity.

I wait a couple of seconds, watching as the onlookers lose interest and begin to move away, then sigh before speaking, torn between feeling sympathy for her and feeling utterly exasperated at her timing and tenacity. 'Look, we've been through this at least a hundred times. Your daughter upped and left Armett House after telling my mother that she was leaving and heading off to Manchester to see some friends. The police investigated and no further action was taken. I'm truly sorry that she never returned home, I honestly am, but her disappearing has absolutely nothing whatsoever to do with my family. Her wages were paid to her as normal that week and we saw no more of her. Today is the funeral of my parents; now you can either pay your respects quietly or you can leave.'

My heart is a pounding drum beneath my ribcage. As I'm speaking, Bella glares at me, her eyes narrow slits. She folds her arms over her chest and shakes her head. 'I didn't come here to pay respects to your family, although your mother, God bless her, should have had a medal for putting up with that man. If I were her, I would have pushed him off the nearest high roof well before now. God knows why she ever married him in the first place.'

'You mean my father?' My heart continues to thrash around my chest; my pulse is racing. I need to stop her. I don't want to hear this. Nobody else in this place needs to hear it either.

'I mean the man who wrecked my life and the life of my poor Katie. He was a creep and a pervert and come what may, I'll have my day in court.'

The slap knocks her backwards. It takes me by surprise as much as it does Bella. She staggers, her palm spread over her cheek. I should apologise. My hand is stinging, my own face on fire. I've never hit anybody before, but her words cut deeply. What type of person insults a dead man on the day of his funeral? For all his faults, I still feel an allegiance of sorts towards him. He was my father, after all. If I don't stand up for him, who will? I insult and berate him every day in my head but Bella has no right to do it in public. Her words are humiliating and demeaning, dragging us innocent family members down into the gutter with him.

I move towards her, my hands now locked firmly behind my back, and find enough courage to hiss in her ear. 'Katie used her bank cards while she was in Manchester. You know that. The police verified the fact she bought sandwiches from M&S and then used her phone to purchase a train ticket to London. What more evidence do you need? She worked as a cleaner at Armett House for my parents. That's as far as the connection goes. Now please leave, otherwise I'll call the police and report you for slander and harassment.'

My heart is still booming in my chest, thudding wildly beneath my ribcage. I feel faint and dizzy. For somebody who hates conflict, I feel I've done rather well and stepped way outside of my comfort zone today. Once the adrenaline stops flowing, I'll wish I hadn't done it, but for now, I feel rather emboldened. I've taken a stand against a screeching old lady who drove her own daughter away from home with her constant criticism and overbearing ways. Katie often complained about how strict her mother was. She went to work for my parents at Armett House to make a bit of money during the summer holidays before going back to college to complete her exams and quite possibly to get away from her mother, who controlled almost every aspect of the poor girl's life. Maybe her tenure at Armett helped her escape, giving her enough money to flee. That's why Bella blames our family: because we enabled her and assisted her, gave her a way out of her dreary and heavily controlled homelife. Don't get me wrong – I hated my father, loathed him even – but insinuating he had something to do with Katie vanishing is ludicrous. Beyond the pale. He was many things but to claim he somehow helped Katie to vanish is unthinkable.

I watch as Bella backs away, her cheek a flare of crimson where I hit her. I glance around and am relieved to see that the few people who are left are too busy talking to one another to notice what just happened. In a few moments, once I've calmed down, I'll go and tell Ezra that I'm leaving. Flo has already left and I can now understand why she made such a rapid exit. After speaking to Bella, I feel dirty and grimy, like I need a long soak in a hot bath.

The slam of the door echoes around the place. Bella has turned on her heel and stormed out. I'm glad to see the back of her, glad that she has taken her accusations elsewhere and left us in peace. Good riddance. Sometimes, I have fond memories of this town and its people and other times, the thought of it makes me sick to my stomach. Being the local allegedly wealthy people who live in the big house has its distinct disadvantages. People love nothing better than to try to tear us down while others remember the summers spent in the grounds of Armett House, the village fetes and paper chases organised by my parents, and think of us with fondness.

Only when I'm certain Bella has left do I pick up my coat and bag and make my way over to where Ezra and Amber are standing.

'I'm off home now. I think I'll take a taxi. I might stay at the house tonight once I've picked up some of my things. That way, I can make a start on my old room as soon as I'm up in the morning.'

'Okay, no worries. I'll call round at some point. I need to go into the office first, let them know that I'm taking the rest of the week off, then I'll join you. The sooner we tackle the place, the better, eh?' He leans forward and gives me a hug.

I almost choke up, tears biting at the back of my eyes. He smells like our father, the same powerful, masculine aroma of aftershave and stale tobacco on his skin and clothes. I feel a rush of love and familiarity without the underlying fear that I always felt in Father's presence. And yet there is something there lately, something dark behind Ezra's eyes. I hope the funeral hasn't unleashed his childhood demons, the ones he has worked hard to contain.

Amber also steps forward and I instinctively move away under the pretence of readjusting the strap of my handbag on my shoulder. She lowers her gaze and links her arm through Ezra's. I have vague memories of Amber from when we were growing up. She was one of the glamorous girls in town. The daughter of a doctor, she was a go-getter. And she did just that. Go get the young, handsome lad from Armett House, that is. Ezra had a few girlfriends before he met Amber but has been with her for over a year now so I suppose they're serious about this relationship and will end up getting wed. Amber came from a middle-class family and in her eyes, Ezra was an obvious match for her. The local lads from the three-bed semis and small council houses just didn't cut it, and my brother did. Her earlier comment rattles around my head, mingling and merging with Bella's remarks about my father's propensity for lurid behaviour. I shut them out. I'm too tired to become bogged down with it all. Jackson Hemsworth was what he was and now he's dead and buried and that's the end of it. I am now free of him. I suppose in a way, we all are.

My cab only takes a few minutes to arrive. I slide into it, grateful to be alone. Crowds have never been my thing. Neighbours and locals haranguing me has also never been my thing. I'm glad to be away from it all.

My first stop is my flat on the outskirts of town. The driver waits while I gather up my belongings. It takes me just a few moments to throw a couple of things into a bag and less than five minutes later, I'm sitting in the backseat and directing him to the road that leads to my childhood home.

'If you can just drop me off here,' I say as we pull up on the busy road next to the large gates that lead to Armett House.

'What, here on the main road?' He stops and stares at me through the rear-view mirror, his dark eyes fixed on mine.

'Yes, here is fine, thanks.' I'm aware there are no other houses close by. The nearest ones are set behind a high hedge on the far side of the carriageway.

'You live in that big house, then?' he says, nodding towards the tall, wrought-iron gates, an imposing scribble of black metal that stands tall and proud.

I glance at the meter and hand him a £20 note. 'Keep the change and thanks for waiting for me back there while I grabbed my belongings.'

I should have directed him to go around the back of the house but I didn't want to be alone with him down a narrow lane surrounded by trees and shrubbery with hardly anybody around. I'm sure he is a very nice and respectable man but after my recent break-up with Luke and subsequent black eye, I'm taking the obvious route of caution and safety. I didn't want him knowing where I lived either but it seems like he knows anyway. I now have to unlock the gates and walk the half mile down the gravel path to the house with him sitting here watching and assessing me, trying to work out who I am and what I'm doing here. Let him watch and wonder. Today has been tiring, the few weeks prior, utterly exhausting. I need a drink, a bath and a long sleep.

The squeaking and groaning of the gate, and the crunch of my feet on the gravel, drowns out the roar of his engine as he disappears out of view. His next fare is far more important than my identity. By the time I reach the front door, he is a dim and distant memory, my mind honed in on why the lights are on inside. Before I can wonder any more, the door is flung open and Flo steps out, wine glass in hand, eyes glazed over.

'They've found her necklace and glasses, Jess. DI Harvey has been here. They've found her belongings but not her. She's still out there somewhere.'

My mind freezes. I think of our mother and feel my chest tighten. I rub at my eyes and take a shuddering breath, trying to shut out the ghastly images that fill my mind; images of Mother struggling to breathe, her body shivering from the cold. The fear she must have felt. Flo and I stand facing one another, a heavy silence between us. For one awkward weird moment, I think that perhaps she is going to burst into tears, something I have never seen my older sister do, but then she clears her throat and rubs at her eyes, weariness apparent in the tremble of her fingers. She smiles and composes herself once more, our usual equilibrium restored. 'Anyway, how come you're here?'

I cock my head to one side and smile. 'To say my goodbyes, I suppose. And to sort out my old room. Why are you here?'

Flo sighs and steps back inside. I move past her and dump my bag on the floor.

'Same reason, I guess. Have you eaten?'

I shake my head. Food hasn't been high on my agenda lately.

'There's some cheese and bread in the larder. And eggs. Why don't you unpack your things and I'll make you an omelette?'

I catch Flo looking at my hips and legs, my recent weight loss evident from the way my clothes are hanging on me. A recent break-up from my violent boyfriend and the death of my parents have all taken their toll. Right now, an omelette sounds perfect.

'And a glass of wine please. One of Father's really, really expensive ones. He owes us that much at least, the old bastard.'

She throws her head back and laughs, and at that moment, any awkwardness between us vanishes. I'm pleased she's here and happy that I'm not alone in this rambling old place. I'm glad of her matriarchal manner and efficiency.

I carry my bag upstairs, every creak of each stair as familiar to me as my own skin. I stop and look around at the large gallery landing above, glancing at the array of paintings and ornate footstools and chairs, and shiver. I have some fond memories of this place. I have lots of dark memories too, the latter taking precedent due to there being so many of them. Flo thinks she is the only one who bore the brunt of our father's behaviour. She has said it before, thinking me and Ezra led a blessed existence, but she's wrong. I was witness to it too but kept the memories tucked away out of sight and all the while, she thought she was protecting me from the worst of what went on. She did her best, she really did, but what use was the comforting words of an older child against the will of a destructive regime that seemed hellbent on destroying us all? She was no match for Jackson Hemsworth. I don't think anybody was. Who could remain one step ahead of the man who wrote and tore up his own rules on a daily basis?

My old room is as I left it. I returned home for only a year after finishing university, the recollections of what went on in this house too dark, too painful for me to battle. I lay my bag on the bed and perch on the chair next to the window to take a few minutes before I head back downstairs for some food and drink. The house now somehow feels lighter, his oppressive presence now absent. Not a happy place but not the fucking miserable abode that it used to be. I may have stuck up for him back there at the community centre because it was a public place and it felt like the right thing to do, but now that it's all over and I can finally think straight, my thoughts are this: I am so happy and relieved that the man who regularly took a belt to us and made our lives so fucking difficult is finally dead. I hope he had a long and lingering, painful death and I truly hope that he rots in hell.

7

FLO

'God, I hate this place.' Jess looks around the kitchen and places her almost empty wine glass on the table with a thump. She pushes away her empty plate and dabs at her mouth with a napkin.

After pushing her food around the plate, she finally gave in and ate every last scrap with me watching and inwardly cheering her on. I'll mention her weight another time. Not now. We need to get reacquainted first, our jobs and day-to-day lives turning us into near strangers.

'The kitchen?' I ask, already aware of what her answer is going to be.

She laughs and picks up the bottle of horribly expensive Sancerre, shaking it lightly and smiling at the fact that it's almost empty. 'No, this house. I do, however, love the fact that this bottle is almost gone. That would really piss him off. The stink however, I do not love.'

'Ah yes, sorry that's the smell of dead rodents. Coops is going to call in tomorrow to get rid of the mice that are already caught in the traps and to put new traps down.'

Jess nods and shrugs. 'Or maybe it's the smell that our father left behind before he died – the pong of his filthy, rotten soul still lingering in our midst.'

My face heats up. I don't reply, unsure if I've the stomach for such a conversation. As adults, Ezra, Jess and I have spoken rarely, if at all, about the behaviour of our father. Maybe we can talk about it tomorrow when I'm less tired, more able to verbalise my thoughts. Or maybe not. Some things are best left unsaid, especially when emotions are running high. Today was the funeral of our parents. Today is also the beginning of the rest of our lives. Time to put it all behind us. I'm hoping to treat this chapter of our lives as a new start, not as a wormhole into our past.

'I rang Ezra while you were upstairs and told him about the police finding Mother's jewellery and spectacles. DI Harvey had already contacted him but I just rang to confirm.'

Jess lowers her gaze and swills the last bit of wine around the bottom of her glass. I notice how white her knuckles are, how tightly she is clutching the stem.

'So that's it then? She definitely went into the river?'

I frown and shake my head. 'Was there ever any doubt that she didn't?' I'm shocked at Jessica's candid reply. Of course our mother jumped.

She juts out her lip in a childish pout and pours the last of the wine into her glass. 'Ignore me. I'm a bit drunk. Did I tell you that I hit somebody today?'

I'm not sure whether to laugh or shriek out loud. 'Hit somebody? Where? At the community centre?' Jess is quiet, reserved. Never violent. I daren't ask. I haven't the strength for it.

'Bella Gardiner. I slapped her across the face.'

I feel myself go faint. I know Bella, we all do. This will only exacerbate our outstanding problems with her.

'Jess, I don't know what to say except, why? What on earth made you hit her?'

She sighs and leans back, her long, wavy hair dangling over the back of the chair like a beige, silk curtain. 'She said some things about our family. About our father and as much as I hated him, I felt duty-bound to protect our family name. So I hit her.'

I nod, not wanting to hear what she is going to say next and yet at the same time, feel drawn to it, like a moth flitting around the light, a desperation to know keeping me interested and alert. 'So what did she say that was so bad?'

'She called him a creep and a pervert.'

A flame rushes up through my body and settles on my face. 'So, you hit her?'

'I slapped her across the face. It just sort of happened.'

Jess sounds tired and weary but she doesn't sound regretful. I think of Bella telling half the town, embellishing the story every time she talks about it until in the end, Jess will be painted as a raging psychopath. As if we don't have enough to cope with.

My legs are leaden as I stand up and contemplate reaching for another bottle. I need a few seconds to think. I need a few seconds to swerve the conversation round to something else. Anything except Jackson Hemsworth. Even in death, he continues to control us.

'I'm calling into the station in the morning to identify Mother's necklace and glasses.' I don't offer an invitation for Jess to accompany me. It's something I would rather do alone anyway. 'It should only take me an hour at most, then we can start clearing this place out.'

She nods, her eyes clouding over. She's drunk. I feel tiddly myself and fancy another glass of wine but don't want to turn up at the police station in the morning reeking of booze, so instead I fill the kettle, grab myself a cup and put a teabag in it.

We sit in near silence for the next few minutes, sipping our respective drinks, talking briefly about which auction house we should contact for the house clearance and whether we'll have a hot summer this year, or a washout. We dance around each other, avoiding the obvious and ignoring the fucking great elephant in the room until exhaustion becomes the deciding factor and we both head up to bed, wearied by the day's events.

I enter my old bedroom, aware that my mother was sleeping here before her death. I called around early one morning before work and caught her coming out onto the landing in her nightgown, hair ruffled, face aghast when she saw me. I smiled and nodded to let her know that no explanations were needed. It had been a long time coming and for all I know, that sleeping arrangement may have been in place for many years prior to me catching her.

The ottoman is full of clean sheets. I spend the next few minutes changing the bed and putting on fresh linen. The rattle and groaning of the old pipes that track across the ceiling of my bedroom tell me that Jess is running a bath. I sigh and rub at my eyes, feeling grimy and gritty. Tainted by standing so close to his dead body. It's hard to believe he's actually gone. Larger than life when he was here and now shrunken in death, his legacy as putrid and rotten as his bloated, waterlogged corpse.

Life will hopefully get easier now we've got the funeral out of the way and some of Mother's things have been found. It has to. It can't get any worse. Fatigue slams into me as I stare down at the freshly made bed. I'm looking forward to slipping between the sheets and closing my eyes, shutting out the dirt and filth and general anxiety of the day.

Mother's most recent reading book and a few of her personal things are still laid out on the bedside cabinet. I clamber into bed and prop myself up with the pillow, then pick the first paperback up from the small pile and glance through it.

She was reading the classic Daphne Du Maurier novel, *Rebecca*.

I recall her introducing it to me many years ago, insisting I read it, and being blown away by the prose when I eventually got round to it. I wonder if Mother tried to see some parallels in her life with this book: the lady who lived in the large house yet often spent her days feeling lonely and full of angst with no idea of what it was she had done that was so very wrong.

I leaf through a few pages, stopping when I find a small, plain, white envelope hidden inside. It drops onto my lap, its contents spilling out onto the duvet cover. A collection of photographs stare up at me, bright, vivid images of a courtyard garden and a villa-style house. It's clearly somewhere in the Mediterranean, each photograph flooded with light, the house having pastel-coloured, faded, shuttered windows and a rustic-looking, crumbling façade. I turn them over, looking for clues on the back as to where they were taken, hoping for a signature or something personal to determine their provenance, but find nothing.

Behind them, still inside the envelope, is a small collection of oldish-looking greeting cards. Inside each one is a tiny, indistinguishable signature and above that, the words, *Love her as I would.*

Something to do with Mother's poetry, perhaps? I'm too tired to put any depth of thought into it. My eyes are heavy, the alcohol and today's events beginning to take their toll. I put the photos back inside the envelope, along with the small cards, and lay them down on the cabinet on top of the book. Maybe I'll take a closer look in the morning when I'm feeling more receptive, more able to wade through the detritus of my mother's rather sad life. Not the kind of sad that meant she was pathetic or inadequate but sad because she was unhappy and I loved her and wanted better for her but didn't have the first clue where to start. With somebody as formidable as Jackson Hemsworth, all avenues were dead ends with no way around them.

Across the landing, I hear the faint sound of Jess's voice as she speaks to somebody on her phone. I pray she isn't making contact with Luke, her ex-boyfriend, the man who with his coercive controlling behaviour, stripped her of what little confidence she had and reduced her to a gibbering wreck. I've watched her grow and become stronger over the past few weeks and months, gradually returning to her usual self.

I flick off the lamp, slide under the covers and wait for sleep to take me away from this hideous and horribly unforgettable day.

8

THE PARENTS

She tried to pull her arm away at the last minute but he was too quick for her, dragging her down with him. He was falling faster than she was, his body heavier than hers. She had removed the rocks from her pockets, surreptitiously discarding them with trembling fingers on the walk to the bridge. He was too distracted to notice, his mind, as always, too full of his own ideas and wants and needs to ever think about anybody else's.

God, she hated him. At that point, she hated him more than she had ever hated anybody in her entire life. The wind and rain cut through her, her thin sweater doing little to protect her body from the damn awful weather. Her glasses fell from her face, whipped away by the wind and gravity. Her vision would be limited, if she survived, that is. She would try, by God she was going to try, but her survival wasn't guaranteed. The bridge felt high, the water below looking dark and cold. The weather was atrocious. He couldn't have timed it better. Everything was working against her. All she had was luck and a prayer, and she didn't believe in either. The strength of the water temperature and the incessant drag of the current would determine her fate. That and her own gritty efforts to stay alive.

She thought of their children: Flo, with her often austere and protective ways; Ezra, with his carefully constructed, polite demeanour that hid his demons; and then Jess, the youngest, the baby of their family. What would happen to them all after her death? And what would happen to Armett House? Their once beloved family home that became a millstone round their necks.

Any more thoughts she may have had were catapulted out of her mind as she hit the water, her body sinking in seconds. She fought against the current. She fought with all her might but her struggles were useless as she felt herself being carried downstream at an alarming speed. Then as she resurfaced, spluttering and fighting to breathe properly, she saw him, his head bobbing about only yards from where she was. Fury raged inside her, white-hot flames that heated up her freezing body. Swimming in such a strong current was almost impossible; her legs dragged from under her as she attempted to straighten them out to reach him. And the cold – it was bone-aching, making it too difficult to move properly, her dexterity already limited.

It was hard to see anything in the darkness without her glasses, and her cries for help went unheard at such an ungodly hour. Nobody could see or hear her. She was the forgotten one. Her husband's helpless victim. But not for much longer.

With a strength that she felt sure had been reserved for this moment and this moment only, she swam towards him, unsure of what she would do when she got there, but certain that whatever it was, it would involve a fierce resistance to whatever he tried to get her to do. Her days of being a victim were over. Her days of kowtowing to him and agreeing to outlandish scenarios because of his empty threats were now a thing of the past. She should have taken a stand a long time ago. Except that she tried and it made everything so much worse. She became trapped, her life whirling lower and lower.

Only as she drew closer could she see it – his flailing limbs and struggles to stay above the surface. Jackson was a strong swimmer. When they agreed to this, she expected him to survive, hoping deep down that the shock of the fall would kill him if the river didn't, but it was clear that he couldn't keep his head up above the water. Maybe he was caught in a riptide? They were near the estuary so it was possible. She prayed that that was the case. If he was in a weakened state, then perhaps she could take advantage and do what needed to be done to end this thing once and for all. And if he wasn't... well, she would have to deal with whatever came next as it happened.

The sounds of his gasps and gulping filled the night air. She approached with caution. Lydia had learned long ago to not trust her husband. He would probably say the same of her, but then he was a compulsive liar and all she was, was a browbeaten wife who had stood by him for too damn long.

Lights flickered in the distance, a line of bright dots where the local industry was located. Factories and workshops and cooling towers, all managed by people working round-the-clock shifts while she and her husband were out here in the freezing, filthy water, fighting for their lives. Once upon a time, many decades ago, ships would sail up and down this stretch of river, the bridge lifting to allow the taller vessels through, but not anymore, all the shipyards now gone, the current industry slowly in decline. Just the two of them now, alone in the darkness.

Her limbs were turning numb from the cold, her body becoming exhausted in no time at all. She used small breast strokes to try and reach him, hoping he had less energy than she did. Hoping she would have the upper hand. But as soon as she grew near, he rose from beneath the water, a monstrous, slimy being like some sort of hideous deep-sea beast, and launched himself at her. Their grappling arms and sodden bodies became entangled as he reached for her head. She ducked and dived, moving away from him, small and more agile than he would ever be, his larger frame hindering his ability to do anything deftly, and slipped beneath the dark water, her chest convulsing wildly. But then she felt it: his hands pushing down on the top of her head. It was like a lead weight, the force he exerted on her small body. Her options were limited, time slipping away. Every second spent underwater was a second closer to death.

Stars burst behind her eyes; her lungs were at bursting point. She couldn't hold her breath for much longer. Soon, she would have to breathe in and then that would be the end of it. The end of her.

Her hands flapped about, legs thrashing wildly, fingers trying to claw at his partly submerged body. She thought of her wonderful children, the life she had led. How she would be remembered. She visualised her veins bulging, her eyes popping out of her skull. Then her mouth burst open and she felt herself sinking...

9

JESSICA

Why, after all this trauma and alcohol, can I not sleep? Perhaps it's the adrenaline still flowing after the upset of the funeral and the realisation that I hit a woman whose daughter has been missing for months. Shame burrows under my skin. I should visit her house and apologise but I doubt she would answer the door to me. All I can do is keep my head down and pretend it didn't happen. I like to think that my break-up with Luke and the death of my parents pushed me to it. I'm not a violent person, so I'm hoping it will pass, this anger and fury that is currently burning deep inside of me. Or maybe there is another reason for it. Maybe I inherited Jackson's violent streak and have more in common with him than I care to admit. I brush that thought away. My parents are dead. Time to move on. No point grieving over things that I can't change. We all know what sort of a man my father was. I am nothing like him. Besides, what is the use of brooding over the past and wrecking the present and a possible bright future?

My phone has been ringing all evening: friends offering their condolences, telling me how sorry they are. Kind but unnecessary. I'm too tired to engage in anything that requires deep emotional connections and soul searching. I just want to clear this house and get back to my normal life. It's not an exciting existence but it's mine and I want it back. Strange how both Flo and I went into teaching while Ezra decided that working in finance was his calling. Good for him. He makes plenty of money while Flo and I are drowning in marking and planning lessons. Outsiders presume we could all be kept people because of who our parents were, but that simply isn't the case. Even if there was enough money to go around, we're independent and don't want to rely on our family for handouts. The last thing I would want is to take anything from my father. The sooner I sever all my connections from him, the better. I will always act like the dutiful daughter in the presence of other people but in my own mind, I'm allowed to hate him. As a damaged daughter, it's my prerogative.

The hot bath has done nothing to calm or comfort me so I slip on my dressing gown and head downstairs, wanting another glass of wine but knowing that I should really do the sensible thing and have tea.

I recoil as I step into the kitchen, the smell an assault on my senses. Damn those mice. I hope Coops gets here first thing and sorts it out. I make my tea and take it into the drawing room where the air is clearer and it's easier to breathe.

My legs are tucked up under me on Mother's favourite chaise longue as I sip at my drink and savour the silence. It doesn't last long. An almighty crash almost knocks me to the floor, the shock of it reverberating through my bones.

Above me, I hear Flo's muffled footfall as she jumps out of bed and paces around the bedroom at speed, then the thunderous sound of her galloping downstairs, her footfall echoing throughout the house.

I'm up and looking out of the window when she comes running

into the room, my face pressed up against the glass, my eyes scanning the courtyard and vast gardens for intruders.

'I should have closed the blinds and shutters before we went to bed. What the hell was it, Jess?'

I spin around and search her face for answers. 'I have no idea. It came from outside.' As I'm answering, I make a move towards the back of the house to the boot room where my wellingtons are stored.

Flo follows me, her arms hugging her midriff. 'I'll grab my coat and check outside. Why don't you do a scan of the inside of the house?'

I shake my head and yank open the big oak door that leads to the room where our old coats and boots are stored. 'The noise came from outside, Flo. Why don't you check the front gardens instead, and I'll take the bigger torch and look around the back?'

She doesn't reply but pulls on her wellies and raincoat without dismissing my idea. I do the same, pushing my arms into my thick, rainproof mac and stuffing my feet into my wellington boots before grabbing both torches and handing one over to her.

The rain has eased up but the ground is still soaking as we step outside, huge puddles strewn across the tarmac and gravel. I swing my torch around behind me and turn around to walk towards the back of the house, casting a beam of light over the stables before I leave. If there is anybody hiding in there, I'd never know. It's a big, dark, old place with lots of shadowy corners. If I were making a run for it, it's where I'd go for sure, but then a random prowler wouldn't know the ins and outs of this big old house and its many outbuildings. Whoever it is that is creeping around the place could be in the greenhouse crouched behind the shelving, or in the shed, the one with the broken padlock that my father refused to get fixed.

'It's only a bloody old padlock and the shed is practically empty. Waste of bloody time and money, Coops,' he would say every time the subject was brought up. And yet he had no qualms about doing his own bits of shoddy building work. I know for a fact he did some work in the old larder and the large pantry and yet neither of them looks any different to me. He was always the same – his way or no way.

So the padlock remained broken and for all we know, there could be somebody hiding in there, waiting for an opportune moment to pounce.

My heart stutters in my chest. I swallow and pull my coat tighter around my neck, sidestepping around the stables and the shed, and the rambling old buildings that should have been knocked down years ago were it not for the fact they are all Grade I listed buildings. Rather than investigate what could be lurking inside, I wave the torch about across the wooded area, my eyes scanning the bushes and shrubbery for anything resembling a human figure. It suddenly occurs to me that I have nothing on me that I can use as protection. I bend down and pick up some of the larger stones that are strewn about the edge of the gravelled path, clutching them tightly in my fist. The heft of them provides me with a modicum of comfort but I would still prefer to have something weightier, something more substantial and threatening.

'The police are on their way!' My voice is a lonely whine, a stretch of nothingness that echoes before vanishing into the cold night air, projecting only my deep fear and not the power and confidence I had hoped for.

My breath mists in front of my face, small orbs that balloon and dissipate as I gasp and try to catch my breath.

The hand on my shoulder almost sends me spinning to the floor. 'Round here, Jess. I've found it.'

'Jesus Christ, Flo! You nearly gave me a heart attack!'

My sister's face is illuminated by the glow of the torch, her skin pallid-looking, her eyes dark and wide.

'Next time, can you let me know you're behind me? Maybe walk on the gravel rather than the grass so I can hear you, eh? I almost passed out with shock.'

She shrugs and takes my hand, pulling me away from the bushes and back around to the front of the house, then down towards the garages where our parents' cars are kept.

'This is what the noise was.' Flo points to a dent in the wooden garage door. Large splinters jut out and there is a gaping hole where the padlock used to be, one of the few that was in decent working order.

I shuffle closer to her, my body shivering from the cold. 'What do you think – an attempted burglary, you reckon?'

'Possibly. Looks to me though, as if those doors have already been pulled open and then jammed back in place.' She points to an overlap in the centre of the wooden doors where they meet.

'Could be. Or maybe one of them was knocked off its hinges and isn't sitting properly?'

'Maybe.'

Flo moves away from me and bends closer, her hands reaching out to touch the hole.

'Don't! We should call the police before we do anything. There could be fingerprints on the handle.' My voice sounds reedy: pathetic and childlike.

'I'm not calling the police if it's just a damaged piece of old wood.'

'It's an attempted break-in, Flo. We need to report it.'

'Right, well you go back to the house and call them if you want, but I'm just going to jemmy this door open and check inside before we jump to any conclusions and alert them. We've got enough on our plates at the minute. I don't think I can face any more of their questions if nothing is missing or damaged inside.' She turns away from me and begins to pull at the large double doors.

She's right. I should wait. I'm just fearful that somebody is still wandering about the grounds, intent on doing something unthinkable to either me, Flo or the house, but I can't leave her out here on her own.

'Hang on a minute,' I say, putting the torch onto the ground, making sure the beam of light is projected our way, 'and I'll give you a hand.'

With doubled strength, it takes only a few seconds to prise them apart. They swing open with a low groan and both Flo and I stumble back. Her hand is placed over her mouth, a shriek held in place. I stumble, recoiling from the sight before me, and fall onto my backside.

My chest is tight and I feel like I can't breathe properly. Flo regains her composure and starts to walk towards the garage. I remain on the wet ground, my mind raking over who would do such a thing. And then I remember Luke and his threats, his escalating violence. His muscle-bound torso and large fists. My vision begins to attenuate and the ground rocks and tilts beneath me.

10

FLO

'It's him. He's here. He did this!' Jess's voice is a strangled sound behind me. Desperate and animalistic.

I think I might know who she's referring to but am more inclined to dispose of the dead creatures before we start apportioning blame.

'Don't touch anything! We need to let the police see them.'

I take a step back. As upset and hysterical as she is, Jess is right. We do need to make that call. I'd rather not, but I know now that we have no choice. The metallic smell of blood wafts towards me. I turn away and let out a small gasp, relieved to not have to look at the dead rabbit with its pink, glistening entrails that have been spread over the windscreen of my mother's car along with a headless pheasant that has been jammed under the wipers. And the amount of blood. It is smeared over the bonnet and across the wide windows. So much of it for two small creatures.

'Come on,' I murmur, leaning down to pull her up off the ground. 'Help me close these doors and we'll go back inside the house and call the police.'

Jess, nods and wipes at her eyes, her face and nose wet with snot and tears. 'Luke did this, I just know it.'

'We don't know anything,' I reply, hoping to God she isn't right and that it's just a deranged local who wants to exact their revenge for some imagined slight, choosing today to do it for maximum effect. Luke is a problem we can do without. 'Let's get inside in the warm and then we'll see what the police have to say, shall we?'

She takes my arm and we shuffle along together, our bodies leaning into one another for warmth and comfort. At times like this, Jess feels like a young child again and my need to protect her is so fierce, it's almost a tangible thing.

Only when we're back in Armett House with the doors locked behind us do I start to ask her what she meant by her comment.

'What makes you think it was Luke who did this?' The phone feels heavy in my palm. I sit down and move my chair closer to hers. 'Come on, Jess. Why do you think it's him?' For all that Luke was controlling and manipulative, killing the local wildlife doesn't strike me as his sort of behaviour. Luke was disgusted by the outdoors, rejecting our invitations to join us for garden parties at Armett House or snarling in disdain when we suggested treks up the hills. Clubs and pubs were more his thing. An argument at the bar over a pint of beer with anybody who dared give Jess a passing glance was more his style.

'He hit me before we broke up. Gave me a black eye. His propensity for violence was growing all the time.'

I also feel like I've been smacked as I digest what she has just told me. 'Hit you? When? I mean... fucking hell, Jess, why didn't you tell me?'

She shakes her head, more tears beginning to fall. 'I was ashamed. He told me it was my fault. I took a week off work under the pretence of having flu and then used make-up to cover it up. It wasn't the first time either. He had started grabbing and shaking me before finally lashing out and smacking me in the face.'

God, I could fucking well scream. I knew Luke was an immature arsehole but didn't know he was violent towards my sister. I hope he isn't wandering about somewhere in the grounds of Armett House because if I catch him, I might just pick up something heavy and hit him over the head with it. Violence isn't my style but for that lowlife, I'll make an exception.

I rest down on my haunches, my face close to Jess's, and take her hands in mine. 'None of what happened, and I cannot stress this enough, was your fault. You had nothing to be ashamed of. Do you hear me?'

She nods, more tears falling, dripping off her chin and onto her knee. 'And to think I hit poor Bella at the community centre. I don't know what came over me. I think it was just the shock of everything that has happened and then I snapped when she started saying those things about our father, that he was a creep and a pervert.' She sniffs and wipes at her eyes. 'So I got really angry and lashed out. Even though every word of what she said is true.'

A buzzing takes hold in my head, filling my ears and making me dizzy with dread. Not now. I can't talk about this now. I swallow hard and ignore the pulse that is thrumming in my throat.

'Right,' I murmur, standing up and pressing the buttons on the phone in one swift, decisive movement. 'I'll call the police now and we'll see what they've got to say about this.'

* * *

The two officers stand staring at the windscreen of Mother's car and the dead animals that are strewn across it.

'What time did you hear the bang?' the taller of the two officers asks.

I look at Jess and then at my watch. 'About two hours ago, I think? Definitely no longer than that.'

'And you didn't see anybody?'

'No. Jess looked round the back of the house and I checked the front. We didn't see anybody hanging around but to be fair, there are plenty of places they could hide.' I sweep my hand towards the large, wooded area behind us.

The two officers nod as they cast their gaze over the dense, wooded area and the many outhouses dotted about.

'It's him. He did it. It was Luke,' Jess says, even though I specifically told her to not say anything until the police had asked all their questions and inspected the damage.

'Luke?' the taller officer says. 'Can you tell us more about this Luke?'

'My ex-boyfriend. I'm sure he's behind this. It's got his name written all over it.'

I want to disagree vehemently but remain silent, knowing it would only cloud the issue and make us both appear slightly unhinged.

They spend the next few minutes taking down Luke's details before letting us know that the forensic team will call in the morning to check for fingerprints.

'It's unlikely they'll find any but you never know,' the smaller of them who I now know to be called PC Winter, says. 'Sometimes, these people just do it for kicks, but we'll take a look at this Luke guy for sure.'

He pulls the doors closed behind him with a dull thunk. 'Once the forensic team have been, you should clear this lot up otherwise you'll have all kinds of vermin in there feasting on it.'

We walk over the gravel track together until we reach their vehicle.

'I'm at the station in the morning on other matters but Jess will be here when the team arrive.'

PC Winter raises an eyebrow at me.

'I'm going to identify some items that we think probably belonged to my mother.'

The other officer speaks, the penny clearly dropping. 'Ah, yes of course. Mr and Mrs Hemsworth. Sorry for your loss.'

'Thank you.' I cringe inwardly at the use of that trite, overused phrase: a collection of words that cover everything but mean absolutely nothing. Lip service to the bereaved is all it is and I think I've had a gutful of hearing it over the past few weeks.

Jess smiles at them and they nod and climb into the car, the tyres of the vehicle crunching on the gravel as they reverse, turn around and drive around the back of the house to the narrow exit that leads onto the back lane.

'Coops will help us clear the car,' Jess says quietly. 'I can't see Jeff Wolf ever coming back here to help out, can you?'

'Not really. Ezra will be round mid-morning I should think, once he's called into his office and sorted out a few things.'

She nods and I notice how tired she looks, dark circles sitting under her eyes, her skin pale and lacklustre. We could all do with a break. Maybe a holiday even, after all this is over. Somewhere with endless warmth and a constant supply of exquisite food and cocktails. I should mention it tomorrow when the forensics team have left and we're feeling less fraught. I don't mind going alone when I travel but perhaps after the dreadful calamity with our parents and her encounter and subsequent break-up with Luke, Jess might be open to the suggestion of both of us going somewhere together. It's a thought I store away for tomorrow when the sun has risen, when we've both had some sleep, and the world feels like a more inviting and welcoming place to be.

11

JESSICA

Fingers of light creep into the room from under the door, slowly filtering around the edges of the heavy drapes. I have no idea what time it is but am suddenly hurled into motion at the memory of last night and the fact the forensics team could be here anytime now.

I quickly shower and get dressed, pulling my hair back into a tight ponytail, glancing in the mirror as I head to the door to make sure I don't look too ghastly. I don't look as awful as I expected but I do look pale and thin. I suppose shock can do that to a person. It will take time to claw back my life, to begin rebuilding a more positive existence without him in it. Without both of them in it. The two men who did their level best to undermine and ruin me, their corrosive behaviours stripping me of every bit of confidence I ever had.

Flo is already up and about, busying herself with making tea and toast for us both. She hands me a glass of orange juice as I pass. I take it and thank her, gulping at it gratefully. My throat is dry after drinking too much last night and not eating enough. I'm lucky I don't have a raging hangover and am just slightly inconvenienced by a mild thirst.

'If you don't mind waiting around here till they turn up to look at Mother's car, I'll head over to the station. I'm hoping it won't take too long. Once I'm back, we can start on the clear-out and go through things together and then when Ezra arrives, we can make some decisions on what to keep and what to sell.' Flo is watching me as she speaks and it's at that point I realise just how much she resembles our father with her dark eyes and full mouth. I don't know how I've missed it until now. It's as if a blindfold has been lifted and things are becoming clearer to me. I take a shaky breath and look away.

'Okay. I'll keep an eye and ear out for them arriving.' I nibble at my toast and gulp down my juice and tea, my throat still as dry as sand.

'Right, well I'm off to finish getting ready and then I'm going to head straight off to the station. I'll take my phone with me in case you need me.' Flo is her usual measured self; always calm and prepared. Ever the organiser and somebody who is full of love and wisdom while I stand in the wings, unsure what to say or do next.

When we were younger, I saw Flo's ways as overbearing. Right now, she is exactly what I need: somebody who can steer us out of choppy waters and back onto dry land. If I had been here on my own last night, I'm not sure I could have coped. I probably would have packed my things and left just minutes after getting here. The idea of Armett House is always better than the reality. In that respect, life at this place has never changed.

'Oh,' she says, turning to face me before she leaves the kitchen. 'Do you remember Mother ever mentioning anything about going on holiday abroad?'

I wrinkle my nose and shrug. 'Not sure. She may have. I know she and Father holidayed in Finland quite a few years back, and of course there was their visit to Japan.' Their leisure time dwindled to nothing in the final few years and they barely spent time together in the house, let alone on a plane in close proximity for hours at a time. 'Why do you ask?'

Flo shakes her head and smiles. 'Just curious. Actually, I found some pictures in an envelope tucked inside her book on the nightstand.'

'And?' I hold my breath, imagining pictures of Mother and Father posing and smiling together, wondering if their marital problems and the cold, distant atmosphere that was ever present in this house was all a ruse.

'Oh, it was just some photos of a villa-style house somewhere in the sun. Shuttered windows and the like. Wisteria climbing up the crumbling walls. Lots of sunshine.'

'No images of Mother or Father?'

'God no. I can't imagine that, can you?'

We both smile and roll our eyes. It's the closest we've come to discussing them in any proper detail. Even after the police contacted us to tell us about their suicide pact, we spoke rarely, Flo, Ezra and I, the shock too great to allow us to indulge in any lengthy discussions about the hows or whys of it. We all have our own stores of knowledge of what they were like. Our own damaged, charred memories. I do wonder if we will ever have a frank discussion about them. I have images of the world spinning wildly off its axis into oblivion if we ever decide to open up that particular can of worms. We've all become so insular, tucking our problems away and dealing with them on our own, that having a heart-to-heart about our parents' unexplainable and often disturbing ways would feel uncomfortable, like talking to strangers at a group therapy session. To be fair, it was our father who was the problem. I just cannot fathom why she allowed it to go on, why our mother didn't up and leave him. There were times when I blamed her as much as I blamed him, for allowing it to continue, for doing nothing when he took a stick to Ezra or when he shouted at me, calling me a stupid little bitch before dragging me by my hair into the kitchen where he slapped me until I cried. Afterwards, she would try to over-compensate by cooking us our favourite food or asking if we would like to go shopping at the weekend, offering us treats and enticements. I would rather she told us all to quickly pack a suitcase because we were leaving him, but then having been in a relationship with Luke, I can also understand how behaviour can be sluggish and insidious, creeping in slowly until it is so far advanced, you begin to wonder at what point everything changed and turned sour.

Flo disappears upstairs and I sit sipping at my tea, staring out of the window, trying to prepare myself for the forensics visit. I won't go back to the garage where our mother's car is stored. I can't face seeing that grotesque mess again. I'll wander around the house, trying to put to memory what we should sell and what we can simply bin while they dust for fingerprints that we all know won't be there. It's a formality, their visit, no more, no less. A box-ticking exercise.

A buzzing noise and accompanying music cuts into my thoughts, a familiar sound that has me searching around for my phone. I stand up and head upstairs to collect it, recalling how I read all the messages from friends last night wishing me well.

My skin flashes hot and cold when I see Luke's name and number displayed on the screen. Two missed calls. I should have blocked him but part of me feared that would make things worse. I sit staring at the screen, unsure what to do next, whether to call him back or just leave it, when it rings again.

Once more, his name flashes up. My stomach plummets. Why is he ringing me now? Our last encounter was less than friendly. He called me a bitch and leaned in towards me, his face touching mine while claiming I had flirted with one of his friends in order to make him look stupid. I had pushed him away. That was when he hit me, lashing out with his fists, and connecting with my face. On instinct,

I trail my fingers over my cheekbone, the memory of it still fresh in my mind. I left his flat that night, saying it was over and that if he ever tried to contact me again, I would call the police. I half expected him to follow me and drag me back inside but he didn't. I received numerous messages full of apologies which I duly ignored. And then just over a week later came the news that Mother and Father had taken their own lives. Contact with Luke and his empty admissions of guilt and requests for forgiveness took a back seat. But now he's back and the thought of speaking with him makes me feel sick to the pit of my stomach. Like a bad penny, he always turns up. I think of him prowling around this place last night and shut my eyes against the wave of revulsion and fear that grips me. This will be why he is calling. It will either be a warning that he plans to return or a ferocious backlash because the police have dared to question him. I answer the call on the final ring and steel myself.

'What the fuck d'you think you're playing at, you mad fucking bitch?'

I swallow and take a deep, rattling breath.

'I had the police here half an hour ago wanting to speak to me about some fucking incident at your precious Armett House. What the fuck is going on, Jess?'

A pulse pounds in my head. Despite sleeping deeply, I feel weary, my bones suddenly heavy. I haven't the strength for this. I consider hanging up but am frightened of the consequences and his possible subsequent visit and snarling seething temper. I'm caught between a rock and a hard place, unsure how to respond.

'Jess? Fucking answer me now!'

'They're questioning everyone we know. It's not just you.' I want to add, *so don't flatter yourself*, but don't want to antagonise him any further. Once Flo leaves, I'm on my own here in the house, frightened and defenceless. I can hear the rage in his voice. Luke would think nothing of smashing a window and hauling himself through ridges of broken glass to get inside to punish me.

This seems to catch him off guard, silencing him for a few seconds. I can hear him panting down the phone and am able to imagine the snaking vein that will be pulsing in his temple and the crooked delve of fury that lodges between his eyebrows when he's angry. The stale tang of his breath as he tries to swallow down his almost ever-present rage. When Luke and I met, he was the perfect gentleman – funny, engaging and polite – but as the months passed, his insecurities rose to the fore with constant accusations of me flirting or not answering his calls and deliberately avoiding him. I did all I could to placate him but my protestations seemed to make it worse. I was accused of patronising him and treating him like a child, acting like a wealthy, spoilt brat. The debutante from the big house. Whatever I did, he found ways to appear like a victim, claiming I was leading him on and living a double life, excluding him from my other activities. So I made various attempts to include him in everything I did, even introducing him to the pupils in my class and letting him speak about his career, and how if they worked really hard at school, they too could grow up to be just like him and get a good job.

'That doesn't fucking matter though, does it? I'm a police officer, for fuck's sake, Jess. You've undermined me and made me look like a fucking idiot in front of my colleagues! It's a good friggin' job I'm with a different force otherwise I wouldn't be able to show up for my next shift without looking like some lowlife fucking criminal.'

If the cap fits, then wear it.

I snap out of my reverie, my skin bristling as he speaks. Hearing him say those words out loud makes it real. Somebody who should uphold the law and yet at the same time, screams at his partner and assaults her. Realising I'm about to burst into tears at any moment, I say goodbye, end the call and block his number. Trepidation courses through me. Blocking him will send him into a near frenzy but I don't know what else to do. It's the only bit of power I have.

I long for Ezra to arrive or for Flo to hurry off to the station and come straight back as soon as possible. I don't know whether Luke is due to go to work or whether he will be off and at home. I used to know his shifts off by heart but have lost track since telling him to keep his distance. Ezra is possibly the only thing that is scaring Luke off. I used his name once to stop Luke bothering me and it seemed to work, but now since this latest event, things may just take an even uglier turn.

Do I think it really was Luke who carried out that awful grotesque act last night or was it the trauma of the day and the alcohol talking, forcing me to make wild accusations? I honestly cannot be certain. If not Luke, then who? Bella's face nudges its way into my brain. I squeeze my eyes closed and rub at my temples, battling against a migraine that is threatening to settle behind my eyes. Not Bella. That simply isn't feasible. But maybe somebody connected to her? Her son perhaps. She could have gone home and told him all about what I did to her. The more I think about it, the more it begins to make sense, the probability becoming stronger and taking a foothold in my brain. He has been excluded from school on numerous occasions and is often seen wandering the streets, hood up, shoulders hunched, and looking for trouble. I should know better than to make uneducated, rash judgements but I'm feeling nervous and jittery. Even if it wasn't Luke, I've now riled him and I'm back on his radar. Right back in the firing line.

Downstairs, I hear the back door close with a deep groan as Flo leaves for the station. I'm all alone in this big old house. I feel more frightened now than I ever did as a child. Perhaps not more frightened. Back then, at least I knew who the monster was. What I didn't know was how to avoid him.

12

JESSICA

Fear rushes through me as I sit pondering over everything. I can hear a noise coming from downstairs. It must be Flo returning. It has to be. Or perhaps it's Ezra, although it's too early for him to arrive. He said he was going to call into the office before coming here. The journey to Durham takes forty-five minutes and that's without him visiting his office and making the same journey back.

I stand up, my legs feeling as light as air, and stride over to the large picture window. I always loved this room as a child. It was my sanctuary. The view looks out over the gardens and many acres of land that Armett House sits in. When I was little, I would dream that somebody would climb the trellis to my bedroom, slip through the large window and rescue me, hoisting me over their shoulder and carrying me off to a place of safety. And now, even as I stand here, nothing has changed. Decades later and the fear is still real. The room has been tainted by the darkest of memories. As grand as the view is and as large as the room is, it's best we sell the place, leave everything behind. Let somebody else take over and start afresh. All we need for that to happen is a body.

Another sound from below. Rather than disguise creaks and

groans, Armett House's size means that every sound is amplified. With oak floors and zero insulation, the tiniest of noises can sound like a bomb exploding.

And then footsteps. Somebody is wandering about downstairs. Was Luke making that call from his car on the back lane, waiting to make an appearance once Flo was out of the picture? A swarm of angry wasps batter at my skull. My throat shrinks, my breathing becoming erratic. I tiptoe out of my room and onto the gallery landing where the sound is louder. I have nothing with which to protect myself if it is Luke who is down there, no makeshift weapons, nothing of any substance or bulk I can use to wield and scare him away.

More movement and noise. Footsteps echoing around the hallway and kitchen. Doors being opened and closed again. Somebody whistling, a melodic, pleasant tune that I instantly recognise.

Coops. Thank God. It has to be him. I know that voice, that pitch and intonation. It's definitely Coops.

The compression in my chest is released, a series of exhalations leaving my throat in a hot rush as I gallop down the stairs and into the larder where Coops is bending down, his back to me.

'You scared the life out of me!' I say, my voice more of a shriek than a greeting.

Coops jumps up and spins round, eyes wide. 'Jesus, Jessica, you scared the life out of *me*!'

We both laugh as he leans into me for a hug, pulling me back to scrutinise my face. 'You look tired, lass. And rake thin. What you been living on – grass?'

I shake my head and smile. 'Oh don't. It's bad enough having Flo telling me off for being too skinny. Don't you start!'

'Right,' he says, glancing down at a dark corner of the larder. 'Why don't you put the kettle on while I sort this out?'

'Oh, you got one?' I am both relieved and horrified in equal measure.

'Well, one dead mouse does not a summer make, but yes, I got one. Why don't you make the coffee while I check the other traps?'

I willingly back out of the area, keen to leave him to it, and fill the kettle, searching the cupboards for clean cups and saucers.

'Once I've done this, I'll go through the list of jobs that need doing. Might even get to mend that broken padlock on the shed, eh?'

I imagine Coops smiling and maybe even feeling slightly victorious that he can now go ahead and take care of things that Father refused to let him fix. That's who Coops is – a drinker of coffee, the fixer of broken things. Including people. I remember one time when Ezra had had a huge argument with our father and was ready for packing his things and leaving home even though he was only sixteen years old. Coops was the one who sat Ezra down and talked to him, giving him sage advice, and persuading him to stay, telling him that tomorrow was another day and that he'd be able to move out soon enough. He was kind, loving and caring. Everything Jackson Hemsworth wasn't.

'You won't know about what happened last night, will you?' I shout to him over my shoulder, my voice almost drowned out by the hiss of our ancient kettle.

'Last night? No. What did I miss?'

'Somebody broke into the garage and placed some dead animals on the windscreen of Mother's car. The police came out and took a statement from me and Flo. The forensics team are calling around this morning to dust for fingerprints.'

I sense Coops behind me and turn to see him looking perplexed. 'Dead animals? What the hell?'

We wait for the kettle to boil, then he takes his coffee and pulls out a chair at the table for me to sit.

'I know. Creepy, isn't it?'

'More than creepy. It's bloody criminal.' His voice is hoarse.

I wonder if he hit the whisky last night after the funeral. I visualise him sitting in his armchair in the shadows of his tiny living room, ruminating over the events of the day. I also wonder if he had an inkling of what our parents were about to do before they did it. He saw them more frequently than we did and was always around the house, tinkering with odd jobs and keeping on top of the grounds.

'Yes, well. It won't be our problem once Armett House is sold.' I sip at my coffee, wincing as it burns the roof of my mouth. 'Maybe whoever buys it will keep you on to look after it? Nobody knows this place and its grounds better than you.'

He shrugs and smiles. 'Wouldn't be the same without you lot here to keep me company. I think I'd sooner retire and be an odd-job man, picking and choosing who I work for.'

Guilt makes me woozy, along with the thought of no longer seeing Coops on a regular basis. 'I wish we could keep the house open but it's just an impossible task, with all the maintenance and running costs.'

'Ah, don't worry. Armett House will be here long after we've all gone. You've been custodians of it, is all. Time to move onto the next phase of your lives.'

We sit in companionable silence for the next few seconds, sipping at our coffee.

'It'll go, by the way. The stench, I mean,' Coops murmurs, placing his cup down next to mine. 'I'll keep calling back in the next few days to make sure all the traps are empty and once we get the last of the little buggers then the smell will start to ease off.'

'Thanks, Coops. Not sure how we'd manage without you.'

He smiles and stands up. 'Right. Off to do a few more jobs. Give me a shout if you spot any of our tiny rodent friends running about the place.'

I spot it behind him: a face staring in at the window, then a fleeting shadow as it disappears out of view. I let out a small shriek and place my hand over my mouth, shock rippling through me.

'Jess? What's up?'

Coops spins around, following my gaze, but the figure has already vanished.

'The window,' I shout. 'There was somebody standing there, staring in at us!'

Before I can say anything else, Coops runs to the back door, pulling at the handle and disappearing outside.

I stand, disorientated, too dazed to do anything. Too frightened to move. Is this how things are going to be now? Are we going to attract strangers to the house? Ghouls drawn to the place by a chilling, macabre story.

My feet refuse to work properly. Taking small steps, I shuffle towards the back door, fearful of what I might find if I head outside.

My palm is resting on the handle when Coops appears once again, his eyes dark, his brow wrinkled with confusion. 'I can't see anyone. What did they look like, this person?'

'I... I'm not sure. It was all so fast. A young guy, maybe early or mid-twenties. Dark hair and dark eyes.' I swallow and rub at my face. 'He was just standing there, staring at me. And then he was gone.'

Coops raises his eyebrows and sighs. 'Aye, well for years now I've wanted to up the security on this place, put up a higher fence and security gates, but your father would have none of it. He was more fixated on doing other jobs that didn't actually need doing. Maybe now's the time to be getting on with it.'

'With all the gossips and sightseers coming to visit after what's happened, you mean?'

A look of resignation is evident in his expression. 'I didn't want to say anything, but yes, that did cross my mind. The whole town and beyond are probably talking about it. It's not every day that...'

I reach out and touch his shoulder, taken aback at the glassy look in his eyes. This is Coops – the tough, working-class guy who rarely shows emotion. He clears his throat and steps away.

'I'm going to go for a wander around, make sure there's nobody lurking. You stay inside and keep the doors locked.'

And with that, he is gone, a purpose in his stride and a look of determination on his face as he closes the door behind him and locks it tight.

13

FLO

The forensics team are just pulling up when I arrive back at Armett House. I say team. It's actually one guy in overalls and what appears to be his young apprentice. I show them to the garage and leave them to it, then head back inside where Jess is sitting on the bottom stair looking like a frightened rabbit. Her eyes are wide, her skin pale and waxy.

'What?' I say, dumping my bag on the nearest chair. The identification process was relatively easy, if not somewhat painful. They were Mother's belongings for sure, but then I knew that before I even took a look at them. I knew it before I even got in the car.

'I saw somebody.' Her arms are wrapped around her knees, her voice a thin, trembling sound.

'Who?' I say, feeling irritated. 'Who did you see?'

'I'm not sure. Coops was in here with me and he ran outside to catch them but by that time, they'd gone. It was a young guy stood there staring in the kitchen window.'

I shrug, unperturbed by it. 'Probably some kid from the local area come to gawp at us after hearing about the suicide.' Saying it out loud causes me to shiver. It still has the power to unnerve me, the fact that both our parents chose to do what they did. I wonder if that feeling will ever dissipate. 'The back fence should have been made higher years ago. We also need cameras around the place. This house is decades behind the times. It could have been anybody, Jess, and if they had wanted to hurt you or damage the place, they would have done it already, wouldn't they?'

She doesn't reply and continues to sit like an errant schoolchild waiting to be reprimanded. Jess is easily scared. I'm not a particularly brave or hardy soul but it would take more than a rogue face staring in the window to be the undoing of me. I walk past her and then stop, remembering her fear of Luke and his unpredictable and violent ways. Guilt shrouds me for being so dismissive.

'I'm sure it's nothing to be worried about, Jess. You've got me and Coops to keep you safe. And Ezra when he gets here.'

She looks up and smiles at me, a weak attempt at masking her fears.

'Anyway,' I say a little too brightly, trying to lighten the mood, 'I'm going to get started on clearing out my old room. Why don't you do the same? You never know, we might stumble across some old things that bring the memories rushing back. I think my old Guides uniform is still hanging up in the wardrobe along with that fancy dress costume of yours that you wore to the garden fete when you were ten years old – the unicorn one. Do you remember?'

Jess musters up a weak smile and stands up. 'Yes. Your Girl Guides uniform is there but the unicorn one isn't. They threw it out shortly after I wore it.'

I stand, puzzled, trying to cast my mind back, convinced she is remembering it wrong. 'Thrown out? Why on earth would they throw it out? It was like a pink, sparkly pantomime horse. Mother spent ages making that costume and you absolutely loved it.'

'Because I ripped it to shreds the following week. I took a pair of scissors to it and tore it apart until it was no more than a pile of glittery old rags.'

The sudden look in Jess's eyes scares me. There is a darkness there. A festering hatred towards something. Or somebody. Her pupils glitter like coal. I don't reply. It's too early after the funeral and everything is still too raw to be led down this rabbit hole.

She speaks anyway, despite my silence. 'I did it to get back at them. To get back at him. I was ten years old. It was the only thing I could do, the only way I had of letting them know how much I hated him.'

My head buzzes. I don't have a reply. I don't want to reply, so instead I walk past her up the stairs into my bedroom and close the door behind me.

* * *

My duties as the elder sibling weigh heavily on me as I begin to sift through my old wardrobe. It's a huge, oak structure that fills an entire wall. Half of it is filled with my mother's clothes but many of mine are still hanging there. I spend the next hour laying everything out on the bed, keeping only a few childhood items and folding the rest up, ready to go into black plastic bags which we'll probably take to the charity shop in town. I imagine we will also need a skip to dispose of the older items. Some pieces of furniture are practically falling to bits whereas some of them are very valuable. They'll go to auction. It's only as I'm thinking this that it dawns on me what an immense task this is going to be, and if we do start sorting the house, what then? With no body, we're in limbo, unable to do anything about selling the house. The thought of the ongoing costs of keeping it running and maintaining the vast grounds and gardens weigh heavily on me.

I slump down on the bed and try to not think about it, turning my attentions instead to the items on the bedside cabinet, my fingers tracing over the photographs I discovered last night. I put them aside and leaf through a couple of small business cards: numbers for gardening companies, decorators and even a seamstress. Nothing of any great importance. They too, are set to one side. I'm just about to take another look at the photos when the landline rings. I pick up the handset next to the bed and say hello.

Nothing in return. I'm met with silence. No breathing down the mouthpiece. Nothing.

'Hello?'

A low rustling sound, then somebody hangs up. I immediately dial 1471 but the number has been withheld. That doesn't surprise me. Faces at the window. Strange phone calls. After a double suicide, we were bound to attract all the crazies and weirdos. I'm not sure how they got the number of the home telephone however, as it isn't listed, but I'm not about to waste too much time and energy worrying about it. We have plenty to keep us occupied in this place. Anybody who chooses to bother us because they have sad little lives isn't worth the effort of me thinking about it.

I spend the next few hours clearing out the wardrobe and emptying chests of drawers, stopping when I locate Mother's diaries tucked away at the back in an old shoebox. A tight band wraps itself around my head. A pulse takes hold in my jaw.

Dare I look inside and read them or would that be a huge infringement of her privacy? Mother was an avid writer when we were children – poems, short stories, once even attempting a full novel and eventually throwing it away in a fit of pique after my father read the first two pages and criticised her prose, thus curtailing her future attempts at writing a full-length book ever again.

I pick up one of the diaries and sit in the chair by the window, opening it at the first page. The words I see written there are a punch to the gut.

Dead. She is now dead and I wish he were too. I would kill him myself if I had the strength.

I take a long, unsteady breath and scan the rest of the entries. Most of them are lists of upcoming events being held at the house to try and raise money for its upkeep – a series of fetes and coffee mornings and even a wine-tasting event hosted by a local vintner. Why Mother didn't keep a separate book for these occasions and bookings is beyond me. Her diary is a haphazard combination of bookings and attempts at poetry and emotional outbursts, most of which are directed at my father.

I would leave if I could but this house is as much mine as it is his. Why should I be the one to go?

Reading it makes me feel marginally sick. We all knew our parents' marriage was less than perfect but to wish him dead? The notion that perhaps the suicide leap was my mother's idea is such an alien concept that it brings tears to my eyes. Something catches in my throat and I let out an involuntary bark. Mother was a gentle soul. Too gentle for him and his shitty, abrasive ways and too gentle to want to kill anybody, and yet here it is, her admissions written down in black and white, and in her handwriting too.

I sigh and turn over the page, and feel myself go faint, the room tilting and swaying around me.

Glued onto the page is an old, grainy photo of me, Ezra, Jessica and our father. I'm probably about twelve or thirteen years of age which would make Ezra ten and Jess about eight. We're sitting on the patio area next to the old shed round the back of the house.

Ezra and Jess, for once, are smiling and waving at whoever was taking the picture, while the faces of me and my father have been scribbled over with a thick, black, felt-tip pen, and then more horrifyingly, gouged out with the words *bastard* and *bitch* written beneath.

The room continues to sway around me. Static fills my head, a loud, wild hiss in my ears. The diary slips out of my hands and falls onto the floor with a thump.

Outside the room, I can hear a noise, everything sounding disembodied. Footsteps coming closer. Then the door bursts open and Jess is standing there, wide-eyed, mouth hanging open. I want to tell her to go away, to just give me a few moments to compose myself but don't have enough time as she suddenly runs into the room and shouts at me, her voice a frightened shriek.

'Downstairs. He's downstairs. You need to come down, Flo. Right now!'

14

FLO

'Who is downstairs?' I think of the forensics man and his young assistant and stand up to look out of the window just as they load their equipment into the car and drive away.

'Him! Bella's son. He came knocking at the back door and barged his way in when I answered.'

My stomach tightens. A pulse taps away beneath my breastbone. Something else that's been thrown our way for us to deal with. Jess swivels on her heel and disappears, galloping back down at lightning speed, turning to look my way when she is halfway to make sure I'm following.

She is standing opposite a dark-haired young lad in the main hallway when I get down there. His shoulders are hunched, hands slung deep in his pockets and she is watching him closely, panic etched into her expression. I can see the arrhythmic pitter patter of her chest through her thin sweater and notice how she is trying to control her breathing, small gasps escaping from her mouth.

'Can I help you? Antony, isn't it?'

He shrugs and glares at me, dark eyes narrowed into tiny slits.

'It's 'er I'm 'ere to see. This bitch. The one who hit me mam yesterday.'

Now it's my turn to feel afraid. He may only be a young kid but he's big enough to cause damage to both of us should he choose to. Or the house. There is plenty of cheap tat in the place but there are also some expensive effects as well. I think of the valuable ornaments and wall hanging fabrics and feel an element of fear begin to creep into the edges of my awareness. This is a Grade I listed building. Any damage incurred would require a whole lot of close guidance and a substantial sum of money to repair it.

'You look tired and hot, Antony. Would you like a drink?' I know it sounds feeble but I need to do something to break this moment, to soften him, get him on our side. 'I think we've got some food as well. Cakes and stuff. Or leftover pizza.' We have no such thing as leftover pizza but I know it's a thing that young lads enjoy. I'll cook him a bloody pizza if it stops him doing what he came here to do. I'll even order one in if I have to. I'll do whatever it takes.

'Yeah. A glass o' lemonade sounds good. Or a beer if you've got one.'

I almost laugh out loud. He is probably only sixteen years old, acting like the tough kid, asking for alcohol at ten in the morning. It would probably choke him and knock him sick.

'Come on into the kitchen, Antony. Let's see what we can muster up, eh?'

He sits down at the table and gulps down the lemonade that I give him as if he is the thirstiest person on earth. I pass him a packet of biscuits and watch as he gobbles down three in rapid succession. I find myself wondering how empty the kitchen cupboards are in his house and when the last time was that he had eaten a decent meal.

'How's your mum, Antony? I've not spoken to her for a while.'

'Pissed off is how she is. Permanently pissed off since our Katie disappeared.' He turns around and wrinkles up his nose in disgust. 'What the fuck is that smell?'

I smile and sit down opposite him. Jess hovers about behind me, pretending to wash pots and make coffee. I can sense her fear from where I'm sitting, the clumsiness of her movements and her erratic breathing a dead giveaway.

'Ah, that's rotting mice, I'm afraid. Big old houses like this often have problems with them. It's an ongoing battle keeping the rodents at bay.'

'Stinks. Don't know how you stick it. I'd rather 'ave a smaller house and no mice.'

I smile and nod and he returns the gesture, his features relaxing, revealing the gentler young lad that lies beneath the rough exterior.

'I was going to call around to see your mum today, Antony, to apologise,' Jess says, her voice taking me by surprise. She sounds more confident than I know her to be. 'As you can imagine, it was a really difficult day for me and my brother and sister. I am really, really sorry.'

'Yeah well,' he replies, scrutinising his fingers before chewing at a ragged nail and spitting it out on the kitchen floor, 'I s'pose it's not every day that people's mams and dads jump off a bridge and kill themselves, is it?'

I suppress a frown, my face set into a hardened smile. He's a young lad, lacking in social graces, uneducated in the lessons of life and how to conduct himself in public. I'll let that one pass.

'No,' I say. 'I don't suppose it is.'

There is a moment's silence before he speaks again.

'She cries all the time when she's in bed, me mam. I can hear 'er through the walls. Sometimes I go out on my bike to get away from it. Easier to ride through the streets in the dark and the cold than to lie there listening to 'er night after night.'

I sense pressure as Jess leans into me, her hands clamped on the back of my chair. She catches strands of my hair as she tightens and slackens her fingers in a rhythmic motion.

Another silence. I can hear my own heartbeat. Can feel every creak of my bones as I stand up and get the lad another glass of lemonade.

He takes it from me and drinks it down in one long gulp again, then wipes his mouth with the back of his hand.

'I 'ave to admit, I came 'ere wanting to smash you in the fucking mouth for what you did yesterday, but it doesn't feel right, hitting a woman, if yer know what I mean.' His voice is flat. No anger. No way of telling what he's going to do next.

'I know what you mean. And thank you for being so open and understanding.' I hold my breath, hoping I've said the right thing, grateful that Jess remained almost silent, allowing him to speak. Any interjections could easily have put him off his stride, sent him spiralling away in another direction. The wrong direction. A path littered with anger and violence.

'Please tell your mum how sorry I am,' Jess says softly, her voice almost a whisper. 'It's not like me to do anything like that. I don't know what came over me.'

He shrugs and stands up. 'Whatever. Anyways, gotta get going.'

I walk to the kitchen door and open it, standing to one side to let him pass.

'You gonna sell this place then, now your mam and dad are dead?'

I grit my teeth and manage another watery smile. There's no malice intended; it's how he is, this young lad whose sister disappeared, leaving their family desperate and broken. Leaving his poor mother a shadow of her former self.

'Possibly. We're going to spend a few days thinking about it.'

'Bet you could get loads of dosh if you sell some of these big pictures and ornaments, eh?'

'Probably not. I'm not sure if you knew our parents but they didn't have a lot of money. They inherited this house but didn't inherit any money to look after it.' This isn't strictly true; they were probably better off than the average householders but not immensely wealthy. I need Antony to be aware of that: that Jackson and Lydia Hemsworth were not cash rich. Part of me worries that Antony will be back with his friends in the middle of the night trying to force open old windows to get inside.

'Right, well I'm off. Good luck an' that. With selling the house and stuff, I mean.' He walks out of the door, his feet crunching on the gravel path, then stops and turns to speak again. 'I reckon she's still out there somewhere. Our Katie, that is. I think she's living it up in a big city somewhere.'

And with that, he is gone, leaving me wracked with guilt and trying to swallow down a rock-sized lump in my throat.

'It's too easy to judge,' I say, closing the door and looking at Jess, a weight of shame bearing down on me. 'He's clearly not a bad lad.'

'Just unhappy,' Jess murmurs. 'They both are, him and his mum. Unhappy and missing Katie. Where do you think she went, Flo? What happened to poor Katie?' Jess wanders back into the kitchen and sits at the table, a pensive look on her face, eyes hooded and dark with unease.

I shrug and sigh. 'I honestly don't know. She could be sofa surfing somewhere in Manchester. That's what half the people in town are saying.'

'And what about the other half? What are they saying?' Jess's eyes bore through me, her voice croaky when she eventually speaks. 'Flo, do you think that our father could have—'

'No, I don't.' I run my fingers through my hair and smooth down my crumpled clothes. 'Come on,' I bark, my voice suddenly brusque. Clipped and efficient. 'We've got a house to sort and plenty to be getting on with. The sooner we get started, the better.'

I head upstairs, my heart leapfrogging around my chest, and perch on the edge of the bed, a tidal wave of exhaustion almost knocking me flat.

15

JESSICA

Once again, we ignore the obvious, sweeping away the detritus of our lives and going about our daily business pretending that nothing is wrong. Except it is. Everything is wrong with this house and this family. Everything, and I wonder how long it will take for Flo to see that. If she ever does, that is. Her blinkers are absolute, forged out of the strongest steel.

I march up to my room, calling through to her as I pass. 'So how did it go down at the station?' I hope we can at least speak about our mother without her shutting me down on the pretence of being busy and absorbed in other more important matters. 'I take it they were her belongings, then? The reading glasses and necklace?' My voice is distant and cool. Deliberately flippant.

There is no reply and then I hear the shuffle of Flo's feet and feel her presence behind me. I turn to see her slim figure framed in the doorway of my room.

'I'm sorry. First the face at the window and then Antony's unexpected visit. They completely threw me.' Her voice has become liquified. Fluid. No more sharp edges. She comes over and sits next to me on the bed. 'Yes, they were Mother's belongings. We can't have them back yet but once they've...' She lowers her head and smiles at me.

'Once they've found her body?'

Flo nods and looks away, her gaze drawn by the view outside, by the vast, rolling lawns and manicured gardens. I think of Coops and how he will manage to keep on top if it all. I doubt Jeff Wolf will ever return and wonder if there is even enough money to continue paying Coops' salary. It's spring, and with summer on the way, everything will be coming into bloom. At least the heating bill for the house will be lower during the summer months. That's if we don't manage to sell it. A house this size with listed status that is situated in over 200 acres of land will take some selling. There won't be a property developer in the country who will want it if they can't knock it down and build 500 or more houses in its place. That's where the money lies and a listed status will curtail their plans for any new developments.

'What if they never find it? What if they never find Mother's body? What then?' My voice sounds reedy and child-like. Desperate, even. That's because I feel desperate and anxious. It's hard to disguise this level of worry. It creeps out of us unbidden, revealing itself in our features and behaviour. Other people have cracked under this level of strain.

Flo shrugs and stands up. 'I honestly don't know, Jess. I wish I had the answer to that but this is new to all of us. We'll all just have to muddle through as best we can.' She turns, bends down and gives me an uncharacteristic hug, her body rigid, her hands warm on my back.

A noise downstairs disturbs us: the sound of the front door opening and feet stamping on the mat.

'Hiya. Sorry I'm late. Got caught up in the office. Anybody fancy a warm drink before we make a start?'

Hearing Ezra's voice is like being coated in honey. He is the best of all of us. And the worst. Poor Ezra often clashed with our father, both too stubborn to back down. He was right to stand his ground. Not like me. I backed down every single time, like the coward that I am. Not that it made any difference. We both carry the scars of Father's rage.

Flo and I go down to see our brother, his face the picture of innocence, unaware of the dead creatures smeared on Mother's car, Bella's son making an unexpected visit and strangers roaming around the grounds, staring in at us through the window.

'Three cups of coffee for us?' he says, already gathering up the mugs and filling the kettle.

We sit at the table, the need to sort and clear our rooms now no longer such a pressing matter.

It takes us ten minutes to fill Ezra in on what's been happening, Flo keen to brush over the subject of me seeing a face at the window. She thinks I'm flaky and easily frightened. She's wrong. I'm tougher than she realises. I've had to be, growing up in this place with the constant feelings of anxiety that swirled in the pit of my stomach. I spent most of my childhood fighting off those feelings of darkness and being fearful of the shadows, never knowing when one of them would materialise into something tangible, its presence brimming with malice and fury.

'Do we have enough money to keep paying Coops?' I ask, thinking about overgrown gardens, broken padlocks and dead mice littered around the place.

Ezra nods and smiles at me. 'If you remember, Mother added me to her account a few months ago. She left more than enough to keep things ticking over. Not a vast amount but there's enough to keep paying Coops and enough to pay the upcoming bills till the winter.'

'And what about their shared account and Father's own bank account?' Flo says.

'I'm afraid we'll have to wait until the will has been read,' Ezra replies. 'I don't have any access to them.' His eyes cloud over. He lowers his head, his fingers clasped tightly around his mug of coffee.

There is a moment's silence. We all know the difficulties with that particular area.

'But they haven't issued a death certificate for our mother yet, have they?' I whisper. 'So we can't sell the house or do anything until that happens. The will won't be activated until they find her. Everything now hinges on the police locating her body.'

'DI Harvey has said we might be able to apply for a Presumption of Death certificate, especially in light of them finding her belongings in the river,' Flo says lightly, as if we're chatting about the weather or the price of bread. 'And besides, we can still clear things out and prepare.' Flo drains her coffee in one long slug and stares off over Ezra's shoulder.

Ezra glances at me. I inwardly roll my eyes at Flo's business-like manner and attempts at being super-efficient. He gives me a half smile and shrugs, both of us used to her competence and brusque ways.

'What about the garage and Mother's car?' I ask, the thought of having to clear it making me light-headed and slightly sick with dread. I should be used to it, having grown up with dead pheasants strung up in the large larder and rabbits caught and skinned in the kitchen for our evening meal, but the fact they have been used to desecrate our mother's car is nauseating. It makes my skin crawl.

'I'll do it.' Ezra finishes his coffee and stands up. 'I hate being in this house anyway and prefer doing jobs outside. This place makes me sick and miserable. I don't know how you two are managing to stay here.'

Both Flo and I ignore his comment. I take his cup from him and put it in the sink. 'I'll sort out the pots,' I say quickly. I guess it's the least I can do if he is going to tackle the most gruesome of jobs.

'Oh, and I meant to ask,' Ezra says as he stands up. 'What's that fucking awful smell?'

'Don't worry about that. It's only dead mice. Coops is coming later tonight to check the traps. He caught one earlier but reckons there are more to be found.'

We all go our respective ways, sorting out things around the house that need doing. Despite Ezra's words, telling us how squalid and miserable this place is, despite all the dreadful things that have happened here both recently and over the years, it feels lighter somehow, as if the heavy blanket of worry that wrapped itself around Armett House and everybody in it is starting to lift. Perhaps it's the lack of our father's presence that is making me feel this way. I even find myself humming along to the radio in the kitchen like a normal person. Like my parents only a few weeks ago didn't carry out a suicide pact, leaving us all despairing and rudderless, each of us scrambling around trying to work out what to do next.

I try to view the positives while I clean the kitchen, thinking of the fact that Luke hasn't made an appearance after his irate phone call and the fact that Antony left here satisfied. Amber is at work so I don't have her hanging around with her sideways glances and thinly disguised barbed comments. We won't have to dance around one another, talking endlessly about nothing because we don't have anything to say, our differences greater than our commonalities. How odd that her mother is more approachable and more prone to kindly chatter than she is. Perhaps Amber would do well to watch and learn.

The light that shines through the kitchen window catches my face, warming me through. I take a deep breath and tell myself that I can do this. I can get through this difficult period of my life. If

Ezra, Flo and I stick together, we can tackle it as a strong family unit. Better together than apart.

The kitchen is spotless by the time I finish, all the pots put away neatly, which seems rather pointless when we're going to clear them out sometime in the near future, but at least it passed the time, stopping me from brooding and worrying about things I can't change.

It's the scuffle of gravel that catches my attention; it's more than your average walk and different to the sound a car makes when approaching. Then I hear voices. Raised voices. Shouting.

I drop everything and run to the back door, pulling it open and dashing outside to where the sound is clearer and more pronounced. It's coming from over near the garages where Ezra is cleaning up Mother's car. Male voices raised in anger, that's what I can hear. Two male voices. Perhaps more.

My heart leaps up my throat as I break into a run and head over to the patch of land where two figures are thrashing about, their limbs locked together, their voices a collective roar of fury.

Sickness wells up in me. I know who it is, this person who is doing his damnedest to punch Ezra's lights out. I know him only too well.

'Luke!' I scream, my legs liquid when I try to speed up to reach them. 'What the hell do you think you're doing?'

My hands are slippery with sweat as I pull my phone out of my back pocket. I take a photo of my repulsive ex-boyfriend while he throws Ezra to the floor and straddles his chest, fist raised over Ezra's face. I snap the image then scream at him. 'I'm calling the police!'

His head swivels round when I shout, his eyes blazing with anger and full of fire. He stops, then squints, realising what I've done. 'Give me that fucking phone, Jess.'

I shake my head and hold it tight in my palm, my fingers trembling when I attempt and fail to call the emergency services. 'I've taken a photo of you attacking my brother. I've already uploaded it to social media. In a few minutes, half the people in Armett will see it. Now leave him the fuck alone.'

Luke clambers off Ezra and makes to stand up but my brother is too fast for him, rolling sideways, raising his fist, and punching Luke on the side of his face before he can get to his feet. Blood spurts out of Luke's nose, turning the gravel a dark-crimson colour. He drops to the ground, lets out a roar and brings his hand up to his face to stem the flow of thick, stringy blood that is oozing from both nostrils.

'Fuck, fuck, fuck!' His voice echoes around the gardens, his pitch low and tremulous.

Ezra is also caked in blood, a graze on his cheek bleeding in thin rivulets and running down his face. His shirt has been torn and his hands are smeared with red streaks.

He catches me looking and smiles. 'Don't worry, most of it is from the rabbit. I was just putting it in the bag when this arsehole turned up shouting the odds about being blamed for doing it. I told him to piss off and he threw a punch. Caught me completely unawares.' He stares down at Luke, who is still on his knees nursing his battered face, too engrossed in his own pain to take any notice of us. 'I'd forgotten what an annoying, miserable fucker he is. You're well shot of him, Jess.'

'Why don't you keep out of it?' Luke manages to say, his voice barely recognisable, thick and distorted by his injury.

Ezra steps back and directs a slow kick at Luke's ribs, not enough to do any damage but just enough to stop him talking. 'And why don't you piss off out of here, little man, eh? Get up on your feet and don't ever come back. If you do, your face will be spread all over the internet as the police officer who goes around attacking people in his spare time. Now be a good lad and fuck right off.'

I watch, stupefied, as Luke scrambles to his feet and heads around the back of the house, clambering over the fence and disappearing into the woodland beyond. I then turn my attention to Ezra, who is standing, watching me.

'What the hell, Ez? Since when did you suddenly turn into a heavyweight boxer? I had no idea.' I knew Ezra could act tough and many in the town think of him as somebody who commands a certain amount of respect, but didn't realise that his talents also included being somebody who can fight off violent intruders. Because that's all that Luke amounts to in my eyes – a deranged and vicious trespasser I once knew rather well. Too well. The thought makes me shudder.

He laughs and wipes his face with the back of his hand. 'I didn't. I just got lucky, I think. Luke is a piss-poor fighter with the strength of a lightweight.' He laughs again and sniffs. 'I'm kidding. Not sure if you noticed but he had the better of me. Probably would have kicked the shit out of me had you not turned up.'

Hysteria takes hold, mingled with shock. We both cackle like children, tears streaming down our faces, my hand leaning on Ezra's chest to keep me upright until eventually, the dam bursts and the tears come for real, my lungs feeling as if they're about to explode.

'Christ, Ezra,' I say, panting to catch my breath. 'Everything is falling apart now they're both dead. What are we going to do, Ez? What the fuck are we going to do?'

16

FLO

'So, he came here shouting the odds because he thinks that we think that he came here and killed those animals?' I dab at Ezra's face with a cotton bud and smile despite feeling both angry and desperately sad. Everything feels distorted, our lives and reputations being sucked into a gigantic sinkhole that has no end. 'That whole scenario sounds like something out of a 1970s sitcom.'

'He won't be back.' Jess is standing by the window, left hand slung in her pocket, right hand at her mouth. She furiously nibbles at a nail, biting and spitting, biting and spitting until there will be nothing left to tear at. 'I've got a picture of him hitting Ezra. I've told him that it's been posted all over social media. He'll currently be scouring every site to try and find it, terrified he's going to lose his job.'

'I hope he does. What a waste of space he is,' I mutter, not caring whether Jess still feels some weird allegiance towards him. 'He deserves to be kicked out on his skinny little arse.'

Jess smiles and goes back to biting her nails, saying nothing. An anxious expression is still etched onto her face, her eyes narrowed in near despair. We may not live together anymore but

I'm still able to see inside her head, to work out what she's thinking.

'He won't be back, don't worry,' Ezra says, his voice raspy. He winces as I try to remove a small piece of gravel from the wound. 'And even if he does, you don't wait, you call 999 straight away. Don't let him try to sweet talk you or give you one of his empty apologies. He's a wanker.'

Jess nods and gives him a watery smile.

'Right,' Ezra whispers. 'I'm back out to finish cleaning the car.' He turns and gives me a cursory nod. 'Thanks for your assistance, Miss Florence Nightingale. You're very aptly named.'

He looks so sad, like the weight of everything that has happened is about to crush him. At that point, I am overcome with an urge to lean in and hug him, but I don't. I suppress my protective streak and watch him slink past me and head back outside towards the garage. His walk and build are so much like our mother's that it pains me to watch him for any longer. I turn away and look instead at Jess. Ezra may be physically damaged but right now, she is the one who is hurting, her scars tucked away, out of view.

'I'm going to carry on clearing out as much of my old stuff as I can.'

She nods and walks with me upstairs in a silent march.

* * *

Later, after Ezra has loaded up his car with half a dozen bags of our old, unwanted belongings, ready for depositing at local charity shops, leaving with the promise of coming back in the morning to help clear the house of the many worthless items our parents collected over the years, Jess and I sit in the drawing room, wine glasses in hand, stomachs full after eating a takeaway from the local pizza shop, and ruminate over what needs to be done. It's early evening and still light outside. I sit with my feet tucked up under me, basking in the small rays of weak sunshine that are coming in from the long, south-facing window.

'It still feels surreal, doesn't it?' she says, draining her glass and refilling it to the top.

I nod and look around the room, desperate to have that difficult conversation about why they did it: what drove our parents to take their own lives in the most public and controversial of ways. The Newport Bridge is a local icon. Our parents lived in a stately home, the only one in town. A large, listed building surrounded by hundreds of acres of land. The two things together created an explosive story. Right now, local people will be sitting at home, shaking their heads, wondering what happened. Wondering how it all went so horribly wrong. I wish I knew. The worst we expected was a divorce, but then the inevitable quandary of who would get the house and who move out would ensue. Armett House originally belonged to our paternal grandfather but after our mother's parents died, she inherited their property and ploughed all the cash from its sale into Armett House's upkeep, including expensive repairs to the roof, chimney and guttering as well as replacing a whole host of rotting timbers. Maybe that's why they ended it the way they did. Maybe they reached a stalemate over Armett House and thought that jumping to their deaths in the freezing river was the only way to resolve it. As far as I can see, the messiest of divorces would have been far easier.

'Do you think they will ever find Mother's body?' Jess sounds like a small child, a deep urge welling up inside her for help and answers. Answers that I simply cannot give.

'I don't know. I hope so. I don't think I want to even—'

The sound of my mobile phone ringing cuts into my thoughts. I use it so rarely, it doesn't initially register with me and by the time I locate it, the caller has hung up. I chat to Jess as I swipe the screen, watching her face while she speaks, and feel myself go faint. When my gaze returns to my phone, the floor seems to slope beneath me, the chair doing its utmost to knock me to the ground, swirling and dipping like a carousel.

'What?' Jess says, her words coming from somewhere remote, her voice distant and ethereal. She sounds as if she is underwater, each syllable a warped gurgle in my head. 'What's the matter, Flo? You look like you've seen a ghost.'

My own voice roars in my ears when I try to answer, my throat tight and dry. I struggle to hold my phone in my palm, my fingers and hands slippery with sweat. 'It's him,' I manage to mumble. 'Somebody must have his phone.'

'Whose phone? What on earth are you talking about?'

She suddenly recoils, jumping out of her chair and backing into a corner of the room. 'Oh God. Is it him? Is it Luke? Is he on his way here?' She pulls at her hair with frantic, sharp movements. 'We need to call the police!'

I shake my head, barely able to verbalise my thoughts. That's because none of it makes any sense. Even saying it out loud makes me feel as if I've slipped into a parallel universe. 'Father's phone. Somebody has just rung me on our father's mobile phone.'

Jess stops with her wild, jerking gestures. Her mouth hangs open, her brow crinkled up in puzzlement. 'No, that can't be right. You must have made a mistake?'

I shake my head, my temples thudding. A spike of pain travels up behind my left eye.

'No mistake. His name came up on my screen. Here,' I say, handing it over if only to confirm the fact that I saw what I saw and I'm not going mad.

Jess takes my phone and swipes it with her thumb, her eyes widening in horror when she sees it. 'Fuck! What the hell is going on here?'

I try to think clearly but my head is pounding, my nerves frazzled. 'I honestly don't know. I can't think straight.'

Jess continues staring at the screen. 'Well, obviously somebody has got Father's phone and is using it to scare us.'

She must be right. After Luke and Antony's visit to the house, I now realise how many irrational, angry people there are out there. The lengths they will go to, to scare and try to knock us off balance. I snap myself out of my stupor and snatch it out of her fingers, my own hand trembling as I call the number back, waiting silently to hear who picks up. Our father is dead. His body is currently buried six feet underground. Somebody stole his phone. I just need to see who it is that thinks it's perfectly acceptable to try to frighten me by using it. I swipe and call back but it immediately goes to his answerphone. Frustrated, I try again but the same thing happens.

'Do you think...?' Jess's words trail off.

I watch her face, scrutinising her expression, waiting for her to express her thoughts and wondering if she dare speak of the unspeakable. Instead, she shakes her head and runs her fingers through her hair before returning to her default habit of chewing at her nails with such ferocity, I am tempted to lean forwards and remove her hand away from her face. The role of being the elder sibling isn't something that is easy to relinquish, the will to control and guide my younger sister always present.

'No,' I say, after waiting a couple of seconds. 'I don't think, so let's not talk about it anymore, eh?'

Her eyes widen and she stops nibbling. Her face softens, her long, fair hair like a silken mane when she rests back on the sofa.

'I'm glad we're both here, Flo. I don't think I would have settled at home on my own. Not with the thought of Luke hovering in the background, maybe even waiting outside in his car. It feels good to spend some time with you. I just wish we were in a lovely hotel somewhere and not this place.' Her eyes roam around the room before coming back to meet my gaze. 'I hate this place, you know. With a passion. I thought earlier that things here were getting better. But they're not. I really thought I could stick being here and banish those awful memories, but I don't think that I can. Every time something positive or nice happens, something horrible takes place. It's as if this house is cursed.'

'Oh, come on,' I murmur, trying to inject some levity into my tone. 'It can't be all that bad. Can it?' A breath is suspended in my chest as I wait for her to reply. As I wait for my sister to finally unload her demons, the ones I have also carried around with me for as long as I can remember. The ones I tried to protect her from. I thought I had succeeded in my mission. Obviously, I was wrong. I wonder if her memories match mine, if we saw the same things, or if she has her own store of thoughts all bubbling up inside, ready to explode at an inopportune moment.

She sighs and stares up at the ceiling. I can see that she is fighting back tears. A lump is wedged in my throat. I swallow it down and turn to face her, ready to hear what it is that she has got to say but rather than speak, Jess lowers her head, stares at the window, opens her mouth and lets out a protracted shriek that makes the hairs on the back of my neck stand on end. She turns to me, her mouth agape.

'There! He's there at the window. Call the police, Flo. We need to call the police right now!'

17

THE PARENTS

She was going to exit the river alone and he couldn't let that happen. They were supposed to do this thing together. She was as much a sinner as he was. He wasn't about to let her live while he sank to the bottom, his pockets weighed down with stones, his lungs bloated with filthy water. So he disposed of the rocks and pebbles as soon as he hit the river, clawing at them frantically before his fingers froze and he lost all co-ordination and dexterity. She had clearly already got rid of hers. That was typical of who she was. And he was purportedly the devious one, the wicked one in their marriage. What he was, however, was a stronger swimmer, but he also knew that the cold could kill them both. No matter how much effort he put into swimming his way to safety, the plunging temperature could see them both off within a matter of minutes. That is if the current didn't drag them out to sea. So he made his move, pushing her down lower and lower, making sure she didn't walk away from this, telling everyone only what she wanted them to hear, his part of the story remaining untold as she rewrote history and pointed the finger at him while he lay in his grave, cold and alone. He would do whatever it took to ensure they went to their deaths together. This was never going to be a solitary venture.

He kept his hands pressed down on her head, counting the seconds, making sure the job was carried out properly. Once he had done it, he would drag her as far down the river as he could. Far enough for her body to be carried out to the North Sea.

Something brushed against his leg. He pulled away. Although a competent swimmer, the thought of eels or some slimy, amphibious creature slithering around his limbs made him recoil. The minute he let go, she emerged out of the water, eyes and mouth wide open, gasping for breath. Shock rippled through him. He thought she was dead. All her initial thrashing and resisting had stopped. He had thought it was over and now here she was, still ready to put up a fight. Still trying to outlive him.

He lunged towards her, hands outstretched, determination coursing through his limbs. Everything was too far down the line to back out now. He had strength on his side. All she had was a steely resolve to survive, and that he could soon overpower.

His palms found their way to her neck, landing on something thin and metallic. That necklace. That stupid cheap necklace that she always wore. It was given to her by their children. The necklace he had given her, she threw away in a fit of pique. A fucking horribly expensive necklace he could ill afford by way of an apology for some long since forgotten argument, ended up in the bin, probably snarled and knotted and now in a landfill somewhere. The windows of Armett House needed fixing, the boiler needed an overhaul and at least a dozen trees were dying and in need of felling – another cost to add to the never-ending list of extortionately expensive repairs that were required for the upkeep of the house – but he spent it on a piece of jewellery for his wife which she then disregarded like an old rag.

With renewed vigour, he ripped the chain from her neck and threw it as far as he could, watching her crestfallen expression with something resembling mild happiness. True happiness would come when he watched her take her last breath and he dipped below the surface of the water, ready to follow suit. Because for all he hated her at that point, the truth was, he couldn't live without her. She was all he had known. He had had his dalliances in the past but for so many decades now, he had loved only her. Everything else was just peripheral and pointless. As he had told her on so many occasions when they spoke of this plan, they ended it together. Neither went back to Armett House without the other. They had too much to lose. Suspicions would be aroused. Tongues would wag. Secrets would come slithering out.

His focus was on her face. He was disappointed to see how much losing that fucking necklace upset her. What about his necklace? What about *him*? He then followed her gaze to where it had landed, a feeling of satisfaction ballooning in his chest, the sight of the dark water, its sheer depth and vastness, amusing him, knowing her precious locket would sink to the bottom in seconds.

A pain shot up his leg, crippling him, forcing him to topple and flail, his limbs thrashing about in the water. He felt himself being dragged under, the cold river filling his throat. This wasn't happening. He wouldn't allow it. He was the stronger of the two. He opened his mouth to take a breath but a sudden yank on his ankle forced him lower and he ended up taking in more water, his lungs ballooning. He gasped and spluttered, his head lolling from side to side as he struggled to breathe properly. He could feel her beside him, her hands pushing him down, dragging at his clothing. She was a weak swimmer. Where the hell had this sudden burst of energy and confidence come from?

With a sudden, guttural roar, he wrestled his way out of her grasp and launched his entire body at her, the two of them colliding in a freezing, slippery tangle, their limbs locked together, body temperatures now dangerously low as they slipped down into the icy depths of the river, sinking lower and lower.

18

JESSICA

By the time Flo turns to look, the face has gone and I am left acting like a hysterical woman. Somebody who can barely hold it together under pressure.

I jump out of my chair and run to the hallway with Flo in close pursuit, telling me to sit back down and not open the door to anybody.

'It's kids from the nearby houses hanging around, Jess. In case you hadn't noticed, we're currently the talk of the town. Whoever it is will have either scaled the front gates to get onto the grounds, or come through the wooded area at the back. All they need to do is leap over the low fence and the beck, and then fight their way through a few low-lying branches and bits of shrubbery and they're here at our front door.'

I spin around, suddenly incensed at being treated as if I'm stupid. 'This is the second time I've seen him, Flo. This isn't some random local child peering in the window. It's a young lad in his late teens or early twenties and although you might not be bothered about it, I am.'

The door slams into the wall when I pull it open, a flood of light filling the hallway. I'm outside and breaking into a run before Flo can stop me, my slippers providing little or no protection against the many jagged pieces of gravel that stab at the soles of my feet. The pain doesn't stop me, curiosity and anger driving me on, making me immune to the hurt and discomfort.

'Jess, there isn't anybody here!'

I carry on running regardless, ignoring her pleas for me to come back inside. Even the stabbing sensation in my feet doesn't slow me down. I'm determined to find out who this person is and what it is they want from us. Staring in once is weird, twice is unacceptable. Even if it is some random local youngster, we need to send out a message that we won't tolerate them wandering about the place, peering in windows and trying to frighten us.

The front of the house appears to be empty. I head around the back and feel my blood still, my flesh puckering with fear. A figure is standing amidst the trees, watching me. It's too dark in there for me to see their features clearly but I just know that it's him. His arms are hanging loosely by his sides and he is standing completely still.

'The police are on their way!' My voice echoes through the grounds before being swallowed up by the cracking of twigs and the rustling of leaves as he begins to move away.

I don't hesitate. I'm on the run towards the woods, the soles of my feet burning from the gravel. The pain doesn't slow me down. I have to find out who he is and why he's here.

He is way ahead of me, dodging and weaving through the bushes and shrubbery, disappearing behind a clump of trees before reappearing again, no more than a silhouette in the distance. I watch him leap and scramble up a small bank and over the low fence that should have been made secure many years ago. Still, I follow him, realising too late that the leap he made was over the beck that lies at the edge of the woods. I land in the water and stand ankle deep in it, the cold and the sludge swirling around my calves. I feel both powerless and infuriated, annoyed at my own stupidity. I played in this stretch of water as a child. I knew it like the back of my hand. I should have been prepared.

I haul myself out of the water and trudge back through the woods, a carpet of leaves and twigs announcing my noisy entry back towards the house. Flo is standing next to the old shed, arms folded, an anxious expression plastered on her face.

'He was only a kid, Jess. You should have just let him go.' She stares down at my sodden socks and damp trousers. 'Why don't you take a shower and I'll throw those clothes into the machine before they become stained.'

I'm too weary, just too bloody furious to reply, both with myself and with whoever it was that keeps on prying on us.

'Come on,' she says, ushering me inside, her arm now resting on my shoulders. 'Get yourself sorted and I'll make us a warm drink.'

* * *

The smell is worse than ever when I come back downstairs, the scent of the shower gel not nearly powerful enough to mask the stench of rotting rodents.

'I'll give Coops a call in the morning, see if he can come back out and empty the rest of the traps.'

'It's not getting any better, is it?' Flo says, sitting down opposite me at the kitchen table and handing me a cup of hot cocoa. She wrinkles her nose and sighs.

'And I'll also ask him to fit some security cameras around the place. I'll call Ezra and tell him to buy them using some of Mother's money.'

Flo sits silently. I know she doesn't agree with my decision but I'm going to do it anyway.

'I'm torn,' I murmur, my hands wrapped around the cup of cocoa for warmth, 'between going back to my flat and feeling a bit vulnerable there on my own, or staying here and having to put up with people hanging around the place and staring in through the windows.'

'Well, I'm staying put until we've cleared out as much stuff as we can,' Flo replies. 'I didn't intend to do it but now I'm here, it seems silly to be to-ing and fro-ing every day.'

'Even though we can't sell the place because we haven't got a will because Mother hasn't been declared dead.' My voice is hoarse, a thin wisp of sound that trails off into nothing.

Flo doesn't say anything in return. I'm simply stating the obvious, voicing my concerns out loud. If the police don't issue a Presumption of Death certificate, then we will be stuck in limbo indefinitely, this house slowly rotting into the ground.

I take a shuddering breath and close my eyes, unable to rid myself of the chill of the water. My feet and ankles still feel cold and my body is shivery despite having had a shower with the thermostat turned up so high, it turned my flesh a shocking shade of pink.

'We can still clear everything out while we wait, can't we?' There is an element of desperation in Flo's voice, as if she is wanting me to say something that will support her statement.

In truth, I have no idea whether we can completely clear this place of its contents. Armett House still officially belongs to our mother and father but who is going to stop us? We all have keys, as does Coops. Some of the things even belong to us: things we left here after we moved out and got our own houses.

'I suppose so,' I say, a wavering note of uncertainty in my voice.

Fatigue crashes into me, unbidden. I yawn and finish my cocoa. Before I go to bed, I want to ask Flo about earlier events: the small (when studied separately), apparently insignificant occurrences that when put together, are enough to cause me a certain amount of alarm – the face at the window, somebody ringing Flo from Father's phone, the dead birds on our mother's car. They all collide in my head. And then of course, there was Amber's warning at the funeral about our family and taking a long, hard look at who we really are and what we did. What *did* we do? I think about how our father treated us: how bad his temper was. The difference in his manner whenever he spoke to Flo. He was gentler, more understanding towards her. I wonder if she noticed. I suspect that one child was enough for him. By the time Ezra and I came along, he had had enough. We were a hindrance. A couple of youngsters who got in his way and spoilt his fun. I know that for sure because he told us often enough. But before I can gather those thoughts and put them into some sort of coherent sequence, Flo speaks, her own question taking me by surprise.

'Do you think our mother treated us all the same? Or do you think that she had a favourite child? Or one she didn't like as much as the others?'

My flesh rucks, a shiver passing over me. How odd that she should say such a thing after my thoughts about our father and how he treated us differently. I don't think I have an answer at the ready and even if I did, I'm not in the mood for a soul-baring session. Not now. Perhaps not ever. Father's strict regime knocked all emotional outbursts out of us. Crying wasn't allowed. Neither was asking questions. Or simply being in the same room as him if his mood was on a downward turn.

'I'm sure we were all the same in her eyes. Why do you ask?' Although curious, I'm quite afraid of what she might say. It's better that we say nothing than we say something indelible, something that will stay scored in our souls and hearts. Something we wish had remained unsaid. Maybe Amber was right and we do need to take a long, hard look at ourselves. Aside from a group therapy session, which is about as likely as winning the lottery, how will we ever unearth our past and find out what the problem is? Why we are so on edge and anxious all the time, as if the sky is going to come tumbling down, the world spinning off its axis into oblivion?

'It's nothing,' Flo says, straightening her posture, her usual calm and collected conduct restored.

'I think I'm going to have an early night.' I pick up my mug and carry it to the sink, tipping out the remainder of the contents and swilling it down with warm water. 'Mother loved us all equally,' I suddenly say, the words blurting out of me, 'but he didn't. He hated me and Ezra. So I guess you're lucky that way. You were spared his wrath. He used his fists on us, hitting us where nobody could see.'

I'm breathless. I didn't mean to say it. It just came out. An unplanned revelation. I don't feel lighter or easier after saying it. I feel weighted down, my body and limbs as heavy as lead.

'I'm sorry,' Flo says as I walk away. 'For everything, Jess. I'm so sorry for every damn thing.'

19

FLO

One minute, we were fine and the next, everything unravelled. How did that happen? I don't know why I'm thinking that. It was me. I made it happen. I ruined the moment with my question about Mother treating us equally. It was that photograph that did it. Seeing my face scratched out. Seeing that word scrawled underneath. Why would she have done such a thing? What on earth did I do or say to deserve it? Even if I had been a truculent teenager, did she really feel that badly about me? I feel pushed aside. Marginalised and unwanted. And I loved my mother so much. Still do.

I wish now that I hadn't asked the question. I think perhaps shock and fear must have played a part. Everything is different, my usual routine skewed and out of kilter. My usual tightly controlled demeanour smudged away by grief and anxiety. I only hope that tomorrow, everything will return to normal, that Jess and I can communicate without any barriers or nasty memories raising their head and fogging up my thoughts. Making me voice things that should remain unspoken.

Distant recollections of the arguments, the raised voices and the cries for help, filter back into my brain. For all I convinced myself that I protected my younger siblings from many things, I know that I didn't protect them from his temper. I couldn't. I was only a child myself. But at least they didn't see what I saw. At least their young, teenage friends weren't subjected to his wandering eye and crude comments. At least they didn't have to change schools to avoid the gossips after one of their friends was caught with him in his bed, his face buried into her bare neck as he whispered things into her ear. Coaxing words of encouragement. Sweet nothings and empty promises used as grooming methods to make them think he cared for them.

Pippa was only thirteen. He was in his forties. She was vulnerable and impressionable. In awe of the purportedly wealthy landowner, too frightened to say no. Too fearful of his dark-eyed stare and powerful presence to refuse his advances.

The memory of it makes my toes curl with shame. I was the one who caught them. Pippa had been staying over for a few days and was used to wandering around the house on her own, so when she went missing, I simply presumed she had decided to go for a stroll somewhere. Mother was out at a fundraising event. It was mid-morning and I was in the garden. Ezra and Jess were in town and Pippa was nowhere to be found. I searched all the outhouses, thinking she was playing a trick on me, and then went indoors to look for her. I could hear his voice, his whispers and gentle coaxing. My skin rippled with horror and disgust as I approached the bedroom, praying I was wrong, yet knowing deep down that I wasn't. I had seen the way he looked at her, giving her sly winks and flashing that smile at her, preying on her sweet nature and unassuming ways.

He should have been prosecuted but Pippa was like a tiny, frightened bird. She just wanted to flee the place. I have no idea whether anybody was ever told but I was too embarrassed to go back to school in case any whispers found their way to me, and he was only too willing to let me look for another one farther away from home, providing me with the money required to travel the extra distance. Blood money. Enough cash to make sure I didn't open my mouth. Mother didn't question it. I told her I wasn't happy where I was and she believed me. I doubt it was the first time my father had bedded a young girl and I'm almost certain it wasn't the last but I for one didn't bring any more friends home after that. How different our lives would have been if he had been discovered and prosecuted. We would have all been free of his ways and our mother would undoubtedly still be here with us.

So, I guess Jess is correct in that aspect. I was spared his temper. Ezra and Jess were not. And of course, he wasn't all bad. When his mood wasn't down in the gutter and his mind wasn't honed in on his next pubescent conquest, he could be happy and playful and brimming with ideas of what we should all do together as a family, but as I grew into myself and developed my own opinions and personality, I could see him for what he really was and found it too difficult to be carried along by his sparkling wit and charm. Those moods were often short-lived anyway and could change in the blink of an eye. And so Ezra and Jess and I lived in a constant state of alert, waiting for the moment when his mask would slip and our lives would once again descend into a form of madness. Mother tried her best but was powerless against his larger-than-life personality. Her effervescent, bubbly character paled into insignificance beside his authoritative ways and dark moods. And now he's gone, leaving us with our damaged minds and blackened memories, almost every thought we have of him stained with images of his roving eye, brooding moods and unpredictable ways.

I shower and climb into bed, doing my utmost to block him from my mind. He ruled our childhoods while he was alive and I'm damned if I'm going to let him continue ruling my thoughts after his death.

Sleep is fitful. I'm plagued with dreams of falling, sailing through the air and plunging into icy waters. I dream of sea monsters and snakes that squeeze the life out of me, wrapping their smooth bodies around my throat tighter and tighter.

I wake with a start, gasping for breath, a banging noise dragging me up out of bed. I throw on my dressing gown and stumble out onto the landing where Jess is standing, looking dishevelled and frightened.

I glance at my watch. It's 1 a.m. 'What the hell is it?'

Jess is trembling. She looks so child-like and helpless with her thin body and long, flyaway hair that I want to reach out and hug her. 'There's somebody at the door.' Her voice is a whisper. 'It's a man and he's shouting.'

Refusing to be frightened or browbeaten into submission by somebody who thinks it's acceptable to try and scare us in the early hours of the morning, I march downstairs and stand with my palm over the door handle.

'Who is it?' I try to inject as much power into my voice as possible.

Nobody replies, just more knocking and hammering.

I put on the chain, turn the key, and pull open the door a fraction, peering out into the darkness. Jeff Wolf is standing there, face contorted with fury. His hands are balled into fists and he is fidgeting, his body continually jerking and moving as if bolts of electricity are coursing through his veins, controlling his movements.

'What do you want?' My words are clipped, my voice sharp, deliberately so to keep him at bay.

In the distance, a figure approaches. Somebody moving quickly, their rapid march soon developing into a run. As much as I try to remain calm, I can feel my chest convulsing. Blood is pounding in my ears and I feel dizzy. One man I may be able to convince to leave; two poses a real problem.

Before I can tell Jess to call the police, the figure calls out, his voice carrying through the darkness.

'Jeff, for God's sake, leave them alone! Come away, man. Just leave them be.'

I clutch at the door handle, letting go for only a few seconds to rub at the pain that is travelling up the back of my neck and around to my forehead.

'Fuck off, Charlie. She's in there and we both know it.'

The roaring and pounding in my ears grows louder. I swallow and attempt to close the door, only to have it pushed open from the other side, the chain clanking in resistance.

'Jess!' I hiss, hoping she is standing close by. I don't want Jeff to hear. It will only antagonise him even further. I push my shoulder against the heavy oak, using my whole body to keep him out, and swing my head around to where I hope Jess is standing, waiting and watching. 'Call the police. Do it now!'

Outside, two voices clash, gruff, argumentative, male voices raised in anger. I close my eyes and take a breath, trying to listen to their incoherent and drunken ramblings.

'For God's sake, Jeff lad. It's just talk in the pub. Besides, it's nowt to do wi' you, is it? Get yourself home and sleep it off. Talk and gossip is all it is. You've had a pint too many and it's got the better of you.'

'Piss off, Charlie. Bella's me neighbour. Gotta say summat for her sake, haven't I?'

My stomach somersaults. *Not this again Please not this again*. It's the early hours. I haven't the energy to deal with this.

More hammering at the door. 'Open up. I know you're in there. Fucking open this door now!'

Then a scuffle. The sound of gravel being kicked around. I pluck up the courage to peer through the opening and out into the darkness. Jeff Wolf and the other man are locked together, Jeff's drunken body wobbling about as the other man grabs his arm and tries to drag him away. Jeff swings a punch and misses. He staggers and falls onto his hands and knees, letting out a stream of expletives as he hits the ground with a crack.

'She's still in there!' he roars as he is pulled to his feet and hauled away down the path. 'Katie's still there in that house. She never left and you know it!'

Inaudible mumbling as he staggers away before stopping and hollering over his shoulder. 'How's your mother's car? Get it cleaned up, did yer?'

A loud hissing sound fills my head. Him. I should have known. Why Father ever allowed him to work at Armett House is a mystery to me. Cheap labour. Cash in hand and no questions asked. It was the perfect arrangement, and if I'm being truthful, Jeff and my father were on the same level, their minds trailing in the gutter. If there was one thing our father disliked, it was people who felt themselves above him, so he gravitated to those who posed no threat to his status and his need to control and assert his authority.

Only when the pair of them are no more than specks in the distance do I dare to breathe properly, my throat and chest still constricted by fear.

I push the door closed and lock it, leaning back on the wood to try and compose myself. I refuse to ponder over his accusations, his wild, unsubstantiated accusations that hold no water, even though Katie has vanished into thin air and our family were the last people to ever see her. I will not make a connection between her disappearance and the terrible, inescapable smell in Armett House. It's not possible. Our father was a damaged, untrustworthy man. A weak man with an eye for young girls. He was a useless husband and a terrible father, one of the worst, but he wasn't a murderer.

Was he?

20

JESSICA

I can't believe what I'm seeing. Flo is rattled. Frightened, even. Her skin is pale and her hands are trembling, her fingers twitching back and forth like the beating wings of an insect that is trapped and desperate to escape. It makes me feel unnerved seeing her this way. It's a new and alien experience and if Flo can't cope with what was going on out there, then I am done for. She is the one I rely on for courage, the one who will look after me.

She stands opposite me for a second or two in complete silence.

'It was Jeff Wolf, wasn't it?' I say, his gruff voice and distinctive northern twang too obvious to miss.

She nods and heads into the drawing room, turning on a table lamp as she passes. 'Come and sit down. I'm having a drink. What about you?'

I nod and lower myself onto one of the armchairs while Flo pours us both a whisky. She goes into the kitchen and puts some ice in each glass then comes back and hands me my tumbler of amber liquid, the clink of the ice cubes against the crystal an oddly reassuring sound. I take a sip, enjoying the peaty flavour and the burn as it travels down my throat.

'He thinks our father had something to do with Katie's disappearance, then?' I say it because it needs to be said. It's long overdue. To my surprise, Flo nods. No preamble. No denials or feeble attempts to cover it up: just a simple nod of agreement. And about time too.

'She used her bank card in Manchester though, didn't she?' Flo says, her gaze roving around the room as if searching for answers, her eyes looking everywhere but at me.

'Apparently so. But then, it could have been anybody using it, couldn't it? No CCTV footage of her. Just a couple of purchases made using her card.'

A silence falls around us, both of us too fearful to voice our thoughts, the ones we've kept tucked away since she vanished.

'And I don't recall Father ever going to Manchester around that time, do you?' My voice is a whisper, laced with anxiety. As much as I hated and mistrusted him, it's hard to imagine him doing the unthinkable and then travelling all those miles to make a few small purchases in a warped attempt to cover his tracks. But then none of us ever imagined it possible that our parents would end their lives the way they did. Maybe we didn't really know either of them at all. Maybe it's time to take off our blinkers and start looking closely at what has really been going on around here.

'I honestly can't remember,' Flo replies. 'It's all such a blur in my mind. Work was manic at the time. I was up till midnight most evenings, planning and marking. The goings-on at Armett House weren't really on my radar.'

Flo is right. We all had our own lives, our own jobs and were busy socialising. Keeping an eye on this place and what the locals were up to hardly mattered to us. No more than it did for our parents to keep us informed of what was going on here. We called in from time to time but nothing stood out as different. Father had his usual mood changes and Mother flitted about the house and garden, trying to be cheerful, a smile plastered on her face in a bid to over-compensate for the frosty atmosphere.

'Oh, and it was Jeff who put the dead animals on Mother's car.'

I feel myself go hot, my cheeks and neck burning. 'Really? He admitted it?'

'More or less. He asked if we got Mother's car cleaned up. That's as good as an admission, isn't it?'

'I suppose so. Either that or he heard about it from the gossips in town.'

I think of Luke and my accusations and the trouble it will have caused him and block it out of my mind. His past behaviour made him an immediate and obvious suspect and that is his fault, not mine.

The clink of the ice in my glass echoes around the room. I can hear my own heartbeat and feel the pulse in my neck as I take another sip of whisky. I have so much to say, so many burning questions that need asking, but no starting point. Just a collection of nonsequential thoughts fighting for space in my head.

'I'll definitely ask Coops to up the security around the house. Even when we leave and go back to our own places, we don't want people wrecking Armett House, do we?'

Flo agrees and drains her drink. We might hate the place but it's a local landmark of historical interest and now it's down to us to take care of it.

'And I'll ask him to check the traps. If he doesn't find anything then maybe we call in the environmental health team. What do you think?'

Once again, she nods. I think she is too exhausted by everything to put up too much of a fight. It feels strange, me making the decisions and leading the way. Empowering. No longer the frightened child but a grown woman who is sick and tired of being browbeaten by those around her.

We finish our drinks and head up to bed, making sure the windows and doors are all locked and as secure as they can be, not realising that the morning would bring further discoveries that would make us question everything we thought we knew about Armett House and the people in it.

* * *

It feels like the first proper warm day of spring, rays of sunshine spreading through the bedroom, a pale golden hue pushing its way through a crack in the heavy drapes. I lie there, basking in its glow and stretch, the sensation of feeling properly rested a wonderful thing. I welcome it, glad to be rid of the bone-aching weariness that has doggedly trailed in my wake for the past few weeks. Even the most pressing of problems feel easier to bear after a deep sleep. And then I remember. I remember where I am, what's happened to us. What we have yet to tackle in this house. I also think of last night and the visit by Jeff Wolf. How it frightened Flo, stirring up something inside of her, stripping her of her usual inner strength. Perhaps she too has been plagued by thoughts of our father. His character flaws and weaknesses. What he was truly capable of.

The floor is warm beneath my feet as I throw back the covers and head into the shower, the blast of hot water an invigorating thing, welcoming me into the day.

Flo is already in the kitchen by the time I get downstairs. She cuts quite the matronly figure, standing at the sink, her hips swaying to and fro while she washes dishes and dries them with her usual vigour.

'There's coffee in the pot,' she says, her voice betraying neither happiness nor gloom.

I thank her and pour myself a cup, almost gagging at the smell that surrounds us. 'Soon as I've had breakfast, I'm going to call Coops about this stench. It's getting worse, don't you think?'

'If you do that, I'll start clearing out the cupboards of old food. If we get rid of it all then there won't be anything here for the little blighters to feed on.'

I sip at my coffee and nibble at a slice of toast from the plate that Flo prepared earlier. My appetite is slowly returning now that the debacle with Luke is behind me and the funeral has taken place. Perhaps the future may just prove to be brighter than I ever thought possible. All we need now is a body. Mother's body. We need to bring her home.

'Have you seen my phone, Flo?'

She nods at the counter top where it sits. I pick it up and call Coops, surprised he isn't already here at the house. Coops is an early bird, up at the crack of dawn and busying himself with the steady trickle of maintenance jobs that a house of Armett's size and age provides.

I glance at Flo, bemused. 'No answer.'

'Maybe he's having a sleep-in now that our parents aren't here. He might be slowly winding down from this place,' she says softly. 'You know, gradually extricating himself from the shackles of Armett House?'

It feels odd to not see him around and the thought of him not being here is hard to imagine. I suddenly realise that I don't like the thought of a team of strangers trailing about the place, some corporate, slick company scouring every nook and cranny, looking for faults that need addressing. It's not the house that I'm attached to. It's Coops. He's always been here. People make places and for all the darkness and fear that Father brought to this house, it was balanced and lightened somewhat by Mother and Coops constantly being around.

I try again, punching in both his mobile and landline number, but receive an answer from neither so finish my coffee and leave my half-eaten toast, then stand up and head for the back door.

'I'm going to go for a walk,' I say as casually as I can, a strange queasy feeling swirling at the base of my stomach.

Before Flo can protest, I am out of the door and heading towards the woods. The same woods the mysterious-looking figure dipped into before disappearing over the beck and out of sight. It's now daytime and the sun is filtering in through the tree-tops, small strands of warm ochre beams highlighting the carpet of foliage and twigs scattered around my feet. No reason to feel frightened or apprehensive and yet a fist of anxiety sits at the bottom of my stomach, a heavy, wieldy thing that is making me feel slightly sick.

Coops' cottage is only a few yards down the lane. I hop over the trickle of water and scramble up the side of the sludgy bank and back onto dry ground. The fence is low and most of it leaning or broken – another of Father's failures. I stride across it and am on the path of the lane in seconds and heading towards Coops' house.

His car isn't on the driveway when I get there and all the curtains and blinds are closed. Undeterred, I head around the back and am spurred on by the fact that the curtains at the windows that look out onto the back garden are not drawn. I knock on the rear door and look in through the window while waiting for an answer. Once again, I call him on my phone and once again, it cuts straight to his answer machine.

I am about to knock again when Mrs Featherstone from next door pops her head over the low fence. 'He's gone, Miss Hemsworth. Left early this morning. I saw him piling his suitcases into his car before heading off at about six o'clock.'

I'm unsure what to say or how to react, so instead, I stand there in silence as if I'm waiting for something monumental to happen. As if I'm waiting, or hoping at least, for Coops to pop his head around the corner and tell me that it's all one big misunderstanding.

'It's odd,' she continues, seemingly unaware that I have been rendered speechless by her revelation, 'because I spoke to him yesterday in passing and he didn't say anything about going anywhere but it looked like he'd packed enough to stay gone for a month or more.'

A dull thudding bangs at my skull. I place my hand on the wall to stop the ground from pulling me downwards onto its cold, hard surface. Above me, clouds obscure the sun, turning everything a dirty wash of grey.

I manage a tight smile and thank Mrs Featherstone, who looks at me with a sympathetic gaze, her eyes sweeping over me, assessing me as she speaks. 'Awful thing, wasn't it? About your parents, I mean. None of us saw that coming.'

'Thank you, and no, we really didn't.'

I make to move away but stop in my tracks when she speaks again. 'He thought a lot of you and your family, Coops did. Spoke about you all the time. He had a real soft spot for you and young Ezra, and your lovely mother. I suppose he'll miss you all and that's why he's putting this place up for sale.'

'For sale?' I spin around and glare at her. 'He's selling this cottage?' My voice cracks, a rush of my usually tightly tethered emotions spilling out.

'Aye. The estate agent was round yesterday taking photographs. I watched her stand over the lane and take some pictures of the outside, asked her what she was doing and she told me he was selling up. They've got high hopes for this old place she said. It's over 200 years old and in a conservation area, which is always a good selling point, apparently.' Mrs Featherstone glances at her own house and smiles. 'Makes me wonder what I'll get for this old place. I could sell up and move to the retirement village up the road, live off the proceeds of my house.'

I can barely speak. She continues with her one-sided conversation but I can't listen to her anymore. Her words are no more than a distant humming sound in my head. Coops didn't mention any of this when we spoke the other day. He certainly didn't say he was going off on holiday anywhere. In fact, he told me he would be back to look at the traps today.

'I think that lassie going missing really upset him as well. He was never the same after that.'

My skin frosts over. 'Katie, you mean?'

She shakes her head, eyes narrowed in bemusement. 'No, if you ask me, I reckon she's in Manchester or London or somewhere big and busy; it's just that Bella refuses to believe it. She can't get to grips with the fact that her daughter doesn't want to come home. It's the other lassie I'm on about, the one that worked at Armett House as a kitchen assistant.'

The sound of a phone ringing somewhere inside her house cuts into our discussion. Before I can say anything in return or fire a stream of questions her way, Mrs Featherstone bids her goodbyes and bustles back inside her house, closing the door behind her and leaving me standing there, dumbstruck and stricken.

21

JESSICA

I walk back to Armett House on rubbery legs, the world swimming and roiling around me. I can't find the energy to attempt to work out what Mrs Featherstone meant or why Coops has gone away without telling us. Or who the other missing girl is. My stomach remains knotted, my thoughts a dark tangle by the time I get back to the house. I step through the door, relieved to be back and yet at the same time, repulsed and sickened by the many occurrences that happened inside this place. At this moment in time, I would give anything to have grown up in a normal, loving household in one of the smaller properties outside of these grounds. Father used to tell us that we were lucky and privileged to live somewhere like Armett House but what he failed to realise was that it is the people who live in the property who make it a nice place to be. Happy, kind, thoughtful people. A house is so much more than bricks and mortar, and large, sweeping vistas of acres and acres of land. A house should be a place of love and happiness. A welcoming sanctuary, not a prison that hides many secrets.

'Any joy?' Flo's voice cuts into my thoughts.

'Hmm? Sorry, what do you mean?'

'Well, I presume you went to find Coops?'

A rhythmic pulse taps at my temple. I try to sound dismissive but it comes rushing out in a panicky stream. 'He's gone. Mrs Featherstone saw him leaving with his suitcases early this morning and now his cottage is going up for sale. I don't know what's going on, Flo. It's making me scared.'

Her laughter is light, like the trickle of water in a babbling brook, making my reaction feel unwarranted, silly and childish.

'He's probably just gone for a break somewhere, and I don't blame him. Armett House must have felt like a dead-weight round his neck at times. He practically lived here. It's about time he had a break from it all and some time to himself.'

'And the cottage?' I say, irritation bubbling up inside me at being dismissed so readily.

'Well, that's up to him. Maybe he's going to retire and move to a little flat in town?'

'But he didn't say anything to us when we last saw him, did he?'

More laughter. 'Jess, he doesn't have to tell us anything. It's his life. He's a grown man and free to do as he pleases.'

Hurt cuts through me, deep into the bone. She's right, I do know that, and yet I feel such a sense of betrayal and discomfort at his absence that I am forced to slump down into the nearest chair. I'm not sure I can muster up the strength to tell Flo about what Mrs Featherstone told me about another missing girl. Surely, we would know about it? People don't just disappear into thin air, do they? I try to convince myself that Mrs Featherstone is an old lady and confused. She's in her late eighties and prone to wild imaginings. Always has been. My main memories of her as a child are of a friendly, but gossipy woman who loved leaning over fences, exchanging titbits of information about local people. She's wrong, has become confused. I keep telling myself that because it's easier than facing up to reality. Easier than plucking my head out of the sand and looking around me at the cold, hard facts that are staring me in the face. Coops is gone and another girl with links to Armett House is missing.

'Ezra is calling over today,' Flo says, wiping her hands on a tea towel and turning to look at me, a slight look of amusement on her face. 'And I'm going to call DI Harvey, see how the search is going down by the river. If they decide to scale it back then I think we should ask about a Presumption of Death certificate.'

I nod, unable to say anything that would sound positive or helpful. The thought of Coops disappearing without any warning and another girl vanishing from Armett House all balloon in my mind, even elbowing aside thoughts of our mother. It's a stupid notion, the one that I'm considering, too outlandish to consider. I can't think about it. I won't. The two aren't connected. Coops is a gentle, sensitive man. He doesn't have an ounce of malice in him. Shame burrows beneath my skin for thinking such a thing. Perhaps Flo is right and he has decided to have a break away from everything. The fact he didn't say anything to us and promised to be back still niggles at me but I push it out of my mind. He is under no obligation to us now our parents are out of the picture, and as Flo just said, he is free to come and go as he pleases. I thought we had some sort of understanding, however. A closer relationship than somebody who just ups and leaves without a word, but that clearly isn't the case at all. We're just his employers: people he once used to know.

I heave a deep, trembling sigh, wishing it were later in the day so I could justify having a drink to calm my nerves, which are currently jangling. Mother was always a reassuring presence in this house, as was Coops, the pair of them doing what they could to counterbalance Father's seesawing moods and aggression, and now they are both gone, a void has appeared. Perhaps I should go back home today to avoid feeling their respective absences so keenly.

There is a feeling of loneliness in Armett House even though Flo is here with me. I thought that not having our father around would ease my worries but it appears that bit by bit, the usual familiarities are all falling away, leaving an exposed, raw wound beneath. So many questions and nobody around to help me work out the answers.

'I'm going to go and empty the post box,' I mumble, the sudden wave of heat that has appeared in the kitchen, choking me.

'The key is hanging up by the back door,' Flo says, her attentions now turned to emptying cupboards of their stores of crockery and piling them up on the counter top. 'I'm going to throw away the broken pots and then stack up the matching sets.'

I nod and leave her to it. Flo is far better at organising household things than I could ever hope to be. If it were left to me, I would send the whole lot off to auction and those that didn't sell would get thrown away.

A blast of cold air greets me when I step outside, the key clutched tightly in my palm. I stride towards the back of the house and then round to the side where the large, black mailbox is. A whole heap of junk mail falls out when I open the box. I sift through it all and place the unwanted items in the recycling bin, then glance at the array of envelopes that are left. Most are addressed to Mr & Mrs Hemsworth and look like bills. I'll pass them onto Ezra and he can sort them. A few look like sympathy cards, addressed to The Hemsworth Family, but one stands out from the others. It's addressed to me and is marked as confidential. My scalp prickles when I stare down at it. It's been many years since any mail has arrived for me at Armett House. For this to come amid the unexpected death of my parents is odd and mildly menacing. I think of Luke and the old snoop of a school acquaintance, Amanda MacDonald and feel a wave of panic wash over me. I don't open it. Instead, I stuff the envelope in my pocket and carry the rest of the mail back to the house. Rather than feel curious, I'm overwhelmed by a sense of panic. This is how my mind works: always assuming the worst. I'll open it later when I'm feeling more positive and receptive to whatever may be inside. I do wonder what Flo would be thinking had she collected the mail rather than me. Would she currently be haranguing me to rip it open, intrigued as to what is inside, or would she simply hand it over, completely disinterested and too caught up in what she was doing to notice or care? I'm probably making too big a deal of it. It will be something minor and inconsequential. Flo has told me in the past that I'm guilty of worrying too much about nothing and not worrying enough when it matters. I think of Luke. She was right about that. I should have spoken to somebody about his coercive and controlling ways but instead remained silent. When you're caught up in the middle of a storm, sometimes it's difficult to see through the dark clouds to the light beyond.

I stop and take a few seconds to think straight. Rather than go back to the house, I decide to take a stroll around the gardens, starting with the small orchard that was set up when I was a child. I move onto the rose garden, which Coops has kept in beautiful condition. Then I walk into an area that was out of bounds for everybody but our father. He called it his private area. His inner sanctum.

I push at the gate, which creaks in protestation, and walk through the low-lying shrubbery. I'm not sure what I expect to see, but what awaits me is less than surprising or shocking. A small lawned area is surrounded by a thin border full of flowers. A lean-to shed sits at the bottom of the area, its door slightly ajar. I'm immediately drawn to it, intrigue at what may lie inside too great to ignore.

The floor of the shed is a series of broken wooden slats. I navigate my way over them, picking my way to the large, ancient-looking cabinet in the corner.

An array of old gardening tools and implements litter the top. I ignore them, pulling out the drawers one by one. Most of them house small tools and seed packets but the bottom drawer catches my eye. It contains a book of Mother's verses. I remember her writing them and a small, local publishing company taking them on and producing a booklet full of her poems. My fingers are trembling as I pick it up and leaf through the pages. Something catches in my throat and I feel as if I have been punched, each poem, almost every word scrawled on in thick, black marker pen with the words *lying fucking bitch* and *deceitful fucking cow* written across the top. I continue leafing through, reading the words, *fucking bastards*, *evil slag* until I can't stomach any more of it and slam the booklet shut.

My heart thrums in my chest. I take the pocket-sized book and leave the shed and the small private area, closing the gate behind me with a bang, then turn back and on impulse, trample on all the flowers and dig holes in the lawn with my heel. What sort of a man would write such things? What sort of a man ignored his children, salting himself away in this small space day after day and scrawling over his wife's treasured poetry that she spent hours and hours writing? A dreadful, wicked man, that's who. Jackson Hemsworth was sometimes happy and caring but more often than not, he was an unlikeable, volatile man who controlled everyone around him, lashing out if anybody dared to defy his orders. I shouldn't be shocked at this hideous find and yet even after his demise, he still finds new and inventive ways to disgust and appal me. Myriad thoughts flood into my brain, all of them tarnished with hatred for him. I don't feel guilty or ashamed for thinking and even saying to others close to me that I'm happy and relieved, ecstatic even, that my depraved and repugnant father is finally dead.

22

FLO

Ezra and Amber march into the living room and sit on the large sofa next to the French windows. I follow and am perched on the footstool, my hands clasped over my knees, when I hear the slam of the back door. Something is different about the pair of them. They appear formal yet relaxed. On edge yet marginally excited. I can't quite put my finger on what is going on here.

'We've come to tell you both something, as well as to give a hand around the place,' Ezra says, leaning towards Amber and placing his long fingers over hers. 'I want us all to sort this place and then we can sell it. The sooner the better as far as I'm concerned.' He looks around, his mouth set in a thin, unforgiving line when his eyes rest on a photo of our father. A fleeting darkness flashes behind his eyes. He sees me watching, a slight flush creeping over his face, then clears his throat and manages a tight smile. I glance at the picture. Strange how we become blind to our surroundings. I should have cleared the place of any photos of our parents. Seeing Father's features staring out at us is a reminder of our damaged past and our present predicament. I want to hug Ezra, to let him know that it's okay to not be okay. That's he can now untether his worries and anxieties, free himself of his heavy, cumbersome burden that sits squarely on his back. But I don't. In true Hemsworth fashion, we sit rigidly and say nothing, keeping every emotion hidden, squashing them down into the darkest corners of our souls.

'Where's Jess?' he says, a slight tic taking hold under his eye.

On cue, Jessica enters the room with a flourish, her expression wild, her hair askew.

She gives us all a cursory nod and sits on a chair at the far side of the room. Something's wrong with her as well. I can't think about that right now. We can speak later, Jess and I, but for now I'm focused on Ezra and Amber, their body language and expressions making me jittery. Whatever it is they're going to say, I wish they would just come out with it. With Jess one side of me, her hands tapping away on her knees nervously, and these two with their anxious expressions, I feel completely on edge, as if something terrible is about to happen. Before I have any time to speculate further, Ezra jumps in and speaks, his voice an exuberant burst.

'We're getting married.'

I feel light-headed, like all the air has been sucked out of the room.

'Married?'

This I did not anticipate. As yet, they still don't even live together. A pregnancy would have been a shock but this has taken me completely by surprise. A thought jumps into my head. A terrible, unpalatable thought that involves Amber seeing an opportunity to have a stake in the profits of the sale of Armett House. I bat it away, that uncharitable notion. She is as good as family anyway.

'Well, that is wonderful news,' I manage to reply a little too loudly. I stand up and lean over to give the pair of them a congratulatory hug. Jess remains seated as if frozen to the spot. 'Isn't it, Jess?'

I hope that my words jolt her into motion but she continues to sit, wide-eyed, her face set into a grimace that is supposed to pass as a smile.

'Yes, absolutely,' she says through gritted teeth, tears welling up in her eyes. 'Huge congratulations to you both.'

I wonder if she is thinking of Luke and her recent break-up, this news reminding her of the hurt he caused her. News that reminds her that like me, she too is single, with no prospects of finding a close partner anytime soon. Or I wonder if it's because she and Amber have never really hit it off? Or maybe, as I first thought when he broke the news, Jess has her own financial concerns for being so reticent about this announcement.

'So when is the big day then?' I give them a wink and stretch my mouth into what I hope comes across as a warm, welcoming smile. I want to be happy for them, I really do.

Ezra pulls his mouth tight and glances at Amber before looking back at me and Jess, his eyes twinkling with happiness. 'Next week.'

'Next week? But how?' Jess says before I have a chance to formulate a coherent reply.

'We've had it planned for a while now. We were going to do it secretly but decided that since the funeral is over, it would be silly to exclude you both. We were going to tell you after the event but thought that some good news would be what we all need right now.' Ezra looks at me, his expression full of hope and longing. He wants us to be happy for him and I'm trying, I really am, but it's come as a shock.

'You were going to get married in secret so you didn't have to invite our father,' Jess says, her voice gravelly and loud, the word, *father*, spat out, as if she is attempting to remove something poisonous from her throat.

I wince and glare at her. 'Jess! What a thing to say.' Embarrassment crowds my mind, flushing my skin a deep shade of crimson. I don't want Amber being subjected to our family's many secrets and feuds.

'Oh, come on, Flo,' she barks. 'We all know it's true and we all know what he was like. I know we're not supposed to speak ill of the dead but he was a bastard and we all hated him.' It doesn't sound like Jess. Her voice is loud and dripping with venom. What happened to my quiet younger sister, the one who wouldn't ever raise her head above the parapet for fear of being shot down? Did hitting Bella act as a catalyst for her morphing into somebody different? Somebody with a propensity for bitterness and violence? I suck in my breath, my windpipe suddenly shrinking, making it difficult for me to get enough air in.

'She's right,' Ezra says. 'Maybe it's about time we started being a bit more honest about our family.'

'I... I don't know what you mean,' I say, flustered, wanting more than anything for this moment to disappear forever. I know exactly what he means and she is right on every score. I just don't want to talk about it. Not here and not now. Probably never if I'm being perfectly honest. I can feel the burn of Amber's stare. Her pupils are boring a hole into my flesh. What must she think of us, behaving like this? It's humiliating. We Hemsworths are fast becoming a parody of ourselves. A laughing stock.

'Look at this.' Jess stands and holds up a small booklet. It looks familiar. I narrow my eyes, realising that it's one of Mother's poetry books: one of the few she managed to get published. 'I found it amongst Father's things in his shed. Take a closer look.' She flicks it open and points to a series of black scribbles. I peer at it and recoil.

'We need to throw that out,' I say sharply. 'Along with anything else we find of that ilk. What's the point of keeping any of it?'

'You're right, Flo. We should throw it out,' Ezra replies. 'But we can also talk about it. No need to hide anymore or dance around the issue. They're both dead.'

His words sting, the sharpness of them, the callousness of his delivery catching me off guard. It's the humiliation I don't like, the admission that something was, or perhaps even still is, horribly awry with this house. With our family. The admission that we aren't and never will be normal.

I try to speak but the words won't come. Jess says something instead. 'Ezra is a recovering alcoholic and I'm a fucking nervous wreck and that man is the reason, Flo. How long are we going to go on pretending? Even Amber knows that there was something rotten about this family. She told me so at the funeral, didn't you, Amber?'

Ezra turns his gaze to his girlfriend, whose skin is now mottled; her pale flesh peppered with pink dots. 'Amber?' he says softly. 'What did you say?'

I'm surprised at how calm he appears to be, how reserved and in control. But then I see his foot tapping, the way his legs twitch when he speaks. He places a large hand on his knee to steady it. When Amber doesn't respond, he speaks for her, looking directly at both me and Jess.

'I've told Amber all about my childhood – our childhood – so she knows everything that there is to know. We don't have any secrets.'

'Not quite.' Amber's voice is a thin squeak, but rings clearly around the room.

My shoulders stiffen, an automatic reaction as I sit, wondering what's coming next. I want to look at Jess to see how she is bearing up but I don't seem to be able to move, my spine fused together with trepidation and dread.

'You don't know everything, Ezra,' she says, glancing at him briefly before looking away and lowering her head. 'Not quite. But I do. I probably know more about your family than you do. Armett used to be a small town when we were all growing up, more of a village really, and tongues wagged. Even living here in the big, stately home, your family couldn't hide everything. It tried and it failed. Miserably.' She lifts her head and looks directly at Jess and me.

Is she smiling? I swear I can see her mouth twitching, amusement at our dilemma evident in her countenance. Amused by the fact she thinks she has some kind of warped hold over us. I visualise myself running to where she is sitting and placing my hands around her throat, squeezing hard until her eyes bulge and her tongue lolls out.

'What,' snarls Jess, 'is the thing that our family tried to hide, Amber? What the hell is it? After all the hints you've dropped, I think we all deserve to know, don't we?'

If Ezra or Amber think as I do, that Jess's sudden flare of anger is disproportionate, neither of them says anything. Instead, Amber nods and briefly stares up at Ezra before dropping her gaze to her lap, as if preparing to unveil a piece of information that will shock us all: something immense and horribly disturbing.

'It's here in this room, the mystery I'm alluding to,' she says, lifting her head and staring right at me. 'The big secret is sitting here next to us. Flo,' she says, her voice crisp and clear and without a trace of shame or regret, 'I'm afraid you're it.' She blinks, her eyelashes fluttering wildly. I rub at my face and swallow, my cheeks suddenly hot. 'Now that your parents are gone, I thought you should hear it from me rather than from some of the old gossips in town.'

I can't breathe. My vision is blurred. I don't react, unable to do anything except sit and wait.

The silence is deafening, the ticking of the grandfather clock behind us the only sound to be heard. I want her to say something – anything – to break this moment, to take the focus off me and bring this conversation to a close, but appear to have lost the ability to speak.

I'm about to stand and leave the room when Amber finally opens her mouth and utters something that turns my little world upside down, my life as I know it, tipped about and shaken violently like a snow globe, the pieces of my life falling around me in a heavy downpour.

'Flo, I'm really sorry to tell you this but Lydia Hemsworth wasn't your natural mother. She didn't give birth to you. You may have called her Mother, but I know for sure that you're somebody else's daughter.'

23

THE PARENTS

Her eyes were open but it was impossible to see anything; the river was dark and murky, her eyes coated with grit. The recent rains had dragged sludge and silt down from the Cumbrian hills and mountains, muddying the water. Still, at least her recent visits to the local baths had served her well, the swimming lessons strengthening her confidence and helping her to hold herself steady against the powerful, raging current.

He was nowhere to be seen, their struggle at an end, sapping her of energy. Every nerve ending sparked inside her, making her aware that he could rise up at any moment and drag her back under into the filthy, freezing depths. She couldn't let that happen and at the same time, wouldn't allow herself the luxury of thinking that it was over, that he was finally gone. It was too much to hope for, the fact that her plan had worked and she had outwitted him and was still here, breathing the precious air around her.

Time had lost all meaning. All she knew was that she had to get out of the icy waters and to a place of safety before hypothermia set in. She was treading water with her limbs turning numb. If she was caught by the current in her weakened state, it could pull her under. She hadn't come this far to be foiled by her own stupidity and lack of clear planning.

She set off for the riverbank using small, smooth strokes in the hope that any passing fishermen or shift workers wouldn't see her. That's when she felt it – a tug on her foot, something pulling at her ankle. Her leg vibrated when she tried to free it; something – or someone – was yanking her downwards back into that cold, dirty water. She kicked back with all her might but the hand clasped around her ankle stayed put, its grip firm.

Fatigue expanded deep within her bones, filling every part of her body. She was trembling and shivering, but refused to give in. Not now. It was almost over. But not quite. If she gave in now, the fighting would all have been for nothing. So she let herself be dragged under, turned to face him and, using her icy fingers, reached for his eyes, pushing as hard as she could, as hard as the water would allow, its resistance slowing her down, deadening her thrust. It wasn't much but it was enough, her fingers reaching his sockets and pressing against the white, jelly-like substance of his eyeballs. He let go of her, and she watched, both horrified and relieved, as he sank to the bottom, eyes open, mouth agape, a trail of thin bubbles emerging from his slack mouth.

And then it really was over. It had finally come to an end. He was gone. After everything they had been through, his vice-like grip on her and her life had been loosened and she was free. At long last, Lydia Hemsworth was finally free. This was the beginning of the rest of her life.

24

JESSICA

Has Amber lost her mind? I feel like I'm wading through treacle when I am eventually able to get up and sit beside Flo, who is sitting rigidly, her face set like stone. My own limbs are heavy and wieldy, my body uncoordinated and lacking its usual deftness as I settle myself in place. God knows how poor Flo feels. I wish I had it in me to grab Amber and lead her out of the room with as much force as I can manage but I think that enough damage has been done to our small family unit for one day. My brother's wife-to-be has taken a wrecking ball to our already damaged lives and smashed what was left of us to pieces. As if we weren't broken enough. I can't begin to comprehend what she is saying. It's impossible. Ridiculous. Unthinkable.

'What the fuck are you talking about?' My voice is low, almost a hiss, my temper unspooling. I'm embracing this new me, the brave, fearless me who has finally found the courage to stand up to bullies and antagonistic individuals.

I expect her to apologise, to look humble, wishing she had never spoken, but she doesn't. Instead, she straightens her clothing and tucks her hair behind her ears, not a flicker of discomfiture or regret in her tone, and clears her throat before speaking.

'Look, I didn't want to say anything, and Ezra didn't know I was going to say this because I'm not even sure he knows about it, but a few people in town have now started talking about it since the death of your parents, and I was really concerned that you would all hear about it second-hand. I would have then had to lie to you all and pretend I knew nothing about it when everyone in town knows that I've known for years and years now.' She sighs and bats her eyelids. 'Believe me when I say, I've thought long and hard about saying this but gossip is now rife and a few angry locals seem intent on talking the Hemsworth family down. This whole thing with Katie going missing has really riled people.'

I can almost feel Ezra's anger as a tangible thing between us. He is sitting silently, a muscle twitching and pulsing in his jaw. He moves his body away from hers, inching away bit by bit until they are no longer touching.

'Do you not think it would've been better to talk to me about this first?' he says eventually, eyes narrowed as he watches her, scrutinising her with a definite look of disdain on his face, as if she were a lab specimen.

Only at the sound of his voice, sensing as I do, the ice in it, does she finally begin to look unnerved and panicky, fiddling with her long strands of auburn hair and shifting about on the sofa. 'I was going to but the time was never right.'

'And it is now? When we're all sitting here together, telling them our good news? What the hell are you thinking, Amber?' He is growling at her, another tic taking hold beneath his eye. He blinks and rubs at his face, his fingers pulling at the soft skin beneath his eyelashes in an attempt to control the twitching.

I grab Flo's hand and squeeze it tight, surprised at how cold it is. How still and silent she appears to be. Flo, my lovely, bossy, over-protective older sister, suddenly devoid of all emotion as she sits here, horrified by Amber's revelation. Clearly embarrassed by this new identity and status that has been thrust upon her by somebody who has stated that she knows our family better than we do. The more I think about it, the angrier I become. Fuck being reserved and frightened of conflict, and fuck my brother's wife-to-be.

'You know what, Amber?' I say, spurred on by the love I feel for Flo. 'You're a spoilt, mealy mouthed, nasty piece of work. And I don't care that you will soon be marrying my brother; as far as I'm concerned, you can take a running jump into the nearest fucking lake. You didn't tell us this because of any loyalty you feel towards us or to spare our feelings and stop us hearing it from any of the locals; you did it because it makes you feel good. Our misery fuels your sense of superiority.' I take a deep, quivering breath. 'Take your nasty snippets of filthy gossip and piss off out of here and don't bother coming back.'

My heart is pounding, perspiration coating my neck and back. I've burned my bridges now and will probably never see or hear from Ezra again but sometimes we need to choose a side. I pull Flo up and begin to walk her out of the room, our bodies melded together as she leans in to me for support, leaving Ezra and Amber behind, drowning in my spilled vat of toxic, anger-infused vomit. I stop walking and pull Flo closer to me as soon as I hear Amber's voice behind me, the words she says turning my blood to sand.

'It was a girl who worked here almost thirty years ago. Your father got her pregnant. As soon as her bump started to show, she was sent packing, your father paying for her to spend her pregnancy holed up in a hotel room somewhere down south where nobody could see her. Then once the baby was born, your parents drove there, gave her a load of money to stop her talking, and brought the baby back here,' Amber hollers after us.

Both Flo and I turn to look at her. For once, at least she has the decency to look upset and out of sorts. And alone. Ezra is up on his feet and pacing around the room, hands slung deep in his pockets, an air of menace about him.

'That was you, Flo,' Amber continues. 'That baby was you. Lydia spent months pretending to be pregnant then you appeared, but my mum worked alongside that girl and knew what was going on.'

'And told as many people as she could, no doubt?' I almost spit the words at her, unable to conceal my contempt for Amber's family, who have clearly worked hard to ruin ours. Our father was a beast. That was enough to contend with and now she is telling me there was subterfuge and lies of such a magnitude, it seems both sickening and improbable that such things could happen. I don't believe it. I won't.

'No!' Amber's eyes widen at my suggestion. 'My mum wasn't the only one who worked at Armett House back in the day. It was a rite of passage back then apparently and loads of people from town worked here. And if it makes you feel any better, my mother doesn't want me to marry Ezra so you're not the only one with family problems.'

'Amber, please stop talking, okay? Don't say another fucking word,' Ezra roars, his face creased with anger.

My pulse races. Something in his expression scares me. I can feel the tremble in Flo's hand, another thing that frightens me. Flo is always calm, measured, considerate. Sometimes flippant, never unduly alarmed or scared. And now here she is, watching Ezra closely, hanging on to me for support. Our roles have switched and I don't know what to do next, how to help her and escape this God-awful scenario.

The thud of Ezra's feet on the wooden floor ricochets through the room, bouncing off every wall. I want to tell him to sit down, to calm down, but the words get stuck in my throat. I wait with Flo, counting down the seconds until at last, Ezra speaks, every word enunciated with precision and lucidity, his voice like cut glass.

'Get up, Amber. We're leaving.'

She stands up, staggering slightly as he grabs at her hand, his touch rough and clumsy, her thin frame no match for his fury and physical strength.

Terror grips me. I try to block their exit but he pulls her along beside him, eyes dark and avoiding mine. I don't think Ezra would ever hurt Amber, or at least I hope he wouldn't, but at this moment in time, I fear for her safety. We may not be great friends but I would never want her to feel frightened or worried because of the behaviour of my brother. I know exactly how it feels to be in that position and wouldn't wish it on anyone. Not even Amber, the person who has just marched in here and ripped apart our lives just as we were trying to piece ourselves back together.

'Stay and let's talk,' I shout after them, my earlier command for her to leave pricking at me, making me feel guilty, but I'm ignored.

Amber spins around and mouths something at me before she is whisked away, the door slamming behind them and echoing throughout the whole house. It's only afterwards I realise that she was silently apologising, but it's too late now. Too late for anything and everything. I've said what needed to be said and so has Amber and now there is no way of taking any of it back.

25

FLO

I feel like a helpless child being led along by a parent, somebody who needs to be looked after while they are at their weakest and most vulnerable. Here I am being mollycoddled by my younger sister because my life as I know it has been snatched away from me and torn to shreds. If I am to believe Amber, everything I thought I knew about my identity is skewed and completely incorrect. And I think I do believe her; that's the problem. The photograph of me and my father with our faces gouged out and those insults scrawled underneath now makes perfect sense. I wasn't hers. I was foisted upon her. A rogue child. The unwanted one.

Before I can stop them or attempt to act in an upright and stoic manner, tears begin to fall. I'm not a person given to weeping and it feels alien to me. Aside from finding out about my parents' deaths, I can't remember the last time I cried. My chest and throat are sore and my face feels hot and swollen after only a few seconds. Jess hands me a tissue and I bolt upstairs, embarrassed by my feebleness, and humiliated by my sudden status of being half of the person that I was only a few minutes ago. Amber is right, I'm sure of it, and if she is right about everyone in town knowing, then I'm not sure I can face any of them ever again. I could scream and deny it and demand a DNA test but I'm not going to. It is what it is and I just need some time alone to try and come to terms with it.

I close the bedroom door and perch on the edge of the bed, my mind raking over the past, thinking about my childhood, trying to work out if there were any signs back then that I wasn't Mother's biological daughter, and can think of none. I do recall clamouring for her attention, always wanting to be by her side, and needing that sense of love to get me through the day, but isn't that what any child does? Children are remarkably astute creatures. Perhaps I picked up on the fact that I was an outlier and would have to work twice as hard for her love and affection. Ezra and Jess were closer together in age and had each other. I was the elder child and craved the company of adults, especially Mother. She was everything any child could ever want from a parent – loving, warm, attentive – and I adored her for it. So no, if I'm being perfectly honest, there weren't any signs that I was different or unloved and unwanted. Aside that is, from that photograph. Had I been rude to her that day? Or perhaps, it had been aimed at my father. I was his child, not hers. A part of him that existed in her life and not a part of her. He certainly did lots of things that could have driven her to hate me just for being his daughter. His behaviour was abhorrent.

My head aches and my back is sore, the muscles in my neck knotted. I rotate my shoulders and rub at my eyes. Time to pull myself together. Who I am now and who I thought I was until Amber's revelation doesn't change the real me, the deep inner core of me that has always existed. I have the same thoughts and values and no amount of gossip and wagging tongues of the idle-minded folk in town will ever alter that.

I brush my hair and rinse my face, shocked when I glance in the

mirror and see how pale I am. How unkempt I look. There are dark
rings under my eyes. My mouth is a thin, parched line, the skin on
my lips flaky and dry. I take a deep breath and close my eyes, a
dream filling my head. A dream of escaping all this horror that is
currently my life. I have a vision of me boarding a plane and
heading off somewhere warm and exotic. Somewhere I can escape
to, away from all this drama and heartache and stress.

The bedroom door closes with a dull hush behind me as I head
downstairs, an emptiness gnawing at my stomach now the shock
has dissipated and the immediate sickness I felt on hearing
Amber's words has settled.

Jess is sitting at the kitchen table, a piece of paper in her hand.
She is absorbed in it and doesn't hear me approach. I'm a ghost in
our midst. A half person.

'What have you got there?' I ask, doing what I can to keep my
voice light and airy. 'A letter from one of the neighbours about
Mother and Father, I suppose? We'll get plenty of condolence
cards.' I surprise myself at how calm I sound. How clear-headed
and poised I appear to be.

She jumps and stuffs it in her pocket, her face flushing pink.
Perspiration coats her top lip, small, iridescent beads of moisture
that she wipes away with shaking fingers.

'No. Sorry, yes. I meant to say yes. Just a letter saying how sorry
they are. I'll throw it away. We'll probably get loads and we can't
keep them all, can we?'

The feeling of light-headedness from earlier returns. She's
lying. I don't know what that letter contains but I do know Jess is
clearly desperate to hide it from me. Are the locals already sending
poison pen missives about my real parentage? Mother is still out
there, waiting to be found, and Father is barely cold in his grave,
and already it has started – people unleashing their bile upon us. It

would be so much less stressful to live in a small, nondescript house with an ordinary family who are too busy working and keeping a roof over their heads to do the stupid, thoughtless things that have happened here at Armett House. What we are now is a target. An object of ridicule. Our parents misbehaved and lied and now we're left to pick up the pieces of their fragmented, deceitful lives.

I would love to take the letter from her but Jess is already on her feet and stuffing it down to the bottom of the bin, making sure it's coated with old teabag and coffee stains, combined with a healthy dollop of old egg yolk. Retrieving it now would make me look ridiculous, like I don't believe her. Which I don't.

'I'll empty this while I'm here,' she says, her voice clipped. 'It's almost full and the collection is this afternoon.'

She lifts out the entire binbag and ties a knot around the top, then carries it outside and drops it into the larger wheelie bin.

Later. Once she has disappeared into her room, I'll rummage around and find it. I don't need Jess's protection from vitriolic townsfolk and I don't want to hear any more fabrications. I've had a gutful of them. I am one huge, living, breathing lie. I refuse to continue with it. We need to start being more open and honest in this house and it needs to start right now.

'I'm thinking of going home later and coming back in the morning,' I say over my shoulder, which is the truth. I hadn't planned on staying here as long as I have. It was an impromptu decision borne out of grief but I now feel it's time to distance myself from the place, to return to who I was before the police told me about my parents' deaths. Before I discovered that I'm not who I thought I was. I need some space to get my head around that fact, some time on my own to come to terms with it.

'I suppose I should do the same really,' Jess replies. She stands at the sink and washes her hands, drying them vigorously as if to rid herself of something terribly unclean that continues to cling to her skin.

'You don't have to if you don't want to. It's just something that I need to do. It's time to move on, to put some distance between me and Armett House. Too many memories, I think.'

She nods, a tacit understanding of what I'm saying passing between us. 'I get that. I might stay a bit longer or I might not. I'll see how I feel later today.'

Jess stays by my side for the remainder of the morning. She knows that I plan on rifling through the bin if she disappears out of sight. We're sorting through items in the dining room when I hear the clatter of the bin wagon rolling up the back lane and only when they make an appearance and empty it, disappearing back down the lane again, does she truly relax, her shoulders dropping, her chatter that little bit easier. Whatever was in that letter will always remain a mystery unless she chooses to tell me. Perhaps it's best I never find out. Sometimes, ignorance really is bliss.

I'm clearing out some of the clutter and Jess is humming to herself, a vague, indistinguishable tune designed to try and lift the mood, when a knock on the door rips us from our cocoon.

'I'll get it,' I say, trying to inject some cheer into my voice. I don't want to spend the rest of the day feeling flat and depressed. I'll try to fight it. It's who I am – Flo the stalwart, the woman who just keeps going against all odds. It's tiring, however, being tough and strong-minded. Just for once, I long to curl up in a ball and wish it all away.

I head to the hallway and pull open the door. Two police officers give me a tight smile, one of them showing me his ID before slipping it back in his pocket.

'You've found her?' My voice feels disembodied. This is just something else we'll have to deal with. Trauma after trauma. It seems as if there is no end to it. I hold onto the doorframe to keep my balance, visions of Mother's barely recognisable carcass filling my mind. 'You've found my mother's body?'

They glance at one another, a look of confusion passing between them, then one of the officers speaks, his voice low and serious.

'I think it's better if we talk inside?'

I step to one side to let them in and close the door, those all-too-familiar feelings of sickness and dread once again taking hold in the pit of my stomach. One step forward, two steps back. This is my life at the minute – our lives: Jess, Ezra and me – never knowing what lurks around each corner. Never knowing what nasty surprise is waiting for us in the wings.

Jess appears in the hallway, her skin pale, her eyes tapered as she stares at the two officers. 'What is it? Is it Mother? Have you found her body?'

'Let's go into the drawing room,' I murmur, leading the way, trying to fight my way through the thick fog that has suddenly obscured my vision. I blink and rub at my eyes. I am so tired of all of this. So terribly and horribly fucking tired.

We all sit down, the male officer pulling at the fabric of his too-tight trousers before lowering himself onto the chair. The female clears her throat and watches me and Jess, her mouth drawn into a tight, sympathetic line. She waits for the other, possibly more senior, experienced officer to speak, trying to look compassionate and understanding and everything a person should look when somebody is being told bad news. I wait, wanting to hear what they've got to say while simultaneously wanting to cover my eyes and ears and shut it all out.

The seconds tick by, each one giving the other awkward, surreptitious glances before finally breaking it to us: the awful, tragic news that our only brother has been involved in a car crash with his girlfriend and that their bodies are currently lying on a mortuary slab at the local morgue, waiting to be identified.

I lean back, the room spinning violently around me. I take a trembling breath in a bid to appear calm, then I close my eyes and feel myself falling...

26

JESSICA

A howling sound fills the room, reminding me of the roar of the sea on a cold winter's evening. I think back to our visits to Saltburn and Redcar as children, watching in awe as the waves bashed against the rocks and the seawall with such noise and ferocity, it had me transfixed and a little bit scared. It takes a second or so for me to realise that the roaring, howling sound is coming from Flo. I make no noise, sitting silently, unable to move. Unable to breathe properly, my reflexes stunted. I want to stand and go to her but fear the floor will fall away beneath me if I attempt to get up.

'No,' I manage to whisper after what is probably only seconds but feels much longer. 'No, no, no. You've got it wrong. There's been a mistake. He was only here a few hours ago.'

Flo continues to howl beside me, her body rocking back and forth in a rhythmic motion that puts me in mind of a clockwork doll that has had its tension wound too tightly and is stuck in this horrifically painful, rigid position, unable to slow down or stop. I want to shuffle closer to her, to put my arm around her shoulders and hold her close but don't seem to be able to move, my limbs locked solid, my mind frozen. So I wait. I wait for my older sister to stop screaming. I wait for this hideous moment to end, for everything to melt away and for somebody to step in and tell me that it's all just a bad dream. But that doesn't happen. This awful time in our lives just goes on and on and on. It's a nightmare without end.

The two police officers do what they can, offering support and telling us that a Family Liaison Office will call to see us later this evening. I nod and thank them, or at least I think I do. My mouth moves and words escape but the world around me has become a hard, rigid place, all the usual rules and norms skewed and out of kilter, and I can't be certain that what I meant to say was what came out of my mouth. I glance at Flo and think of a professional who will guide us through this torrid time. We both need the possible support a Family Liaison Office may provide. A warm smile, a shoulder to cry on. Somebody who can answer our questions and talk us through the formalities. With my usually stalwart sister struggling to cope, I feel rudderless, a lone ship trying to navigate through unchartered waters. At least after the death of our parents, we had each other. Now there is just me and Flo. Flo, my usually austere elder sister who has been reduced to somebody who no longer resembles the person she used to be – the strong, decisive, authoritative woman who took charge and helped us cope in a crisis. I'm on my own here and have no idea what I'm supposed to do next. Ezra is dead and Flo is a wreck. I need to step up, be twice the woman I was. Twice the woman I thought I could ever be. She is in there somewhere. I just need to dig deep and find her.

I show the two officers to the door and by the time I get back, Flo has calmed down. She is sitting there, looking utterly stricken, eyes pink and swollen, her face a ghastly shade of grey. Shock, a drop in blood pressure, that's possibly what is causing her deathly pallor. I make her a cup of tea with sugar and then hand her a glass of brandy. To my surprise, she drinks both, the colour gradually returning to her face.

'God, Jess, what are we going to do? I'm totally unprepared for it,' she says when she has finished. 'It's all such a terrible shock.' And then she makes me cry by apologising for being upset.

We lean into one another, the warmth of her body a reassuring thing, and sit like that for a minute or so, not speaking, just taking the time we need to come to terms with the fact that our parents and brother are dead and now there is just the two of us.

After throwing away the letter earlier in the day, I was going to tell Flo about its contents but it can wait. It could possibly prove to be too much for her. One thing at a time. We can live minute to minute if we have to. If that's what it takes to heal and make it through the day, then that's what we will do.

'Stay here with me, Flo,' I murmur, as we finally separate and move apart. 'You can't go home. Not just yet. We'll both stay here at Armett House together until things are a bit clearer.'

I'm not entirely sure what I mean by things being clearer, but I had to say something, and Flo nods at me and smiles, understanding my intentions fully. Living in separate houses at the opposite end of the town at a time like this seems silly and pointless. And awfully lonely.

'I need to know what happened,' she says, her voice croaky with grief. 'About the car crash, I mean. I need to know how it took place and why.'

I nod. We're both thinking the same thing – that Ezra's anger at Amber's revelation somehow contributed to the car colliding with something or spinning wildly out of control because he was too troubled and tormented to concentrate and keep his eyes on the road.

I tap Flo's hand. 'I'm going to run you a bath.'

She doesn't try to stop me. I head upstairs and only then do I feel the loss of my brother, the gaping void he has left in our lives. Armett House feels huge with only two of us left to fill it. The sooner we get rid of this rambling old place, the better. And at some point, I am going to have to tell Flo about that letter. But not yet. I just need some time to wrap my head around it, to comprehend what it is that Coops was trying to tell me.

The water is hot as I watch it gush into the old, ceramic tub. I sit on the edge and trail my hand through the pure white silken bubbles, wondering what the future holds for us. Wondering if there are yet more dark secrets about to emerge, crawling out of the woodwork of Armett House like venomous spiders, ready to feast on what is left of us, gnawing and biting and not stopping until they reach our bare bones.

It isn't right or fair that one family should have to endure this amount of heartache but then, life doesn't work like that. Happiness isn't doled out in equal measures and feeling sorry for myself won't solve anything. What I need to do right now is be as strong as I can be, for both me and Flo.

I call down to her that her bath is ready and watch as she trudges upstairs, her face drawn, her arms hanging limply by her sides. It pains me to see her like this. I want the old Flo back. I swallow and fight back tears. I want Ezra back and I want our mother back. I even feel more than a modicum of sympathy for Amber and for her poor mother. Christ, this is all such a fucking dreadful mess.

'Give me a call if you need anything,' I say as she enters the bathroom and begins to pull off her sweater. I step outside and close the door behind me with a muted click then stand for a few seconds until I hear the gentle movement of water as she climbs into the bathtub and settles there.

Coops' letter and the car accident swirl around my mind. I'll need to let him know about Ezra's death but don't have a forwarding address. He said he would write again. I hope he doesn't wait too long to get in touch. Since receiving his note, it's now apparent that I need to let him know sooner rather than later, especially since my suspicions about Mother have now been confirmed; suspicions that she is alive and well somewhere and didn't drown in the river that night. She is currently hiding out at an unconfirmed location waiting for Coops, her lover of many years to arrive and join her. I was right. All that time and I knew that I was right. Mother is alive and well and even as I'm thinking this, Coops is probably by her side comforting her, wondering what they're going to do next.

27

FLO

The hot water kind of soothes me, but it doesn't erase the images from my mind – images of Ezra and Amber, their lives slowly ebbing away in a twisted piece of metal, their cries unheard as they waited for somebody to help them. It doesn't erase the image of my parents struggling to breathe in the freezing, grimy water in the dead of night. It will take a lot more than a hot bath to expunge those visuals. I think perhaps only time will ever be able to do that. Years down the line, I might be able to smile and enjoy life again but right now, everything feels so far out of my reach, I may as well be on another planet. I'm not sure how I would have coped today without Jess. She's been a tower of strength. It should be the other way around. I should be the one supporting her but after Amber's disclosure, I was left weakened, my inner core already decimated. I didn't have anything left in reserve that I could draw on in order to protect myself.

'Everything okay, Flo?' Jess's voice floats in from the landing. Her soft, wonderful voice. What on earth would I do without her now?

'It's fine, Jess. I'm fine, really. I'll be out soon.'

'I'll make us a hot drink. See you downstairs.'

The shuffle of her feet across the rug followed by the all-too-familiar clip clop as she walks across the hallway and into the kitchen gives me a strong sense of comfort.

I lie there a little longer until the water cools, at which point, I climb out and dry myself, pulling on a dressing gown and tying it tightly in the middle to stop whatever is left of me from falling out. I feel completely hollow, my insides gouged away by grief and shock.

The smell of something sweet is wafting around the kitchen as I enter. Jess hands me a mug of hot chocolate which I sip at, grateful for the sugar that floods into my bloodstream, giving me an immediate hit.

'I suppose with Coops gone, we'll have to call somebody about the mice, won't we?' At this moment in time, dead rodents are the least of my problems, but there is no doubt that the smell is getting worse.

Something in Jess's expression makes me feel less than secure. Does she think I'm being uncaring, suggesting such a thing when our brother has just been fatally injured? Maybe I am.

'Or perhaps we could leave it. It's just that—'

'No, no, it's fine. You're absolutely right to suggest it,' she cuts in. 'We need to get it sorted. The smell is hideous. It's definitely getting worse.'

My eyes follow her movements: the way her face changed when I spoke about Coops' absence, the fluttering of her hands – a sign that she is nervous. Something isn't right here but I'm not sure I have the energy to probe. It's as I sip at my hot chocolate and look up to see her staring at me, her cheeks flushed, teeth nibbling at her nails again, that I know there is something wrong. Something she isn't telling me. We know each other too well to think we can put on an act and hide things, although I have to admit, Luke being violent towards her completely blindsided me.

'What?' I say, blowing on my drink and watching the tiny tendrils of steam that curl up from the cup, warming and moistening my face. 'What's wrong? I know there's something. I know you too well. I can tell when you want to say something.'

She shakes her head and smiles. 'Honestly, there's nothing. It's fine. I'm fine.'

'No you're not and no it's not,' I reply, my throat sore and constricted. 'Nothing is going to be fine for us for quite a good while yet, so let's not make it worse by keeping secrets from each other, eh? We need to stick together, you and me, Jess. It's a big, scary world out there and with a rapidly shrinking family, it's better we face that scary world together rather than alone, don't you think?'

She nods, eyes suddenly heavy with unshed tears. It's draining carrying around dark secrets. They can weigh a person down, pushing them deep into the loam.

I pull out a chair and pat it. 'Sit down and talk. I promise you, whatever it is you're going to tell me, it can't be any worse than what we've already faced, and if it is, then so what? The sky has already fallen in on our world. We may as well be squashed under it together.'

A small sob escapes as she lowers herself into the chair, her whole body beginning to tremble. I brace myself, my aching brain too befuddled to try work out what it is she is about to tell me. What can possibly be more dreadful and upsetting than losing our parents and brother in such horrific circumstances? Whatever it is, I will put on a brave face and be ready to hear it.

'He's gone to see her, Flo. Coops has gone to be with her,' is all she can say in between crying and blowing her nose, each word coming between a series of sobs and hiccups.

I consider asking who she is referring to but am sure that I already know. Maybe I've always known and closed it out of my mind, refusing to entertain the idea. It's outlandish and ridiculous and horrifying. It may also be illegal.

'Where is she?'

Jess shakes her head. 'I don't know. All he said in the letter was that our mother had contacted him and wanted to see him. It's been going on for years apparently, their affair. He apologised and said he would be in touch soon enough and that was it.'

I'm torn between feeling relieved and being angry, but if I'm honest, there are also feelings of euphoria in there too. She's alive. Our mother – she may not have given birth to me but she is still my mother – is out there somewhere.

'Do you think she even jumped?' I whisper. 'Or do you think she watched him fall and then fled the scene?' I look at Jess for answers but she shrugs.

'I don't know any of the details.' Her eyes widen, her mouth is limp with horror. 'God, I've just had a horrible thought: will we have to tell the police?'

My head pounds at the thought of it. 'I'm not sure. Let's give it some consideration before we do anything. She's clearly done this for a reason.'

'Which is?'

'She doesn't want to be found.' I place a cool hand over my forehead to alleviate the thrumming sensation there that is starting to make me feel queasy. 'And besides, what would we say? That we think she is out there somewhere and we only have the word of a man who has also disappeared?' I shake my head and sigh. 'No, let's just wait, see what happens next.'

Jess bites at her lip, her earlier show of strength now dissipating. 'Why do you think she doesn't want to be found? She could have clambered out of the water and come back here, couldn't she?'

This I don't understand. Jess is right. What or who is she hiding from? Us? Or is there something more sinister going on here? I'm suddenly struck by a possible notion. 'What if she's had some kind of breakdown? What she has gone through is traumatic. She could be struggling to cope and has got in touch with Coops because—'

Jess begins to nibble at her nails. 'Because she trusts him more than she trusts us?'

'No, I don't think that's it at all. She has her reasons; we just don't know what they are as yet.'

The knock at the door drags us out of our thoughts. Jess stands up and answers it. I can hear their low chatter and then the clip of footsteps as she leads whoever it is back into the living room.

'Flo, this is Josie, the Family Liaison Officer who wants to ask us a few questions about Ezra and Amber.'

I must look ghastly but if Josie is perturbed by my appearance, she has the good grace to not show it. Jess tells her to take a seat, asking if she would like a tea or a coffee.

'Coffee would be great if it's not too much trouble? White, no sugar.'

Jess disappears into the kitchen, leaving us sitting together, the atmosphere strained.

Josie smiles and looks around the room. 'What a fabulous period place this is,' she says softly. 'When was the house built?'

'1720, I believe. The stables and outhouses came after that but the main part of the house was built over 300 years ago.'

'It's magnificent,' she replies, her eyes travelling over every piece of furniture before coming to rest on me.

'Sorry,' I say hurriedly. 'I look a bit of a mess, I'm afraid. Not the best of days, or even weeks, as you can imagine...'

She nods and briefly dips her eyes, glancing down at her lap before looking up again as Jess comes back into the room carrying a tray that contains three mugs and a plate of biscuits.

'Here we are. Coffee, white and no sugar.' She hands one to Josie and one to me and places the tray on a nearby table. 'Help yourself to biscuits. All a bit plain, I'm afraid. We haven't had time to do any grocery shopping.'

Josie smiles. 'It's absolutely fine, no problem. A drink that's warm and wet works for me.' She takes a sip and holds the mug on her lap, clasped between both hands. 'I just wanted to ask you a few questions about your brother, if I may?'

We both nod. I tense my muscles, my spine rigid, waiting and wondering what's coming next. I don't want any graphic details. I want it to have been sudden, no long, lingering, painful death. No crying for help that didn't arrive.

'Can I ask what his mood was like after he left Armett House?'

I feel her eyes bore into me and glance at Jess, who clears her throat and puts down her coffee cup, the porcelain making a loud clunk on the table.

'Not great, I'm afraid. As you can imagine, we've all been under a great deal of pressure these past few weeks. Why do you ask?'

Josie gives us both eye contact and keeps her poise and expression friendly but neutral. The consummate professional.

'It's just that we've been given some dashcam footage from a witness,' she says, her voice soft and measured. 'And it appears that your brother and his partner were arguing in the car.'

Jess and I sit and wait for what is coming next. I count my breaths, trying to control them. Trying to stop the trapped groans and cries from finding their way out of my throat. I watch Josie's face, trying to guess what it is she is about to tell us.

'And from what we can see, he was angry, shouting at her, at which point she lashed out and slapped his face which is when he seemed to lose control of the car, missing an oncoming vehicle by only a couple of metres before colliding with a brick wall.'

An argument. A slap. A brick wall. Those words ring in my head before I squeeze my eyes shut and place my palms over my face, my trapped emotions rising from deep in my abdomen, and escaping as a muffled hiccupping sob.

28

JESSICA

'It's my fault.' Flo's eyes are heavy with grief and exhaustion. 'This is all my fault.'

I stand at the window and watch Josie's car pull away, wondering how long it will be before our dirty secrets are fully aired in public. It won't be long before the local press decide to print a seedy piece about Ezra and Amber's death. They were at least considerate enough to not put the story about our mother and father on the front page, relegating them to page four, but have since compiled numerous articles about Armett House and its past, claiming our family inherited the house by illicit means, passing each piece off as gentle humour.

'It most definitely is *not* your fault,' I say, as emphatically as I can. 'Amber was only too keen to tell us what she knew when she was here, and from all accounts, she hit Ezra while he was driving. If we're going to blame anybody, then we blame her.' I'm not sure I really mean what I just said, but I'm angry and need to find a target for my grief and fury.

We sit in silence for a few seconds. I can hear my own heartbeat thrumming in my ears, then out of the blue, Flo suddenly pipes up, 'Why you? Why did Coops write to you and not me or Ezra?'

I gulp and run my fingers through my hair. 'I don't know, really. I honestly don't know.'

I do know but don't want to alienate Flo even further. Coops and I always got on really well. I was closer to him than Flo and maybe even Ezra; that's why he addressed the letter to me. Just like our father favoured Flo, Coops favoured me but to say that at this juncture would be hurtful. Flo already feels like an outsider. I'm not about to punish her even further by pushing her out of the family circle, although at the minute, putting some distance between us and the Hemsworth family may just prove to be beneficial to both of us. Our family name feels tainted, cursed even, our torrid secrets eagerly clawing their way out of the shadows and into the light.

'We need to organise his funeral,' Flo murmurs, her eyes heavy, as if even speaking is too tiring for her.

'We need to identify his body first. I'll go. It's not a problem at all.' Flo doesn't say anything and that's when I realise, she doesn't have any fight left in her.

Ordinarily, she would bustle her way in and take charge. This new, hollowed-out Flo really scares me. I think perhaps some medical intervention might be useful but not just yet. For now, we can be content with just the two of us here. We can live life at a slow pace, take each day as it comes. Tomorrow, I will call our respective schools and let them know this latest development, tell them we'll be taking more time off, and then I can focus my attentions on looking after my sister, do what I can to make sure she doesn't deteriorate any further, either physically or mentally. We'll look out for each other from hereon in. That's just how it's going to be.

'It was her who called the other day. It was our mother on the phone. I'm sure of it,' Flo says softly. 'Somebody rang and there was silence at the other end of the line. The landline number for

Armett House isn't listed anywhere. It had to be Mother. And the call on Father's phone. That was her too, trying to communicate but being too scared to say anything.'

'You might be right. If only she had spoken. How lovely would it be to hear her voice again.' And it would too. For all the heartache her actions have caused, I would give anything just to be able to listen to her gentle tones, the sound of her soothing platitudes telling us that everything was going to be all right in our world, even if it isn't. I want those reassurances; I want to be that little girl again with somebody around to help protect me. It's like wading through thick mud having to get up and face every day not knowing what new ordeals are lying in wait for us.

I sit down and lean my head back on the sofa, a sudden fatigue hitting me hard. Flo stands and gathers up the cups and the plate, stacking them back on the tray in a messy pile. She starts to head out of the room, her movements quiet and gentle. Then a loud, piercing scream and an almighty clatter as the tray crashes to the floor, the crockery smashing into a hundred tiny pieces.

'The window!' Flo shouts. 'There's somebody staring in the window.'

I'm up on my feet and tearing out of the room, wrestling with the door handle to get outside to catch him. This time he stays put: no running off into the woods, no disappearing into the darkness. It's him. The same young guy. I didn't imagine it. It wasn't one of the locals come to gawp at us. It was him; it was always him.

'Hey!' I march over and grab his arm, not caring about his size and the fact he is clearly much stronger and way more agile than I am. 'What the hell do you think you're doing? This is private land and you're trespassing.'

He makes no attempt to flee, standing completely still, his hooded eyes surveying me with frightening precision.

'My sister,' he says, his accent heavy, his voice deep and raspy.

'She come here. She work here. She now gone. I need to know where she go.'

My head buzzes, a hissing line of static filling my ears. 'Your sister? I'm sorry but we don't have any young girls working here. We don't have anybody working here anymore. Whoever it is you're looking for, she definitely isn't at Armett House. You need to leave.'

'She no come home. I come here, look for her.'

To my horror, tears well up in his eyes. I stand frozen for a couple of seconds then soften my resolve and reach out to touch his shoulder. Flo and I have shed enough tears to drown an entire village. I can't bear to be witness to any more.

'Look, why don't you come inside for a short while? Just until you're ready to pull yourself together.' Even as I'm saying it, a loud, inescapable voice in my mind is screaming at me to not let him in. I don't know who he is or what he is capable of. He is a stranger in our midst and after what we have endured, I would do well to exercise caution and yet something in my gut is telling me he is harmless. Mrs Featherstone's words are also clanging loud and clear in my head: what she told me about another young girl going missing from here. Acid swills in my gut, scorching my innards. I should turn him away, tell him never to return. I could go back inside and pretend none of this is happening. Except it is. Armett House isn't a fortress. This thing isn't going to go away. If I ignore it, it may even get worse. He could go to the police, tell them his sister disappeared from here and with Katie's absence, alarm bells would ring and the police would arrive and scour the place.

Before I can change my mind, I find myself gesturing for him to step inside. He does so and stands in the hallway, looking around at the wide, sweeping staircase and parquet flooring, eyes wide with admiration.

'This is nice house. Very nice indeed. You work hard and make plenty money, yes?'

A hot flush inches its way up my throat, burning my face and ears. I wipe at my forehead with shaking fingers and guide him into the drawing room, keen to avoid the smell of the kitchen and the mess of the broken crockery in the living room.

'Take a seat,' I say to him, wondering if I can trust him to not pocket any small ornaments while I go and let Flo know what's going on. I berate myself for thinking such a thing and tell him I'll only be a minute while I go and get my sister. Hurt and grief has made me wary and sceptical of everything and everyone.

Flo is busy sweeping up the shattered pieces of pottery and wiping down the wooden floor when I go to fetch her.

'He's inside. We need to speak to him together, I think. He seems harmless but is convinced his sister used to work here.' I'm not sure why I'm even bringing Flo into it rather than speak with him alone except for the fact that we will have strength in numbers. 'Bring a phone just in case,' I say, nodding to Flo's mobile that is nestled amongst the cushions of the larger leather sofa.

She picks it up and follows me through to the drawing room where he is sitting, hands clasped together on his lap, the same position as when I left him.

We sit opposite, my stomach roiling with anxiety.

'This is my sister, Flo and I'm Jess.' I turn to Flo and speak softly, attempting to communicate with my facial expressions. 'This young man has come to speak to us about his sister who he believes once worked here.' I widen my eyes and then turn around to look at him.

'Yes. Is right. She work here for nice people, sending money home for long time and then all of sudden – nothing. No phone messages, no money. Nothing.'

'Right, sorry,' I say as clearly as I can. 'I didn't catch your name or the name of your sister?'

'Right, yes. I forget important information. I am Andrei and my sister is Cristina.'

'Okay, Andrei. The thing is, we don't have anybody working here now. You see, our parents died a few weeks back. Apart from us living in the house while we empty it and put it up for sale, there isn't anybody else around. Nobody cleaning or helping out in the kitchen. Not even a gardener. Nobody at all, I'm afraid.' My voice echoes around the room, a tinny, distant sound that brings more tears to his eyes.

'I am truly sorry for your loss. I only come here to ask because this is last place Cristina come to in England. She work here for a few months, then nothing. No texts. Nothing at all. My parents, they very concerned so I travel here from Romania to find out where she go.'

I sigh and ball my hands into fists, what ragged nails I have left after biting most of them to the quick, digging into my palms. What on earth am I supposed to say to this poor young man to alleviate his worries? Perhaps his sister did work here for a short while but she clearly isn't here now. I don't want to appear dismissive or cruel but I am exhausted and all out of ideas.

'Have you contacted the police?' Flo suddenly pipes up.

The small bones in my neck click and creak when I spin around to stare at her. What is she suggesting? 'The police?' I shriek, my voice loud and reedy. 'Why the police? Perhaps she just moved onto another town to find work?'

'Why not the police?' Flo replies, her voice laced with annoyance.

I want to scream at her that she knows fine well why not. Because they will come here and ask questions that we have no answers to and with all that we've got going on, that is the last thing we need. They are currently still dredging the river for a woman we now know is still alive. Our brother's body is lying on a mortuary slab after a fight with his girlfriend who revealed that half the town know about Flo's dubious parentage, and now she is seriously suggesting that this young man call the police to inform them that his sister disappeared after working here at Armett House. I realise that Flo is suffering and possibly still in shock, but has she completely lost her mind?

'No,' I say as firmly as I can. 'He doesn't need to call the police. We have enough on our plates at the minute, Flo.' I glance at Andrei, who is watching us intently, an innocence in his eyes that tugs at my heartstrings. I know only too well how it feels to lose somebody close to you. I'm not a monster but what I am is a believer in protecting what little family I have left.

'Have you asked anybody in town if they have seen her? Or perhaps put a shoutout on social media? To be honest, I don't think the police will even do anything at this point. Where was she living while she worked here, Andrei?'

'Living?' he says, surprise etched into his features as if I have asked the strangest question ever. 'Here? Cristina live here with your parents. They kindly offer her room to stay and now she is gone. As you say in your language, she disappear into thin air. Like puff of smoke, poof! Cristina, my sister, she now gone.'

29

FLO

My stomach leaps about, knotting and unknotting itself as Jess and I stand in the doorway and send poor Andrei on his way. I can feel the heat of Jess's body next to mine and am able to detect her anxiety and annoyance. I brace myself, knowing what's coming next.

'The police?' she shouts as we close the door and lock it. 'Flo, the bloody police? I mean, what were you thinking? Have we not got enough to deal with at the moment? Ezra's body is barely cold, our mother is God knows where with Coops, and not dead in the river as everyone thinks. Our father has only been in his grave for a few days and now you're seriously suggesting we get the police involved? Sorry to sound aggrieved and maybe even slightly aggressive, but what the hell?'

I shrug, unperturbed by her outburst. 'It's the right thing to do,' I say quietly, turning and shuffling off to finish clearing up the broken pieces of crockery. 'What would you suggest we do?'

'We?' she spits. '*We* aren't involved in it at all. It's not up to us to actually do anything. As much as I feel sorry for him, Andrei and his sister aren't our problem. She clearly isn't here anymore. You and I, however, have yet another funeral to organise, a body to identify and a house to clear and sell. That is, if our mother decides to stay in hiding letting everyone think she's actually dead.'

Jess is right and yet I feel driven to help that poor young man. He was clearly upset and we both know how difficult it is to live with that feeling of not knowing where a family member is. Only a few days back, I had visions of Mother being dragged out to sea by an unforgiving current, her lifeless, distended body caught up in a North Sea storm, battered about by howling winds and rain, so I know how great that sense of loss and uncertainty is, how it can take over your life.

'I'm so tired of it all,' I whisper. And I am. My head is fit to burst, crammed full of so many emotions, I feel like I can hardly breathe: grief, fear, anxiety, sorrow, shame, guilt – they are all there, vying for pole position in my brain.

'I know, I know.' Jess lowers her voice, softening her posture and features, and guiding me back into the living room. 'I know you are and I get that, I really do. And I'm sorry for shouting. Look, why don't you sit here and I'll finish clearing up,' she says, bending down and picking up the brush and dustpan before I can protest.

'I just want to help him. I want to do the right thing,' I say, my voice barely more than a whisper. Where has my usual strength gone? I feel as if a strong breeze would blow me away. Is this what shock and grief does to a person? I need to regain some energy, get my former gusto back. I don't want to spend every day floating around this house, a ghost of my former self, somebody who has no point or purpose. My mother is still my mother despite what may or may not have taken place all those years ago. Ezra is gone and although she is putting on a good show of being brave and unaffected by recent events, Jess still needs me. We need each other. I've got to get my head together and start thinking straight.

I lean down and wrap my arms around her. She stops sweeping

and turns to smile at me.

'Well, that was unexpected! Is that forgiveness for me giving you a telling off?' She laughs and waves the brush at me.

'Not sure really. I just think we need to take a deep breath and perhaps start again?'

'Yes,' she whispers, going back to the final clean up. 'You're right.' She sighs and stands up. 'If Andrei decides to go to the police, then we'll just handle it like we've handled everything else. We're made of stern stuff, you and me, Flo. And if he doesn't, then it isn't our problem and he has possibly gone elsewhere looking for her.'

I smile at her, our equilibrium once again restored. Everything isn't right with the world, but it is at least all right with us.

'I don't know about you, but I'm worn out.' She looks tired, deflated and beaten.

'You should have a nap,' I say to her. 'A small thing but it helps.'

Jess nods and takes the dustpan into the kitchen, depositing the shattered pieces into the bin with a clunk. 'Will you be okay down here on your own for a while?'

'Absolutely. You go ahead and relax a little.'

I slump down into a chair and rest my head back, thinking about Andrei's sister, thinking about our parents, and thinking and weeping for Ezra. I know I should feel sorrow for Amber but everything is still too raw, her words still tattooed into my brain. She didn't have to tell me. If we found out via other means, she could have said that she had remained silent to try and protect me. As it is, those words led them down a crooked path from which there was no return and now we're all being punished for it. She left us without our brother and for that I don't think I can forgive her. Not yet. Perhaps in time but not just yet.

The room is deathly quiet, the ticking of the old grandfather clock in the far corner the only sound to be heard. I savour the silence, thinking of where Cristina could have disappeared to. Maybe like Katie, she is one of many teenagers who simply take off, keen to leave the small-town life behind and find excitement in the big city. That's what I tell myself because it's easier. Easier than believing the other narrative that is running riot in my head. The narrative that something is terribly awry here. That our father did something unspeakable to those girls. I knew he had a penchant for younger females and remember the way he treated Ezra and Jess, how he once slapped Jess across the face for 'looking at him the wrong way' and the time he locked Ezra in the garage, refusing to allow him food for almost two days because he forgot to clean the boot room when asked. Ezra was twelve years old at the time. So if I'm being truthful, maybe our father did have it in him to do the unthinkable. If he could be that cruel to his own children, then what special torture could he inflict on people who were not part of his family?

A chill passes over me, my skin prickling. I shiver and pull a blanket off the back of the sofa, wrapping it around my legs for warmth, wondering why my father's wrath was reserved only for my younger siblings, why I escaped without any lasting scars.

Upstairs, the floorboards creak and groan as Jess moves about, reminding me that I'm not alone. Thank God for her being here with me. Armett House is too big a place for one person and still overly large for two.

I slink down into the cushions, my eyes heavy, my limbs leaden and limp. I guess shock can do that to a person and today has been a day jam-packed full of shocks and dark, inconceivably dreadful surprises. My eyes are heavy and I struggle to keep them open, sleep pulling closer and closer into its clutches.

Visions soon begin to fill my mind: dark water, people swimming peacefully while my parents thrash about, their voices raised in horror as they cry for help. Then Ezra, standing, watching on the riverbank with Amber by his side. He takes a step towards the water and with a sudden surge of energy, pushes her in and watches her sink to the bottom. I cry out but nobody sees or hears me. I cry until my voice is hoarse and my throat is sore. Then I turn, surprised by the wave of heat that hits the back of my neck, and see that I am somewhere different, somewhere that isn't the north east of England but clearly a place that has a Mediterranean feel to it. A place with rustic buildings that have shuttered windows. I glance around and see a figure in the distance walking towards me through a haze of heat, the approaching person saying something to me that I cannot hear. I call to them and hold out my arms, waving to attract their attention. And then she is there, my mother, standing directly in front of me, her features melting in the intense heat, her voice warped, her words woolly and incoherent, apart that is, from the final few utterances. 'Mine, Flo. Always be mine.'

I sit up, my head pounding, eyes gritty, and rub at my face. I know then at that moment, where she is. Those photographs, a memory resurfacing. It all begins to make sense. A memory of Mother telling me how she would love to buy a small villa in Malta, a place she visited as a youngster and immediately fell in love with. Father refused to go there. Father refused most things, sometimes out of spite but mainly because he liked to control people. It was his way or no way. But for years, Mother used to reminisce about that childhood holiday, chatting to me and Ezra and Jess about how one day, she would go back there. And now she has. I know it for sure. Our mother is in Valletta in Malta and if my instincts are correct, Coops is also there with her.

I drag myself out of my state of inertia and run upstairs as fast as my weakened legs will allow, banging on the bedroom door once I'm up there, hollering through to Jess with a dry, husky voice.

'I've found her, Jess. I've found our mother. I know exactly where she is.'

30

LYDIA

She peers out from a crack in the doorframe and sees his silhouette stretched out over the sun-dappled, cobbled street, the shape of him speeding up her heart, pushing it around her chest with such strength and ferocity, she feels sure it will burst out of her chest at any given moment.

The door gives a quiet groan as she pushes it open a fraction, careful to not show her face, stepping back instead to one side to let him pass. Only when it is closed and locked behind him do they embrace, their bodies melding into one, arms firmly clasped around one another's necks.

'You made it. You're here,' is all she can say, her voice weak with relief. 'You're actually here.'

He gives her a long, lingering kiss, his whiskers rubbing against her skin.

'I left early. An hour's drive to the airport and an easy, three-hour flight and here I am.'

'Here you are,' she replies, nuzzling her face into his chest, his familiar scent making her woozy with happiness and relief.

He drags his case out of the living room, up the stairs and hauls it up onto the bed. She stands behind him, watching his movements, scrutinising his face for any signs of reticence. She shrugs that thought away. He wouldn't be here if he had had any second thoughts. He has done it; he's risked the clacking tongues of locals and finally joined her.

'The cottage is up for sale.' He lifts his clothes out of the case and lays them on the chair next to the bed.

It's dark in the room, the shutters keeping out the unrelenting midday heat, and it's small, but it doesn't matter. They're together. Despite all the odds, he is here by her side. The past has shown her that large houses don't necessarily equate to a happy family life. She has sacrificed everything to be with him: her status, money, her home, and her children. A stab of guilt cuts at her at the thought of Flo, Jess and Ezra, her three wonderful children. She will write to them once the initial furore has died down. She has already made a few calls but was too cowardly to speak, to tell them what was really going on. But she will soon enough. She will tell them everything: why she did what she did, that it was never about abandoning them. It was about abandoning her past, leaving their sins behind them. It was about severing all ties from *him* without any repercussions. It was always about him. But not anymore. He's gone and she is here. They are here. Together. The future lies ahead of them and although there will undeniably be many hurdles thrown their way, they can clear them together as a couple. The indescribable feelings of loneliness she experienced whilst living with Jackson evaporated the minute she saw his body disappear beneath the water. That was the moment she began to live again, the exact point when she knew that at long last, she was completely free.

31

JESSICA

My eyes are just closing and I'm sinking into a welcome sleep after reading a few pages of a book I found on a shelf when I hear her. I'm rudely hauled into wakefulness. I sit up and listen to Flo's near hysterical shrieking outside the bedroom door. Something about our mother. I slide off the bed and put on a fluffy bathrobe then open the door.

'She's abroad, Jess. Mother is abroad with Coops.' Her breathing is ragged, her words coming out in truncated gasps. 'Malta. She's in Malta with him.'

I tie my belt tighter around my waist and take a step closer, placing my hand on her shoulder.

'Slow down, Flo. What makes you think such a thing?' I rub at my face with my other hand, lethargy fogging up my thinking. I long to sleep for a hundred years and wake up refreshed, not bogged down by this new weariness, this bone-aching lethargy that has me in its grip.

'Because I had a dream. I woke up and put it all together in my head. I found some pictures a few days ago on her bedside cabinet of a villa with shutters and now it all makes sense.'

I suppress a sigh. It obviously makes sense to my poor, befuddled sister but her logic doesn't make any sense to me. It's tenuous and fantastical.

'Are you sure? I mean, I'm not doubting that your dream seemed real but making that connection is quite the leap, isn't it?'

She bats away my hand and shakes her head. 'I'm right, Jess. I know I am. Wait here and I'll get the photos to show you.'

Flo shuffles off to her bedroom and returns seconds later clutching a fistful of pictures which she thrusts at me. I take them, leafing through them one by one, studying the possible location and trying to work out why Flo has jumped to such a conclusion.

'Can't you see it?' she says. 'Do you not remember how she used to talk about her holiday in Malta when she was younger and how she would have loved to return but our father wouldn't go? The only holidays they went on were the ones he booked. Mother never had a say in it and always hankered after going back to Valletta.'

I think that perhaps I do recall such conversations but they obviously resonated more with Flo than they did with me. I was much younger, my mind honed in on other things. I was in survival mode, trying to dodge the beatings and protracted rants and the imagined slights and behaviours that existed only in my father's head.

'But she could be anywhere, couldn't she? It doesn't have to be that particular country.'

Flo shakes her head, her mind made up. 'She's definitely there. I just know it. And Coops is there with her.'

It's easier to agree than put up any resistance or opposing opinions. Mainly because I don't have a counter argument. I just hope that wherever our mother is, she is happy. I also hope that she eventually gets in touch. We feel her absence keenly, and I would also like to let her know about Ezra. So much has happened since she left. She wouldn't want us to be floundering like this, me and Flo living here in this place with no purpose or sense of direction. This isn't who we are or how we want to live our lives.

'Well, I suppose we'll just have to wait until she gets in touch, won't we?'

Flo nods. I hand back the photographs and turn and head back into the bedroom. I hear her traipse downstairs and then I lie back down on the bed, glad to have some time to not think about anything. I pull up the covers, close my eyes and let myself drift away.

* * *

I sleep for half an hour or so and wake with a start, feeling groggy and out of sorts. My movements are ponderous and clumsy when I head downstairs, my body and limbs as solid as iron. I have a snack and read a few more chapters of my book, my eyes still heavy. After two cups of tea, some tidying up and a lot of talking about anything and everything, we have an early night and I awake the next morning to sunshine flooding into the room. I enjoy lying there basking in its warmth until I remember with a jolt that today is the day when I will be going to identify Ezra. I wonder if Amber's parents will be there and hope that the police have the good sense to keep us apart. I'm not angry at them; after all, none of this is their fault and they have also lost their daughter. It doesn't get any worse than that. Losing a parent or a sibling is traumatic. Losing a child is an unthinkable trauma that no parent should ever have to suffer. It's just that I'm feeling low and filled with dread. Everything feels over-whelming, life now an uphill struggle. I haven't the ability to speak to anybody who isn't family or a police officer. I don't think I can summon up enough energy to even pass on my condolences or show gratitude if anybody shows me any sympathy. I hope that Flo doesn't try to come with me. She isn't up to it. Yesterday, she appeared to make some progress but her odd suggestion as to our mother's whereabouts has made me think that she still isn't her usual self.

I think about Coops' letter and wish I hadn't thrown it away. It was a rash move. I was feeling anxious and jittery and didn't know what else to do. I panicked and now I have no evidence that our mother is still alive or where she is, aside that is, from the wild imaginings in Flo's head.

I borrow Flo's car and after a meagre breakfast of half a slice of toast that stuck in my throat like a large piece of sharp gravel, I make my way to see Ezra. I can't think of him as a body. He is still Ezra, my brother. A compassionate and yet deeply damaged man.

The roads are almost empty. I'm thankful for it. I'm not completely focused. Had there been a rush of traffic, I'm not sure I would have coped. It's a short journey and I pull up in the car park after only a ten-minute drive.

My breathing is laboured, perspiration breaking out on my back and around my hairline as I step out of the car and head towards the entrance of the mortuary. I take a few seconds to steel myself. It's Ezra, my lovely brother. *Not a broken, bruised corpse. Not a damaged, dead body. It's only my lovely brother. No need to be scared.*

The whole process takes only a matter of minutes. He looked alive, not the pale, blue-tinged dead body that I expected. The sheet was pulled up to his chin, the injuries to his abdomen that killed him, concealed. I stared at him, willing him to move, waiting for him to open his eyes and tell me that it was a dream. A nightmare. It was as if he could have sat up at any moment and turned and flashed me one of his enigmatic smiles. I could hear his voice telling me that everything was going to be okay, that me and Flo were going to manage just fine. It felt easier than I had anticipated but I'm glad that it's over.

And then I see her, standing in the distance watching me –

Diana, Amber's mother. My feet are glued to the floor. I have no idea what her reaction is going to be if she approaches me. Did the police also tell her about the argument in the car? Is she going to blame Ezra? Take it out on me, shouting and causing a scene? My chest convulses. I inhale deeply, taking in a lungful of air to keep my breathing in check.

My blood turns to sand as I watch her walk towards me, her feet click-clacking on the tiles of the long corridor. I prayed this wouldn't happen, that our paths wouldn't cross, but here we are, about to stand face to face, both of us grieving, our emotions stripped bare.

Her face is pale, devoid of any make-up, and her eyes are heavy with exhaustion at the tumult of feelings she is clearly enduring. I inhale rapidly, readying myself. But then she does something that catches me off-guard. No shouting. No acrimony or bitterness. She leans forward and hugs me, her arms pulling me close to her until I can hardly breathe and am forced to extricate myself.

'I hoped I'd see you here,' she says, stepping back and surveying me, her eyes sweeping over my face. I nod, simply because I don't know what else to say or do. If she notices my shock or awkwardness at her presence, she doesn't show it. For a brief moment, we stand like two lost souls, each of us locked in our own misery until she breaks the silence, the words she says blindsiding me.

'She messaged me, my Amber, before they set off in the car. She let me know me that she had told you about Flo.'

I say nothing, knowing the words I choose will feel wrong, misshapen and jagged. So I let her continue, her eyes brimming with tears.

'I tried to talk her out of going ahead with the wedding. I tried to stop her having a relationship with Ezra. I want you to know that. It was the right thing to do. The only thing. She railed against it. We fought and Amber is – was – a headstrong girl.'

At this point, I open my mouth to say something, fury sparking inside me, but she holds up her hand and smiles. Something in her expression is telling me to back off. There is a gentleness about her, a smoothness in her eyes and stance as if she is made of cotton wool, her outline and solidity blurred and softened by grief and pain.

'Please, I don't want to cause any arguments. You've been through enough, and my reticence wasn't anything to do with Ezra. He was a wonderful young man. He would have made any wife proud. It's just that...' She stops mid-sentence and takes a long, juddering breath, her jaw trembling as she bites at her lip and fights back tears. 'The story Amber told you was partly true. There was a young girl who worked at Armett House and had a child by your father, but it wasn't a friend of mine. That young girl was me, Jessica. I'm Florence's biological mother.'

The world slows down around me. I need to sit down. I feel Diana's hand on my elbow, her fingers holding me firmly while she leads me to a chair. I unzip my jacket, heat rising off my skin. I shiver as a blast of cold air bursts beneath my flesh, cooling me down again.

'Ezra and Amber were half brother and sister.' The words feel alien to me. I rub at my eyes, my body trembling and quivering. I feel empty, my veins full of air, my muscles limp and liquid. 'I'm afraid so. I'm really sorry. I tried talking to Amber but she was so in love with him, so smitten, that anything I said was dismissed. I told her the story about a young girl as a way in, a way of softening the blow before I broke it to her properly. But of course...'

'You didn't get chance.' I finish the sentence for her.

Two broken families. That's what we are now. Two broken families and my father was the one who broke us. How much hurt can one human cause?

'Am I supposed to tell Flo?' The words that I say echo in my head. I don't think I would know how to break it to her. She's been through enough.

Diana shakes her head. 'Do we need to do that now? I feared for Amber and Ezra's children, if they had any.' She sniffs and stares off down the corridor, eyes glazed over. 'That was why I broached the subject with her. Perhaps we can let Flo know another time when things have settled down? I just wish that Amber...' Tears well up in her eyes at the mention of her daughter's name.

I agree with her suggestion and we part with short, stilted promises to keep in touch. Whether that will happen is anybody's guess. Whether Flo eventually finds out is another thing I also must consider. What is to be gained from telling her? As far as we are both concerned, our mother is our mother. And I'm pretty sure Amber was either exaggerating or lying when she said everyone in town knows about it. Would Diana really want everyone gossiping about her? It's highly unlikely. She is a reserved lady, the epitome of elegance. Amber embellished the story to give credence to her revelation, a justification of sorts for breaking such devastating news.

I head to the car and slide into the seat, grateful to be alone with my thoughts. This day was supposed to be about Ezra and now I have a whole load of other problems to consider, information packed into my head that I don't want, like the fact that Amber was my half-sister. How could we have shared genes and yet be so very different? Then again, there are plenty of siblings who are nothing alike, who despise one another and rarely speak, if ever. I also wonder how Diana felt about my father, whether she cared for him or whether she was aware with the passing of time that she was just another notch on his bedpost: one of a long line of young girls who fell for his charms, not realising that they were in fact, being groomed. I saw the way he was around young women. He was charming and benevolent, traits he rarely displayed with his own family. What he was in reality, was a predator. I hope Diana hates him. I know I do.

And then I think of Ezra. Today, I wanted to keep my thoughts focused on him and him only. He deserves my full attention. He deserves that much and more. Leaving him there was the hardest part. Growing up, Ezra and I were so close. We loved and got on with Flo, but she was on the periphery of our lives, the age difference between us too great to bring us together as playmates or as friends. We existed in the same family. We lived in the same house and yet witnessed and endured different traumas.

I shake those thoughts away. Another time perhaps, when my mind is clearer. Time, they say, is a great healer. I hope whoever thought up that adage is correct. I don't want to go through the rest of my life feeling like this, as if I'm made of brittle glass, ready to shatter at the slightest knock or provocation. If there is anything positive to come out of this sorry mess, I want it to be that me and Flo emerge as stronger people. Tougher and resilient than we've ever been. After all, whatever happens in the future, it can't be any worse than what we've already been through. We've experienced the worst of times. Life can only get easier.

The engine kicks into life, an easy tune on the radio helping to calm me. It feels as if it will be a long time before I can smile again. A genuine reflexive smile, that is. Being in a position where I can laugh feels like a million miles away but it's out there somewhere, a point I can aim for. A destination I want to reach.

I have an internal monologue going on in my head on the way back, words I say to Ezra to tell him how sorry I am, and how much I miss him. I want him to know that he was loved. Always loved and cherished. That's all any of us ever want, isn't it? To feel wanted and cared for. As children, Ezra and I always tried to overcompensate for our father's hatred towards us. I would stay with him and hug him while he wept after yet another beating and he would do the same for me, each of us telling one another how special we were and how it wasn't our fault. I'm not even sure our own mother knew the extent of Father's harshness towards us. There was a point when I was convinced that we deserved it, that we must have done something terribly bad and that Flo was a better person than either of us could ever hope to be.

It wasn't us, I say as I turn the corner and pull up onto the gravelled driveway, the slight screech of the tyres announcing my arrival. *It was never our fault, Ezra.*

I say it because as I was driving, after speaking with Diana, a rogue thought came to me in a rush, a notion unleashing itself into my brain like a whirling vortex, slamming into my skull and knocking all the air out of my lungs. It makes sense, this idea, as warped and outlandish as it seems, and the more I think about it, the more it appears to fit, to have some sort of backward logic to it. It niggled me for some time after receiving Coops' letter, why he chose me and not Flo or even Ezra. I park the car and sit for a few seconds, trying to sift through everything in my head. It's got to be the only explanation. I climb out and stare at the expanse of manicured lawns and ancient trees in the distance, almost certain now of why our father hated and resented us as much as he did.

32

FLO

'I've rung Environmental Health. It was permanently engaged. I'll try again in an hour or so,' I say to Jess as she walks into the kitchen and wrinkles up her nose at the smell.

I should ask how it went, I know that, but can't seem to find the right words: words that don't seem awkward or clunky or dismissive. What is the right way to ask how your dead brother looked as he lay on the slab at the mortuary? What is the right way to ask your sister how she felt as she saw him, confirming that it was definitely Ezra? I fear that if I utter his name, more tears will come and if they do, I don't think I'll be able to stop them, so instead, I walk over to Jess and place my arm around her shoulder. A physical touch is easier than a flood of tears. We lean our heads in, our temples touching, the slight heat of her body and the soft, sweet air she exhales, a welcome reminder that I'm not alone in this dreadful tempest.

'Come and sit down. I'll make you a cup of tea.'

'Coffee, please,' she murmurs. 'And a strong one too.'

I nod and catch her eye and for now, that is all we need to do or say to get through this moment. She looks drained, hunched over and exhausted.

'I think it should be a small affair. Us and close friends only,' she says as I bustle about behind her, scooping coffee into the pot and finding cups. 'The funeral, I mean.'

I know exactly what she means. It could be a chance for many of the locals and the reporters to intrude, muscling their way in and having their say; all those idle gossips offering simpering smiles and hollow platitudes whilst simultaneously dragging our family name further into the gutter. Neither of us can face that. Not again.

'I agree,' I reply, putting her cup down in front of her. 'As small as possible.' I almost add that it's what Ezra would have wanted but that would be a lie. In truth, neither of us know what he would want. Dying wasn't on his radar. He was planning his wedding, not his funeral.

We sit and sip at our coffee. There is no need to say anything. The silence is comforting, not awkward or difficult. It's a time for reflection. Jess speaks first, her voice barely more than a murmur.

'I was thinking, what you said about our mother being abroad. Perhaps you're right. I wonder if there's any way of finding out exactly where she is in the city without triggering an intervention from any of the authorities?'

I shake my head and sigh. 'I have no idea. I mean, who would we ask? It's not every day somebody who is presumed dead, boards a plane and disappears, is it?'

Jess manages a small smile, her mouth twitching at the corners as if being happy is a painful and undesirable undertaking. 'No, I suppose not. I guess we'll just have to wait for Coops to write again.'

'If he ever does,' I say.

She nods. 'Yes, if he ever does.'

We go about our respective ways, each of us too exhausted and numb to even consider emptying Armett House of its contents.

'I'll contact a private pest company,' I say, after trying Environmental Health once more and not getting through. I find a number and make an appointment for somebody to call next week.

'Next week?'

'Yes, I know,' I reply, hanging up, annoyance rippling through me. 'It's a good job we don't have an army of them scuttling around the floor.'

Jess disappears and I know she will be calling the undertakers. She has taken it upon herself to organise Ezra's funeral, and I'm not about to stop her. We each have our own roles and neither of us questions it.

We spend the remainder of the day milling about doing very little and yet strangely achieving an awful lot. The kitchen is spotless and I take it upon myself to wash and dry our laundry, hanging out the bedsheets and towels.

I'm in the drawing room, leafing through an old book, reading the same few lines over and over, my mind too distracted to concentrate, when Jess comes clattering down the stairs, phone in hand, her mouth agape as she stares down at it.

'What?' I mouth, unprepared for yet another piece of horrific, stomach-churning news. My skin is too thin at the minute. I can't take any more shocks or setbacks.

'It's her,' Jess shrieks, her voice reaching a pitch that could shatter glass. She holds up her phone and points at the screen, her bitten ragged nails displaying how on edge she is. 'She's back. It's all over social media. Katie Gardiner is bloody well back in town!'

* * *

For once, it's not us, although in a way, it is. Katie's reappearance certainly takes some of the heat off our family, or what is left of us, and will remove the eyes of suspicion that were fixed in our direction, but at least it will give the locals something else to talk about. I doubt we'll get any apologies for the wild accusations that Jeff Wolf made. He would sooner choke on his own saliva than say sorry for what he said and did, and as for Bella and the constant gossip over the past few months that has fuelled the fiery tongues of the rest of the town, well, she will probably be too relieved to even give us a second thought, and that's how it should be. All she will be focused on is her daughter's return to the fold.

'It was exactly what everyone suspected,' Jess says, her eyes still glued to her phone. 'She's spent the past few months sofa surfing in Manchester and London but come back home now that her money has run out.'

'Living off the cash in hand that Father paid her?' I say, cocking my head at Jess and raising my eyebrows.

'I don't doubt it, so we'll still shoulder some of the blame. The Hemsworth name will still get dragged through the mud from time to time.'

We both give a half smile, Jess widening her eyes and giving me a knowing look. At least we can relax a little, knowing some of the gossips will now be focused on Katie instead of Ezra. Maybe we'll be able to keep his funeral small and private after all, everyone else's attentions now focused on her. Katie is also now one less thing to worry about. We still have unresolved issues but not having her disappearance hanging over our heads is a positive. A small one but a positive all the same.

'Shall I make us both something to eat?' I say, standing up and making my way into the kitchen. I'm not particularly hungry but we need to eat something to keep our strength up.

I try to avoid glancing at Jess's protruding hipbones and chiselled features as I pass. Her skin is like tissue stretched over bare bone, her face and shoulders sharp and angular. Only as I open cupboard after cupboard does it become apparent that we have let things slide. Each one is empty save for a couple of packets of out-of-date powder soups and a box of stale cereal. We have bread but nothing in to make a sandwich, having lived on buttered toast, coffee and alcohol since getting here.

'You know what?' Jess says as she stands behind me, a note of enthusiasm in her voice. Perhaps not enthusiasm, but not the shock and misery that has trailed in our wake for what feels like an age. 'I'm going to go and get some food. We're down to nothing. The cupboards really are bare.'

'I can come with you, if you want?' I don't want and am relieved when she shakes her head and smiles at me.

'No, honestly, it's fine. If I'm okay taking your car again, I'll nip out to the local supermarket and fill a trolley. I'll be back in no time at all.'

'Here, take my bank card. I'll pay.'

Again, she shakes her head and leaves before I can protest. We can sort out the finances later. I'm relieved to stay inside. Leaving the house and having to face people is so low on my agenda, it is practically subterranean. Already, I can visualise those sideways glances from locals, the whispers and the clacking tongues as I pass by. The faux show of sympathy and pointless, simpering, banal talk. I haven't the energy for any of it. I would rather stay here in the safety of my childhood home. Father is no longer here. All the ghosts of the past have died with him. I'm safe here at Armett House.

I decide to give the kitchen one last clear out in readiness for Jess coming back. The smell has strengthened even in the last hour, catching me unawares and making me gag. I cover my face with a tea towel and stand for a few seconds to get my breath.

The pest control company aren't coming out until next week and I don't think we can wait that long, not if the stench is going to get worse day by day. Once again, I grab my phone and call as many as I can, only to be told they are busy. Either that or their numbers ring out or are permanently engaged.

Enough is enough. They're only dead mice. I'll sort it myself. Jess is out buying our food and having to face neighbours after a traumatic morning at the morgue. The least I can do is clean up the place and freshen up the air we breathe. I fling open windows, take a deep, juddering gasp, and decide to search for the source of the hideous stink that is worsening daily, taking over the whole house.

My stomach heaves and my chest convulses when I head into the old larder, the place where the smell is the strongest. Something is different in here but I can't work out what the change is. I switch on the light and stare around. The shelves are as I remember them, old, empty tins stacked high to the ceiling. They most likely contain old nails and screws although why they are in here as opposed to the garage or one of the outbuildings is anybody's guess. Father always did dance to his own tune, refusing the advice of Coops and any builders who carried out work on the house.

I pace to the far end of the space where the shelving stops, and turn to survey the whole area, my eyes roving around the small room. From this perspective, it all looks the same. So why do I get the strongest sense that something is amiss here?

Taking short steps, I head back over to the door and then turn. That's when I notice it. The larder is smaller. When I was a child, I used to come in here and fold myself under the lowest shelf, where I would sit and read for hours at a time. Something about the small space made me feel safe. Now this place makes me want to run away and hide.

Once again, I head to the far end, tapping with my clenched knuckles as I check for false walls. I reach the end and press at the plaster, then bang my feet on the floor. Something gives beneath me. I scan the nearby shelves. One of the larger tins looks big enough to do some damage. An old catering-size tin of beans catches my eye. I pick it up and swing it against the wall, putting my whole weight behind it. The wall cracks and splinters, eventually giving away to a dark space behind. I continue battering until there is a hole big enough for me to peer through.

The stench hits me square in the face when I lean forwards to try and see through to the other side. I step back and don't waste any time in pulling at loose pieces of plasterboard, my fingers working ferociously until they begin to bleed.

As I'm clawing my way through, the memory of a bigger space comes to me: perhaps another two or three feet beyond the plasterboard. Once I've pulled away enough of the false wall, I try to manoeuvre my way in, forcing one of my legs through, my foot twitching as I attempt to find solid ground. Hot and impatient, I push my body farther in and hurl myself forwards in a bid to tear away more of the thin plasterboard, my fingers tearing and scraping, the top half of my body tipped forward. I give one last final push and let out a shriek as I find myself falling into a void of darkness.

33

JESSICA

All eyes are upon me, or at least that's how it feels. It's difficult to shake off this mantle of anxiety. I feel exposed and vulnerable, as if every emotion that is swirling around my head is visible to the naked eye, my worries and issues writ large on a placard above my head.

The supermarket is busy, bodies bustling about, trollies piled high, baskets swinging from people's arms as they traipse up and down the aisles, surveying the produce and throwing items in with more than a degree of impatience. I quickly fill my trolley full of basics. I don't buy any wine. I plan on drinking what's in Armett House, making sure we finish all of our father's precious bottles that he stored away. Not once did he ever offer any to guests, let alone his own family. What is the point in having such a huge store of vintage wine if it doesn't get opened and drunk?

I sigh and shut my mind off to him. Ezra is the one who deserves all my thoughts, not that horrible old bastard who demanded so much from those around him yet gave so little in return.

My thoughts are a muddle, my emotions a tension of opposites when I think of Ezra and Father – one a loving, considerate human being and the other a cold, hard-faced horror of a man. It's then that I hear the voice behind me.

'I heard about the accident. I just want to tell you how sorry I am.'

Amanda MacDonald. Oh God. My scalp prickles. Perspiration breaks out on my face and neck. Not her. Please, not her again. I can't face her tittle-tattling and gossip, her probing questions that always, without fail, contain hidden meanings, her radar tracking for anything untoward that she can twist and deliberately misconstrue.

Counting to three, I take a deep breath and compose myself before spinning around to face her. The one thing that immediately strikes me is her expression. As always, she is almost impossible to fathom, her eyes hooded, a faux smile plastered on her face, like an actress rehearsing her lines. I wonder if anybody ever gets to see behind that mask to the real Amanda underneath.

'Thank you for your kind words,' I say, edging my trolley along to try and leave her behind. She hooks her handbasket further up her arm and walks alongside me, her face angled towards mine. I can smell her breath – a strong garlic odour – and an underlying aroma of something bitter. Perhaps the acidic bite of bile.

'Poor Ezra and also poor Amber. Two families devastated.'

I nod, my face heating up on hearing her words.

'Yes. We are devastated. Thanks again for your condolences,' I say as we reach the checkout area.

'Still, it's one less thing for you to worry about with Katie coming back, isn't it? Did you know she's back in town?'

A breath rattles in my chest. 'Yes, I heard. There was never any doubt in my mind that she would come back.'

I start to transfer my groceries onto the conveyor belt. She continues to stand close to me, her breath growing more and more rancid by the second, the heat from her body making me hot and restless. Why is she still here? I have a strong urge to push her away, the image I have in my mind of me watching as she falls to the floor with a loud clatter so powerful, it feels real.

'It's still not over for you though, is it? I mean, I wonder why Damien Cooper's cottage is going up for sale? It's such a terrible shame. The skeletons are still falling out of that cupboard onto you, aren't they?'

I throw more groceries onto the conveyer belt, a glass coffee jar clattering its way down before coming to rest against a spread of softer items that cushion its noisy, rocking motion. My breathing feels loud and laboured. Stupid Amanda MacDonald and her constant probing and toxic tongue. She is the very worst of us – a sour individual wrapped up in beige, inoffensive clothing that disguises the deeply harmful poisons at its core. At this moment in time, I hate her more than I've ever hated anyone. More than Luke and more than my father. At least I knew what to expect from them. Her particular brand of venom is harder to detect, her words hidden within the guise of a harmless young woman whose only crime is to dress as if she has just stepped out of an Agatha Christie novel. I pray she doesn't say anything else to me because if she does, I'm not sure I will be able to hide my contempt for her. She's like a predator, having a feeding frenzy on the remains of my dead family. One push, that's all it would take to knock her to the floor. Just one quick push.

It turns out that I don't need to do or say anything to make her leave me alone because like a hungry wolf waiting to savage its next victim, she spots one of Amber's close friends in the distance and makes a beeline for her, the tip tap of her feet as she leaves the most welcome sound I've heard in a long, long time.

I finish loading my items and then bag them up and pay the cashier, keen to get back to Armett House. The place that was once my prison has now become my sanctuary, providing safety and protection from the horrors of the outside world.

As I leave, I turn to see Amber's friend, whose name escapes me, launch a blistering attack on a poor, unsuspecting Amanda. I'm torn between feeling pity for her and wanting to give a loud cheer. Perhaps she will learn something from this incident and tread more carefully in the future. Grief is raw and unabating and trying to prise gossip out of people when they are at their lowest ebb is an atrocious pastime. I hope Amanda now realises this and keeps her distance.

Unfortunately for me, she doesn't. I'm loading up the car when she arrives and stands right next me, flustered and red-faced.

In my peripheral vision, I can see the lump in her throat as it bobs up and down, her mouth slack with shock and disgust. 'She always was a cow, that Julia, wasn't she?' Amanda's voice is a near shriek, her timbre ratcheting up my annoyance levels even further.

'Her close friend has just died. What do you expect?' My voice is low, measured and controlled. Lacking in emotion or compassion for her self-inflicted plight.

'Well, all I said was that at least Amber died with the person she loved. Is that so very bad?'

'Yes, it's fucking well bad, you weird, old gossip monger. She was only twenty-five years old, for God's sake. There is nothing positive to be said about her death! Now please go home and think before you speak.'

If I expect Amanda to glibly accept my insults and go home, I'm way off beam. Not that I did expect it. Just hoped.

Her voice is hoarse, each word, each syllable clipped and slightly demonic as she moves even closer to me and speaks into my ear. 'The whole town is fed up of your family and their warped ways. I survived your father's frantic clutches. Many didn't. And you're the one calling me weird? Maybe take a closer look to your own faults before you start looking for flaws in my character. Because when I use the term *father*, I use it very loosely.'

I stare up into her red, pulpy face, wondering how hard I would have to hit her to break something.

She smiles, her face slightly crooked, her mouth lopsided. 'Take a look in the mirror, Jessica. Ask yourself who you really are.' Another twisted grin, her eyes twinkling with joy as she tears apart my family right in front of me. 'There are none so blind as those who cannot see.'

And with that, she is gone. Fury ripples through me, the fact that I've allowed myself to be niggled by her words. She has slithered beneath my skin and is currently nestling there, watching me squirm. It's not just her statement that has riled me, though. It's the fact that she might be right. I had this thought after coming back from the morgue as I pondered over our father's treatment of me and Ezra. What if he isn't our real dad? What if our mother also had her own share of extra-marital affairs?

A headache sets in behind my eyes. I slam the boot closed and open the driver's door, eager to get out of this place, to leave its tawdriness behind. I should have gone elsewhere, shopped farther afield. I could have avoided the likes of Amanda but as it is, I put myself in harm's way and am now being forced to obliterate the memory of her and her words. At least I've got Father's wine to drink when I get back. I can console myself with one of his hideously expensive ones, drinking it and draining the entire bottle. It's the only bit of power I have or will ever have over him, the man who ruined, or attempted to ruin my life.

It takes only a few minutes to get back to Armett House. I drag the bags out of the car and dump them on the kitchen counter, calling out for Flo to let her know that I'm back. When there's no answer, I assume she is upstairs so I unpack and put everything away.

I call again, my voice louder this time, wandering around the place, my voice a lonely echo. Outside. That is where she'll be. She must have gone for a walk in the gardens. It will do her good to get out of this place, to escape the smell and the confines of these walls.

Ten minutes later, I've made us both a sandwich when I hear a sound: a low, scuffling noise. Scratching. Perhaps even a distant moan. It's hard to pinpoint but I'm almost certain it's coming from somewhere near the kitchen. I tear around the place, my voice losing its edge of control.

'Flo? Where on earth are you?'

I stop and listen out as I stand near the old larder. There is something for sure, some sort of rustling, as if it's coming from beneath me. I think of scurrying mice and rats, then look down and bang my foot on the floor, waiting and listening. I hear it again, a muffled noise. Somebody moving about. Somebody trying to speak.

'Flo!'

I spin round, my thoughts fogged up with fear. A cellar. I seem to recall we had a cellar under the kitchen but feel sure that our father sealed it up many years ago. I cast my mind back, trying to recall where the trapdoor was. Not in the kitchen. The flagstone flooring has been down in here for years and years, perhaps even a century or longer.

I'm panting now, my skin prickling, my nerve endings sizzling like hot oil.

It comes to me unbidden – the memory. Me and Ezra hiding in the larder when we were children, doing what we could to escape our father's clutches, his growing temper something that drove us to seek out new and inventive ways of hiding ourselves away. So we chose the cellar. It was used rarely, a dark, dank place that reeked of decay, and yet it didn't frighten us half as much as Father's belt did.

The door to the larder is already half open. I step inside and am glad of the overhead light that helps to dispel the dark demons that are perched on my shoulder at the sight of the place. I brush away those memories – the sound of his footsteps as they grew ever closer and the accompanying stomach cramps that folded me in half at the thought of being found – and head towards the gaping hole at the far end of the room. At some point, a false wall has been put in and already the stench is overpowering. I know it then, the thing that I have refused to consider even though it is patently obvious. The thing that has lingered in my mind since speaking with Andrei that I banished from the forefront of my mind – that somewhere in the bowels of Armett House lies the dead body of Cristina with my sister lying close by.

34

JESSICA

'Down here, Jess. I'm down here. Get a torch!'

My feet twist beneath me, my gait rickety as I head back into the kitchen and go through to the boot room. I grab two heavy torches and hold them tightly, as if my life depends on it.

I'm back and down on my knees, shining a light through the ragged hold and into the darkness within seconds.

'Are you okay, Flo? No broken bones?'

'I don't think so. But I need to get out of here, Jess. You'll have to come in and help me up.'

The thought of clambering down there makes my flesh ripple with dread. Distant, dark memories nudge their way into my brain: Father's roars, the way his eyebrows bunched together when he was angry. The sickening clack of his leather belt as it snapped together while he hunted for us.

He's not here anymore. The monster is dead.

I swallow down my fears and misgivings. Even in death, he continues to control and taunt me. I think about my slap, how I reacted to Bella's words at the funeral. Maybe I'm more like my father than I care to admit. Maybe I inherited his propensity for violence.

Or maybe he isn't actually my father.

A surge of heat flares across my face, sweeping around my neck, making me sticky and uncomfortable.

No.

That can't be true. I tell myself that even though the more I think about it, the more it feels like it could be a real possibility. Also, I am not a violent person. I refuse to go down that route. I was under pressure. Bella had goaded and insulted me. I reacted badly and it won't happen again.

I make my way towards the end of the larder, then bend down and peer through the broken pieces of plasterboard, squinting into the place that was once my hiding place. I sweep the torch around and gasp when I spot Flo lying on the floor in a crumpled heap.

'I've hurt my arm and my ankle. I think they might be broken.'

My immediate reaction is to gag. The smell is revolting. Unearthly. Worse than anything I've ever encountered. I think of poor Flo being stuck down here, in terrible pain, and want to hug her.

'Give me a second,' I say, prising myself through the hole, the torches suddenly heavy and unwieldy in my grip. 'I'm going to gently throw these down. Is there anywhere soft I could aim them at so they don't hit the floor and break?'

'I don't know. It's really dark down here and I can't reach the light switch.'

I stop shuffling and crouch down on my haunches, sweeping the beam of light around the area. My first reaction is to shriek at the sight before me but know that such a response would alarm Flo. She has been sitting here in the dark and is probably unaware of what surrounds her, so I close my eyes and take a few deep breaths, steeling myself in readiness for standing amongst the vast array of dead rats that lay scattered around the cellar. Not just a couple or even a dozen. Maybe fifty or more. Or perhaps I'm on red alert, my mind overplaying things, but I don't think so. At least we now know the source of the smell. Later, once I've sorted Flo out, I'll come down here and clear them away. I will shovel them into a black sack and burn them at the bottom of the garden in Coops' old dustbin that he used for disposing of garden rubbish. But before that, I have to tend to Flo, see if she needs hospital treatment. I pray she doesn't but if she does, then we'll just have to deal with it the way we've dealt with everything else that's been thrown our way.

Over in the far corner is a pile of old rags. If I can aim the torches at it, and they land without smashing, then I can wiggle through the hole and drop the couple of feet to the floor below. I take a swing and throw them. They land on the intended target, sending a pile of dust swirling into the dim, murky air of the cellar. I cough and lever myself through the hole, dropping onto the floor without too much trouble, then pick my way over the scattering of rats and collect the torches. Something about the pile of rags catches my eye. I turn away, my efforts focused on Flo and getting her out of here.

'I tried to find where the smell was coming from. You were busy getting us some food in so I thought I'd do my own investigative attempts at finding the source of the smell.'

I point the beam of light at her face and hold the other one beside me. Her eyes follow the ochre trail, her gaze landing on a dead rat beside my feet. She glances at me then looks to where she is lying. Beside her lie two more dead rodents. She squeezes her eyes closed then opens them again and lets out a sharp laugh. 'At least we've found them, eh? The rancid, stinky, little blighters.'

'We certainly have.'

'Well, they look fairly well fed. Makes you wonder what they were living on, doesn't it?'

I swallow and run my fingers through my hair. I don't want to think about that aspect of their existence. I think of the pile of rags in the corner, the shape of them and on impulse, march over and kick them aside. Nothing but dust. That's what is underneath. I'm not sure whether to feel elated or disappointed.

'Yes, well,' I say gruffly, heading back over to where Flo is lying, 'let's concentrate on getting you up and out of here, shall we?'

After letting out a series of small moans, we manage to get her up on her feet. She limps along, her hand clutching mine.

'Isn't there a door somewhere down here?' I scan the area with the torches and spot something resembling an easier way out. Having to hoist up an injured Flo isn't going to be a simple procedure.

'There's a crawl space. The door is on the other side of it, but I don't think I can manage it, I'm afraid.'

I don't reply but know that mine isn't a rogue memory. I do recollect that there is another way in here. Ezra and I used to clamber down the trapdoor but Father would come in via another entrance and it wasn't through the crawl space.

'Sit down here a second, Flo. I'm just going to have a quick sweep around this place, try to find an easier route out if I can.'

I lower her onto the floor where she sits, looking both bewildered and grateful. I sweep both torches across the walls and locate the light switch. Within seconds, the entire area is flooded with a yellow hue, its glare bright enough to bring on the wildest and most painful of migraines.

'What's that over there?' Flo points to a row of wooden planks that are propped up against the wall.

She's right. I seem to recall a door in that vicinity. This cellar has lots of dark corners and rooms that branch off from the main area so if there is no door behind these planks then I'll have to clamber around and conduct a more thorough search. With no ladders, getting Flo back up through the old trapdoor feels almost impossible.

Not wanting to waste any more time, I march over and pull the planks away from the wall, my heart thrashing about my chest. Behind them is indeed, a door. I'm not sure what I expected to see – something more sinister, perhaps. Something that once seen, could never be unseen. But it's just a door. I'm not sure whether to feel relieved or mystified. Armett House has a predilection for deceit and disappointment. In this house, anything is possible.

I try to work out why a false wall was put in place in the larder and why this door was hidden from view but am not sure it's worth the effort. Father was a master of deception. A manipulator and a proven liar. I can't begin to work out the machinations of his mind but know that whatever his intentions were when closing up this rat-infested cellar, it won't have been innocent. If poor Cristina isn't down here, then where is she? I pray she has taken herself off somewhere, her feelings bruised by Father's ruthless ways as he ran roughshod over her feelings.

The door gives easily, more easily than I expected, which suggests it has been used recently, and we're greeted by a spread of light. As carefully and gently as I can, I help Flo up to her feet. She winces but doesn't cry out in pain.

'I can actually stand on it. Most probably a sprain.'

I glance down at her foot. It's straight but swollen. 'How's your arm?'

She takes a couple of sharp breaths and nods. 'Not too bad. I didn't pass out so maybe they're not broken after all. I think it was the shock more than anything. That fall was unexpected. It took the breath right out of me. I expected to get a firm footing when I clambered through that hole. I didn't expect to step into thin air.'

'Yes,' I say, as I hold her tight and guide her though the door that leads out to the back of the house near the old back entrance that decades and decades ago was used by the staff at Armett House, 'well, we know who to blame for that, don't we? Father and his pathetic attempts at DIY.'

I'm being overly jolly, masking the truth. I'm not going to open up to Flo about my suspicions. She probably has her own. Besides, there was nothing in there but a whole host of dead rodents. They must have been poisoned, but by whom? Did Coops do it? Something in my gut says not, but I have no evidence to point to anybody else doing it. Killing rats wasn't Father's style. He left those sorts of dirty jobs to the maintenance staff. And if Coops did poison them, then he would have known they were here and cleared them away. Unless it was Jeff Wolf? He would most definitely have left the job half done, and yet I don't believe he did it either.

The light causes us to squint when we eventually get outside. I shield my eyes with my free hand and turn to face Flo. Slightly pasty looking, as if all the blood has drained from her face, she smiles at me, a spread of colour gradually returning to her pallid cheeks.

'Thanks, Jess. I feel like such a bloody weakling.'

'Ah, that you are, but you're my weakling.' On impulse, I lean forwards and plant a light kiss on the top of her head.

We only have each other and I need to remember that. Unless our mother decides to get in touch, that is. Until that happens, we have to stick together no matter what.

35

FLO

I don't know how I would have got through these last few days without her. Quiet, reserved Jess has stepped up to the plate and managed brilliantly.

'There. How does that feel?' She presses the cold compress into place and gently elevates my foot onto a small stool.

'Much better, thanks.'

'You've got a whacking bruise on the top of your arm.'

I stare down and can see a large, purple welt below my shoulder. It hurts like hell but I can rotate it fully. No breakages, thank goodness. No lasting damage.

'We'll keep an eye on it. If either your ankle or arm get any worse, I'll take you to the hospital.'

Dread bites at my innards. Hospitals, morgues, police stations. I've had a gutful of them and am sure Jess feels the same way. All I want to do is stay here with her. At some point, I'll need to go home to my own place, but not just yet. Despite its torrid history, there's a modicum of comfort to be had from staying here until all this is over. Whatever *this* is. *This* is possibly the most challenging thing that can happen to a person, losing my parents and brother in the space of just a few weeks. But I'm here. I'm functioning and breathing. I'll survive it. *We* will survive it together, me and Jess.

'Right, I'm going to make us both some dinner. It's about time we had a decent meal inside of us.' Jess stands up, her expression authoritative. It's so good to see her brimming with confidence again. 'Here you go. It might help take your mind off the pain.'

She passes me the TV remote and shuffles out of the room. I thank her and switch on the television, glad of the background noise. Any form of distraction is welcome. Because my mind is beginning to make mad suggestions. Why was the cellar boarded up? Why was a false wall put up and the door disguised with planks of wood? It's as if somebody was trying to stop anybody getting in. And yet, there was nothing down there. Except those dead rats. Perhaps Coops or our father did it to hem them in, stop them getting into the house. That's the only explanation I can think of. Or maybe it was to stop somebody from getting out.

I swallow and shut my eyes, my head aching. I spend the next ten minutes or so watching a crime documentary about a killer in a neighbourhood who fooled everyone into thinking he was a good Samaritan when in fact, he was the Devil incarnate, slaughtering people as they slept, just for kicks. Just because he could. I turn it off just as Jess enters the room carrying a plate of food balanced on a tray.

'Right, it's not much but it's the best I could come up with in such a short space of time. Chicken stir fry with teriyaki sauce and noodles.' She hands me the tray and the aroma of the food is quite possibly the best thing I have smelled in a long, long time.

'Thanks. The painkillers are kicking in and my stomach is empty. This looks wonderful.'

We sit and eat in companionable silence, the clink of our cutlery on the plates the only sound to be heard. It feels like an achievement, to be sitting here, eating. A small step towards some sort of normality. Then I think of Ezra's funeral and feel my stomach tighten.

'I know exactly what you're thinking,' Jess says. She stands up and takes the tray. 'Because I'm thinking it too.'

I raise my eyebrows and purse my lips. 'That we shouldn't be sitting here eating and feeling relaxed while our brother is lying in the morgue?'

'Exactly that. But we have to keep our strength up. We've got a few more weeks to get through and we have to do it for Ezra. Be the best we can be under the worst of circumstances.'

I nod. She's right. Of course she is. It's just difficult. My earlier clear-headedness dissipates, replaced by a fog of sadness and confusion. I'm tired. I think that maybe the shock and the painkillers are influencing my thinking. My eyes close, the weight of them too great to fight. I don't even hear Jess leave the room. I sink into oblivion and stay there for the next few hours.

* * *

The house is silent when I wake with a start and drag myself upright. Outside, daylight is fading, the sky beyond the gardens a wash of pale violet, the clouds dark and bruised. The pain in my ankle rises, reminding me that I'm not quite on the mend. The pain in my shoulder and arm is less violent, more of a deadening, numb sensation.

'Jess?' My voice is a thin, lonely echo that streaks away into the ether.

The ticking of the clock heightens my sense of solitude. Still weary, my body trying to throw off the mantle of sleep that is pressing down on me, I sit up and shout her name again. 'Jessica!' I emphasise the hard consonants in a bid to get her to hear me but am met with a wall of silence.

My bladder nags at me, a sudden stabbing sensation in my lower abdomen that forces me to shift about in my seat. With no idea where Jess has gone to, I attempt to stand up, the deep ache and throbbing in my ankle eye-wateringly painful. I hobble out of the room, calling out for Jess as I make my way to the downstairs cloakroom. Walking on my foot is good. I don't want it to stiffen up. Even damaged limbs need exercise and movement.

Five minutes later, I am back in the chair and there is still no sign of Jess. The lamp next to me casts an eerie glow around the room when I turn it on, its tessellated pattern stretching across the ceiling and walls like a hundred sets of monstrous, watching eyes. I flick on the TV and turn up the volume to drown out the roaring silence that is filling my head. Where the hell is Jess? I convince myself she is upstairs napping because to think anything else is too frightening. I suddenly crave her company like a junkie after their next fix. This isn't me. It's not who I am or who I used to be. Events of late have rendered me weak and powerless, sapping me of all energy. I sit and ponder over Amber's revelation, thinking about who my biological mother is. Does she ever give any thought to me? Or was I a nuisance to her – somebody who impinged on her life, curtailing her freedoms? Maybe she was glad to get rid of me.

I sigh and rest my head back on the cushion, tears biting at the back of my eyes. I won't cry. Sitting weeping won't change anything. I'm almost on the precipice of a deep void of self-pity, the drop beneath me dark and endless, when I hear Jess calling through the house, the apparent crack in her voice telling me that something is wrong, that Armett House hasn't finished with us quite yet, that there are more dark secrets waiting to creep, monster-like, into our world and shred what little dignity we have left into tiny, unrecognisable pieces.

36

JESSICA

I head out while Flo is sleeping, her gentle snores assuring me that she will be in a deep slumber for the next hour or so. The combination of a solid meal and the painkillers have knocked her out. Going back down into the cellar has been on my mind since getting Flo out of there. I want to clear up those rats and make sure the place is properly sealed up so the chances of any more rodents getting in is non-existent. If, on the off chance, we are issued with a Presumption of Death certificate and we can put this place up for sale, the last thing we need is for a surveyor to unearth an infestation of rodents. All old houses have problems with pests of one sort or another, but hundreds of rats are bound to put off any serious prospective buyers.

Brush and shovel in hand, and with two thick plastic sacks tucked under my arm, I head outside, entering through the same door we exited. I flick on the light and begin to sweep, depositing the dead vermin in the sack with a sickening thud, the mass of their collective bodies stretching the sack to capacity. I'd like to say I did it without feeling sickly and dizzy but that isn't true. The sight of them made my head buzz and my legs heavy and unsteady.

It takes me five minutes or so to collect them all. I tie up the sacks and take one last look around the cellar, checking every corner, even staring up at the low ceiling for a sign that something – anything – untoward took place down here, but can see nothing. I slam the door shut behind me and lock it, vowing to never go in there ever again.

The weight of the two bags is stomach-churningly heavy, each one swinging in my hand as I transport them over to the old bin, ready to be burned. I had forgotten how far down the garden it is. Coops insisted it be far enough from the house to not cause any damage should something highly flammable ever be accidentally thrown onto it. I am almost there when I spot something else along the way that always frightened me as a child – the old well. Whenever Father was in one of his rages, I used to imagine that one day, he would get so angry, he would throw either me or poor Ezra down there and nobody would ever find us. I stop for a second or so, then shiver and stride past it, still too afraid to stoop over and look down into its murky depths.

I drop the bags on the grass and rub at my face, weariness weighing heavily on me. It's been a long day/week/month/year. And it's not over yet. I think of Ezra and his funeral and am overcome by a need to slump to the ground and hammer my fists against the charred lawn. But I don't. I have things to do. Things that will no longer get done by anybody else. All of a sudden, it's my job to do what Coops used to do, like disposing of the dead rats from the cellar. The sooner I get this fire going, the sooner I can get back inside.

Except I don't have any matches. I turn, ready to march into the old shed to collect them, and stop, my eyes drawn towards something on the floor next to the ashes of a previous fire. It's the glint that catches my attention, an incongruous twinkle of something shiny amidst a pile of grey cinders. I jam my hands beneath my

armpits, their sudden clamminess making me hot and agitated. My
movements feel jerky and ungainly when I bend down to try and
scoop up the item. It's a ring. I don't recognise it and can see that it
is sitting on or attached to something dark and oily looking. My
hands shake and my eyes mist over when I grab at the gemstone in
the middle, lifting it out of the pile of black dust and grime before
letting out a shriek and falling backwards, my limbs working furi-
ously to distance myself from it. It falls from my clutches, dropping
next to where I'm slumped. I don't want to believe it or look at it,
and yet can't seem to tear my eyes away. Next to where I have fallen
is the ring with a finger still attached to it. A barely recognisable
blackened and burned finger, but a finger all the same.

My insides heave. I swallow and take a few deep breaths, trying
to stem the involuntary reaction to bring up everything I've eaten.
Tears and snot mar my vision. I wipe at my face with my sweater
and stand up. It's difficult to think straight, to work out what I
should do next. I wish I had the thought processes of DI Harvey, the
ability to think clearly and block out all emotion.

Gloves. I need some latex gloves and something in which to
place the charred finger. My legs threaten to fail me when I turn
and run towards the old shed, my pace shaky and off balance.

The door gives way with a heavy groan and I'm greeted by an
array of rusty old gardening tools and a thick mesh of cobwebs that
I have to fight my way through to get what I need. I can't find any
gloves but instead pick up a trowel and an old glass jar.

Everything feels dulled and out of kilter as I walk back to the
burned remains, my senses deadened by my unwanted find. The
grass beneath my feet is spongy and uneven. The slight breeze cuts
at my skin like sharpened knives.

Slick with sweat, my hands tremble when I slide the trowel
beneath the scorched finger. It drops into the jar and my stomach
convulses at the sight of it lying there, a dismembered body part,

still attached to the jewellery it wore when she was alive. Because it is most definitely a she. *Was* a she. This is the finger of a female. I'm not a forensics expert but the size of it and the design of the ring all point to this once belonging to a woman. Perhaps a young woman. One who once worked here. I swallow and stand for a moment to catch my breath and gather my thoughts. What next? Do I tell Flo and upset her even further? Or do I do the most despicable thing ever, and hide it? That would be a terrible thing to do, but what if I were to hide it only until after Ezra's funeral? It may be a terrible act of dishonesty but it is also an act of deep kindness, sheltering my sister from more trauma and worry until the time is right to let her know what I have found.

It doesn't take me long to come to a decision. I carry the jar back to the shed and put it up on a high shelf, covering it with containers of weedkiller and packets of seed. It can be a problem for another day. Right now, I have two bags of dead rats that I need to burn. One difficulty at a time.

I find it rather alarming how quickly I'm able to forget, concentrating all my efforts on the black sacks and their contents, not on the finger of a dead girl whose remains are possibly at the bottom of the bin I'm about to use.

Something stops me. What if she is still in there? If her finger didn't burn then perhaps there are other body parts that are still intact and recognisable. My head spins. I take a deep, ragged breath. Disgust at my own behaviour swells in my chest. What on earth am I doing hiding things? If I get found out, I risk being arrested, losing my job, my reputation. It would make the death of my parents look like a walk in the park. This is another human being. When did I become so thoughtless, so bloody hard-faced and cruel?

With mechanical precision, I drop the bag and peer inside the bin. It's too dark to see anything properly. Even in daylight, the burned contents are almost impossible to distinguish. I run back to the boot room and grab at a torch, thinking how odd it is that I've needed the use of them so much in the past few days. More than when I ever lived here. When I lived at Armett House, I craved the darkness and the shadows. They gave me anonymity, places where I could hide. Now they seem full of peril. Fear lurks around every shadowy corner, salting itself away in the darkness, waiting to strike when I least expect it. Death does that to a person, I guess. Makes them fearful of every single little thing. And here at Armett House, we're surrounded by it. Death is everywhere, its sharpened claws digging into us, trying to draw blood and sap us of our strength. And it's working. That's the worst thing – it's fucking well working. Both Flo and I are on our last legs, our energy draining away hour by hour, minute by minute.

For reasons I cannot explain, or perhaps because I am fast becoming suspicious of everybody and everything, I glance behind me to make sure nobody is there, to make sure Flo isn't awake and making her way over here. Then I turn on the torch and steel myself, leaning over the bin and shining the beam downwards. I hold my breath, squint into the light and recoil. A chunk of air is wedged in my chest. I gasp and clutch at my throat. A wave of heat passes over me, followed by an icy chill. It can't be. I've got it wrong; my nerves and brain aren't functioning as they should. I've had a shock and my thinking is skewed, that's what it is.

My breathing slows down. I count to ten and take another look inside the bin, convinced I've overreacted. Maybe I have. At the bottom is something that isn't immediately identifiable as anything human or non-human. After my earlier find, I'm inclined to opt for the former but hoping for the latter. I've had enough shocks for one day.

I don't have anything to use. I can't pick this thing out with my bare hands, so I reach into my pocket and grab an old tissue and with a pincer-like grip, extract the burnt item. It's a spherical shape and I can already see that it's not a skull. I let out a wild laugh of relief. This scenario is both comical and horrific. It looks like some old leather football that didn't burn properly. I drop it on the grass and turn to look in again just one last time. I'm not going to dig too deep, just give it another cursory glance before dropping in the two black sacks and setting fire to them. Then I'm done here.

The smell of smoke takes my breath away as I peer once more into the blackened, charred remains, but it's not just the stink that knocks all the air out of my lungs. The big old football was clearly put in there to disguise what lay beneath. I don't reach in to remove it. I leave the burned hand where it is before falling back onto the grass and letting out a shriek. The pain of falling doesn't hurt me. I'm beyond feeling anything physical. It's the horror and dread that consumes me, bulging within my veins. I try to stand up but the ground tilts violently, tipping up and down and side to side. When I do eventually manage to stand up, my body folds like a pack of cards and before I can stop myself, I fall, stars exploding behind my eyes, white sparks hitting the back of my skull like rapid gunfire. I close my eyes, wishing I could disappear into the heavens, wishing I was anywhere but here at Armett House.

It's a gasp, Jess's voice, when she finally enters the living room and starts to speak. She looks drained, her face pale, her eyes hooded. I clench and unclench my jaw, waiting. Watching. Ready to listen to what she is about to tell me. It's not good. I might be injured and removed from what is happening, my mind temporarily fractured, but I'm no fool. Recent events haven't beaten me completely.

'I don't want you to get upset, Flo, but I think we need to call the police.'

A slight stuttering of my heart, that's how it begins, the panic that I can feel as it gains momentum, slithering through my body and twisting at my guts. I take a few deep breaths to try and stem it. This could be nothing. It could be everything. I go through the motions of being calm, nodding at her words and looking composed when all the while, I'm on the cusp of going into a meltdown.

'What's happened?' My voice sounds ethereal. There is a clanging in my head. I bite at my lip and curl my hands into fists, my nails digging into my palms.

'I found something. You don't need to know what it is. I can deal with it. I just wanted to keep you up to speed with what's going on for when the police arrive.'

'But I don't know what's going on if you're not going to tell me.' A voice in my head is screaming for me to remain in ignorance. And yet I can't. This is my family, our house, and therefore also my problem, whatever this thing is that she has found.

Like a frightened child, she perches on the edge of a footstool, hands placed over her knees as if to keep herself upright.

'Is it to do with the dead rats in the cellar?' I ask, not sure whether I really want to hear the answer. I know that it isn't. It's more than that. Much more.

'Yes and no.' She sighs and paws away a rogue tear with her bunched-up fist. 'I went down there to clear them up and when I went to the old bin to burn them, I found something. Something awful.'

Silence. Only the sound of my heartbeat as it pummels at my sternum.

'Jess, you either will tell me or you won't but sitting here like this in some kind of purgatory is killing me. Please, just come out with it.' I'm ready to hear this and I'm not ready. Whatever my feelings, it needs to be said.

'I found some burnt body parts in the old bin that Coops used to use for burning garden rubbish.' Tears explode out of her. She puts her head in her hands and rocks back and forth. 'Christ almighty, Flo, what are we going to do? What the hell are we going to do?'

* * *

We're back to how things always were – me leading the way, telling Jess that everything will be all right even though we both know that it won't. I'm not sure things will ever be right again in our little world. We've been shaken about and turned upside down, our lives rocked violently. We are now in freefall with no safety net to catch us.

Outside, a team of police officers are combing the gardens. It didn't take them long to arrive once I made the call. DI Harvey made an appearance a few minutes after the rest of the officers, brisk and efficient and brimming with questions that she fired at us with military-like precision. She barked out a series of orders to a group of officers standing in the hallway before turning her attention to us.

'It's not our mother.' Those were Jess's first words to her when she sat down and began asking us questions. 'I don't know who it is but I don't recognise that ring so it's definitely not her.'

DI Harvey simply nodded and wrote something down in her notebook, then added. 'I want you to tell me from the beginning, exactly what happened.'

So Jess and I told her. We gave a full recount of the smell and the larder with its false wall and the cellar and the rats. We told her about my injuries and Jess's clean-up mission. Which is when she discovered the burnt body parts. We didn't tell her about our suspicions as to where our mother is. Perhaps later. That's our assumption. It's not a fact.

'We're scaling back the search for your mother.' DI Harvey stands up and sniffs loudly, brushing away an invisible piece of cotton from her trousers with slim fingers, her body language telling us not to bother her with minor trivialities or to question her motives.

'But this isn't her,' Jess says, irritation creeping into her tone. 'Our mother is still out there.'

'Once we've completed our investigation here then we'll have a clearer picture of what has taken place.'

It's futile arguing with either of them. Both their minds are already made up. And I know that Jess firmly believes what she is saying. She believes what she saw. Me? I haven't seen anything and so am willing to wait and see what the results are. What if it is our mother? Are we really going to dismiss that fact so readily? Maybe we should at least explore the option that she never really entered that river and Coops is lying to us. That he hasn't gone to see her and is covering his own actions. If he was involved in this then he obviously would make up a story about going to see her, letting us think she's still alive. There is, of course, one other blatantly obvious answer: that it is poor Cristina out there and her brother was right – she never left this house. I think about mentioning it to DI Harvey, telling her about Andrei's visit here but my nerves get the better of me. Speaking of it would open another can of worms and I'm not sure I can face it just yet. My stomach is a vast pit of hot, bubbling lava that scorches my innards as I go over every possibility again and again and again. It could be her. I would rather it be Cristina than our mother. I know that is a terrible thing to think, but for all of our mother's lies and deceit, I still want her back. We both do. I stop and take a shaky breath. I don't want it to be poor Cristina. Of course I don't. I would rather it wasn't anybody. I just want our mother back as much as Andrei wants his sister back. It's like some cruel, macabre contest, waiting to see who the poor unfortunate soul is that met their end in such a foul and demeaning way.

DI Harvey turns to face us, her expression unreadable. She's good, I'll give her that. The consummate professional. I wonder if her colleagues regard her highly or if they're just a little bit frightened of her imperious ways.

'We're going to go through the house as well, looking for anything that might help us with our enquiries.'

Jess and I glance at one another, wondering what's coming next. Are we supposed to move out and vacate Armett House so the police can tear it apart in a bid to discover the identity and fate of the poor individual who ended up losing their life and being partly incinerated at the bottom of the garden? I look down at my foot. I'm not in a fit state to go anywhere right now.

'Is there anywhere else you can both stay while we conduct our investigation?'

My stomach sinks. All of a sudden, moving out and allowing the police free rein of Armett House makes me feel woozy, trepidation gnawing at me, stippling my skin.

'We've each got our own places. We can go back there,' Jess says, suddenly accepting of it all. She looks weary, her eyes heavy with resignation.

DI Harvey glances at my foot.

'There's enough space for both of us in my house,' I sigh. 'When do you need us out by?'

* * *

We don't have much to pack. Just a few small items of clothing and not much else. The crime-scene tape is put up as we load up my car.

'We might be able to identify the remains from the DNA but I doubt we'll get any evidence worth speaking of. The fire will have destroyed it all.' DI Harvey is standing next to my vehicle, her willowy frame towering over me while I wedge myself into the passenger seat. 'And we'll also need to ask you some more questions so don't leave town, will you?' She stares at my foot and manages a wry smile.

I don't return it but instead, raise my eyebrows and nod. Jess slams the boot closed and slides into the driver's seat.

DI Harvey taps gently on the roof of the vehicle and walks off in the direction of the group of people that are milling about in white hazmat suits. A tent has been erected around the bin and the shed. I watch as Harvey pulls on some overshoes and latex gloves and disappears inside. Jess fires up the engine and we make our way around the back of the house and onto the narrow lane that leads past Coops' house.

38

JESSICA

When is the right time to inform a police officer that you think your purportedly dead mother is still alive? Before they begin testing the remains you've just found? Or is it during? Perhaps it's after, when the results come back and it's clear to everyone that those body parts belong to somebody else: a complete stranger. The longer I leave it, the harder it is to unload this heavy burden. It's not as if we know where Mother is. All we have are our own theories. And that letter. The one I threw away. I still don't know why I did that. Panic, I think. I was overcome with anxiety and panic. It was a stupid move. I made a mistake and now I need to find a way of telling DI Harvey that we think our mother is abroad somewhere with her lover. The world is a big place. Flo thinks Malta. I think anywhere but here. The police would have the means to check. She used her passport. There will surely be a record of it somewhere?

And then there's Coops to think of. His face jumps into my mind. It's impossible that he had anything to do with those remains. At least I hope that's the case. But our father – who knows? He had many sides to his personality, most of them charmless and forceful. I didn't think it was possible to loathe him anymore than I already did and yet here I am, hoping his death was a lonely and painful one. My hatred for him is screeching through my veins and boiling my blood. If he was responsible for this atrocity, then I'll banish all thoughts of him from my head from here on in. He doesn't deserve to be remembered in any capacity. He deserves to be forgotten forever, languishing in the fires of hell.

'Do you really think it could be her?' Flo asks. She looks crestfallen, a deep sadness behind her eyes. 'Cristina, I mean. We should have gone to the police earlier. What if they think we're hiding something?'

'We are,' I snap. My teeth tug at a loose piece of skin on my lower lip. I grind and bite until it breaks, the sting causing me to wince. 'We haven't told them about Coops' letter and his disappearance. Or our theories about where Mother might be.'

We're sitting in Flo's living room, the light streaming in through the slats of the pale-cream blinds. She lowers her gaze, wringing her hands together in her lap. 'The longer we leave it, the more suspicious it looks.'

She's right. I know that. We have had, however, a lot to deal with. That could be our excuse when we do finally make the call: that life got in the way of order and common sense. I think even the most hardened of police officers would find it difficult to point the finger of suspicion at us after the premature deaths of three members of our close family. Four if you count Amber. I catch a sly glance in Flo's direction and think about her features, trying to see if I can spot any resemblance to Amber or Diana. That's another secret I'm holding onto – my sister's true parentage. Will there ever be a right time to tell her or is it a secret I should take to my grave? I don't think Diana will ever approach Flo to tell her, so why should I? Let sleeping dogs lie. Flo adored our mother as we all did, even though she was weak and ineffectual against Father's harsh regime.

I'm about to pick up my mobile when a ring tone cuts into my thoughts. My screen is blank. I look at Flo and nod. For a brief moment, she looks taken aback, her eyes wide with alarm.

'It's yours, Flo. Where's your phone?'

Gently nudging her body to one side, I lean down the side of the chair where she is seated, then pluck out her mobile and watch as DI Harvey's name flashes up on the screen. I show her it, unsurprised when she shakes her head and turns away. It's all too much for her. Everything has just become too much to bear, her skin too thin, her emotions too brittle to take on board any more baggage.

My finger is hot and damp when I slide it across the screen and speak. 'Hello? This is Jessica, Flo's sister. She's currently resting. What's the latest?'

I feel faint. I'm warm and sticky and yet freezing cold at the same time, fire and ice meeting and clashing inside of me as I listen to what she's got to say. DI Harvey's words float around my head. The old well. I should have known. It had always been a place of terror for me. And now my fears have become reality.

I thank her and place the phone down on the coffee table, going over how I'm going to break this latest piece of news to Flo without upsetting her even further. There's no easy way to say it, no way of softening this blow and making it appear less repulsive and hideous than it really is, so I just come straight out and bark out what DI Harvey has just told me.

'They've found something in the old well.' I clear my throat and try again. 'Someone. They've found someone in the well at Armett House.' My feet tap on the floor, a fast, arrhythmic motion that I can't seem to control. 'DI Harvey wanted to come here to tell us but I insisted she tell me over the phone. It's her. It's the rest of Cristina, I just know it. She hasn't said anything about who it might be, but both you and I know. We need to tell them our suspicions about our mother, and Andrei's visit, and we need to do it now.'

There is a moment when everything around us becomes thick

and gluey, our lives playing out in slow motion. My tongue feels too big for my mouth. My voice is disembodied, an underwater gurgle that swells in my throat.

'I'll call her back, ask her to come and see us after all.'

Flo nods, her eyes glassy with unshed tears. I want to hug her. I also want to shout and rage and bash my head against the wall until I'm too numb to think or care anymore. This shouldn't be happening – any of it. I have a funeral to plan. That is also an aberration.

Thoughts flood into my brain as I sit staring at the phone. Is this why they did it, our parents? Is this why they jumped off that bridge? But if Father was guilty, why didn't Mother just go to the police? The unthinkable creeps its way into my brain. I expel it. No. I won't think that thought. It's not possible. Father was the monster in the marriage. If Mother was guilty of anything, it was that she was his enabler, and it was fear that made her that way. Fear of his brutality and a fear of losing everything, including her home, if she were to challenge him.

I call DI Harvey, wondering how to make it all fit together, this bizarre and implausible story. Words balloon in my mind – so many, all of them clunky and warped. I think of how I'm going to break it to her without appearing deceitful. And how I should say it. With a degree of humility and sadness to convey to her how fucking awful it has been for me and my sister. We deserve some under-standing and compassion. We're doing what we can to clamber out of the dark hole we have found ourselves in. There is no rulebook for this, no way of knowing what is right and what is wrong.

She answers on the third ring, her voice clipped. That efficiency and methodical attitude again. I wonder how she relaxes when she's at home. Or is she a workaholic, permanently on duty and obsessed with her job, with few friends and no close family, those she did have now severed from her busy schedule?

There is no easy way to say any of what I'm about to say, so I state the facts as they happened, trying to not inject any emotion or inflection into my voice. Just cold, hard facts reeled off as I remember them.

'Thank you for letting me know, Jessica. I wish you'd let us know earlier, but as you've just said, with everything you've had going on, these things can slip one's mind.'

I don't know if she's being disingenuous or completely sincere. She's a hard one to read. It's not as if we've broken any laws. Everything that has happened and our sentiments about it are all just supposition and guesswork.

'I suppose you'll be able to check to see whether Mother has travelled abroad?'

As I'm saying it, I think of her and Coops and the police banging on their door in the early hours and hauling them out of bed, wide-eyed and scared witless. Wondering who it was that gave away their location.

'We'll conduct a thorough enquiry,' is all she says.

'We had a phone call from our father's phone.' I blurt it out, the memory hurtling into my brain at lightning speed. How could we have forgotten? With everything that's happened, it's a wonder I've remembered it at all.

'From your father's phone? To where?' She sounds breathless. It's good to hear that she's human after all.

'It was Flo's phone, the one I'm using now to speak to you.'

She hangs up after telling us that she'll be round in the next fifteen minutes to collect the mobile. This is it now. We're close to finding Mother. The police will be able to check her location when she made that call. A tension of opposites stirs within me deep within my abdomen. I've let her down, given away her secrets, and yet relief also settles in me, a warm, comforting thing. We couldn't have carried on as we are. All this deceit is too large a cargo for anyone to withstand. Even halved between Flo and me, it's too wieldy. We're buckling under the strain. Flo is already slipping away from me and I need to catch her before she disappears completely.

I don't know what the sentence is for faking one's own death and for assisting somebody with it. I only hope Mother and Coops will forgive me for what I've just done.

39

FLO

It's a relief. I know Jess and I should feel guilty, but right now, what I feel is liberated. The shackles of deception have been cutting into my flesh and I'm relieved to be rid of them. Already, I feel lighter, less fraught. I'm not sure our mother will feel that way when the police eventually track her down. It's time for this to be over. She will be able to explain her reasons when she comes home. A sliver of anticipation slides over my flesh. We may even have her back in time for Ezra's funeral. That is, if we ever have the time and strength to arrange it. Jess is on the phone now, speaking to the undertakers before DI Harvey arrives. Keep it small. Small and dignified. That's all we can hope for. Anything else would feel grotesque. Like a monster rearing its head. I have no idea what sort of funeral Amber's parents have in mind for her and whether we are expected to, or should even attend. I'm going to let Jess sort that out. I just want to focus on getting Mother home. It's a point to aim for. I realise there will be other hurdles to clear, legal routes to navigate, but she will be here, with us. Not snarled up on a riverbank somewhere. Not washed out to sea, but back at Armett House. The place we all love and hate in equal measure. The discovery of the finger has settled it in my mind. I have ideas as to what went on, why our parents did what they did, but won't formulate any concrete notions until the investigation has been completed. I don't have enough energy to keep raking over what took place within these walls. That's for the police to decide.

The knock on the door comes only a few minutes after Jess hangs up. I've already placed my phone on the table, ready for DI Harvey to take. I won't miss it. It's more of a hindrance than anything else. Unlike some of my friends and colleagues, I don't spend each and every minute of the day glued to it.

'You should have let us know sooner.' That's her opening gambit as she marches into the room and stands there, hands slung in pockets.

'Are we on the naughty step, then?' Jess runs her fingers through her hair and musters up a half smile.

Harvey sighs and shakes her head. Smiling is possibly a step too far for her, especially since we've neglected to tell her about the call. 'You could have saved us hours and hours of man-power. We've had divers combing the river for days now.'

'We weren't certain it was her,' I manage to stutter. 'We thought it could even have been kids who found Father's phone somewhere.'

'We've also had a lot on our plates,' Jess interjects. 'It's difficult to think straight when most of your family have died in quick succession.'

At least DI Harvey has the good grace to nod and lower her eyes. She picks up the phone and drops it into a plastic Ziplock bag before sealing it up and taking a few steps back. 'Off the record, where do you think your mother might be?'

I suck in my breath and widen my eyes a little.

'Off the record?' Jess barks. 'Does it matter if it's on or off the record? You're going to try and find her anyway.' Jess is losing patience. She's tired.

DI Harvey shrugs. 'I was just wondering. And this Damien Cooper guy—'

'Coops.' Jess's voice is a sharp snap.

'Okay, this Coops guy, was he the only maintenance man on the grounds? We're going to need a list of all the staff who worked at Armett House.'

I sneak a quick glance at Jess. Her face is flushed. Do we even have a list? That's not how our father ran things. A lot of people were paid cash in hand. I think of Cristina and briefly look away.

'If you do a search of Father's study, they should be in there. To be honest, Ezra helped out around Armett House more than we ever did. He would have been the one who could have answered your questions.' Now Jess sounds sad. Sad and forlorn, as if it's just sinking in, the fact we won't see our lovely brother ever again. I often wondered why Ezra didn't turn his back on the man who made his life so difficult, but I also know that he spent many years trying to impress our father, doing what he could to be viewed as a capable young man when all Father ever did was belittle him and drag him down with barbed comments and insults. As Ezra grew bigger and stronger, Father knew that violence would be met with a backlash so he turned instead to insults and disparaging remarks, finding fault with everything Ezra did. And still Ezra helped, chatting to Coops, asking for assistance when he wasn't quite sure how to fix things, being his sociable, upbeat self when deep down, he was suffering, drinking more and more in a bid to blot out the past. All any child ever wants is to be loved. We got it in shedloads from Mother but even that couldn't compensate for the absence of kindness and care that should have come from the man who called himself our father. We were a nuisance. The unwanted ones. I was treated slightly better than Jess and Ezra. He was much harder on them.

'This Andrei – can you give us a description of him? And a surname would be good if you've got it.'

'Sorry, no surname. Again, you might find it in Father's study. All we know is he was from Romania. Dark hair and brown eyes. Average height. He was wearing jeans and a navy-blue hoodie. Your average young man, I'm afraid.'

DI Harvey nods and thanks us. She leaves with the promise of being in touch and the warning that we should contact her immediately if we remember anything else.

A silence descends once she has gone.

'I think we should we consider ourselves well and truly told off, eh?' I say.

Jess laughs, her eyes creasing up at the corners, a flood of colour in her cheeks. 'Indeed. Maybe we should get in trouble more often if we're able to laugh about it.'

I hug her, my arms locked tight around her neck.

'My God, Flo. You're choking me. Is that your plan? See me off and inherit *all* of the Hemsworth fortune?'

Hysteria takes over and, in the end, I'm not sure if the tears are from all the laughter or the large sphere of sadness that has taken up residence at the base of my stomach. Both Jess and I wipe at our faces and sit forlornly, the moment bringing a brief easing of our troubles.

'And you know what else?' Jess says.

'What?'

'I didn't get to burn those dead rats. Some poor, unsuspecting forensic investigator is going to open those bags and get the fright of their life.'

I shrug and jut out my bottom lip. 'Ah, so what? I'm sure they've been faced with a lot worse.'

I can feel brief glimpses of the old me coming back. The old Flo dips in and out but she's still there, lurking. I just need a little more time to come to terms with everything that has happened and then I'll back, as strong as ever. Different. Dented even, but I *will* be back to normal soon enough. I know it for sure.

40

JESSICA

Sometimes, even our adversaries can have their uses. The thought comes to me in the middle of the night. Poor Cristina's brother deserves some closure. Even if it isn't her body that the police have found, he has a right to know what's going on.

After an early night and dipping in and out of sleep, I'm now sitting up in Flo's spare room, unable to shut off thoughts of what the forensics team have unearthed in that well. If the police don't find out where Andrei is, I know somebody who might have a clue to his whereabouts: Amanda MacDonald, the oracle of Armett. If she doesn't know, then nobody will. Armett may be a fast-growing town, many of the new residents oblivious to our family's presence here, but Amanda has eyes and ears everywhere. I'm not prepared to go knocking on her door, but I am prepared to visit her place of work. I know that she is a receptionist at the local council offices. I could go there in the morning under the pretences of sorting out some things for Armett House, and then feign friendliness, see what she is prepared to reveal. She may take umbrage after our recent spat but that's a chance I'm willing to take.

I lie back down, comforted by this idea. Doing nothing doesn't feel right. Five minutes of contrived chat with Amanda. I think I can manage that. It's the least I can do for another poor soul who is missing his sibling. God knows, I understand how that feels, how debilitating that endless grinding sensation is that refuses to leave, drilling its way deep into your bones.

My eyes begin to droop. Another weight has been lifted. Another hurdle cleared. Now we've just got Ezra's funeral and the inquest to get through. And Mother's return home with Coops. Then and only then, we might just be able to be left alone to grieve.

Breakfast refuses to stay down, becoming lodged in my gullet. After a few swigs of coffee, I place my plate in the sink and leave Flo's house, arriving at the council offices at 9.30 a.m. with a thick, brown envelope tucked under my arm. I recall a colleague once telling me that if you want to look efficient and have nobody question why you're aimlessly wandering down a corridor at work, carry a large bunch of documents or a clipboard and they'll assume you're doing something really important. With that thought in mind, I open the door and step inside, wiping my feet on the mat to give myself a little more time before approaching the front desk.

'Fancy seeing you here.' She sounds like the cat who has got the cream, our previous encounter seemingly forgotten.

I look up to see Amanda watching me. 'Yes, we seem to have a habit of bumping into each other.' I do my best to appear friendly and relaxed. 'I'm here to sort out a few things for the house.' I slide the envelope out from under my arm and hold it aloft. 'Just a few queries about council tax.'

She smiles knowingly. 'Ah okay. You'll need to be on the second floor.'

Without any delay, I smile and take a step closer to her. She cuts quite the authoritative figure, sitting there behind her impossibly tidy desk. I'm prepared for a snub but hoping for assistance. 'Actually,' I say softly, continuing with my smile and cocking my head to one side conspiratorially. This is Amanda's forte: partaking in idle gossip. It's her reason for living. 'While I'm here, I was wondering if I could ask you about a visitor that we had at the house last week. I know that you're a popular person in town and have loads of friends so thought you might be able to help me out.'

If she has seen through my lies, her face doesn't show it. If anything, her eyes have an extra sparkle to them, her spine suddenly that little bit straighter, as if somebody has just injected an extra helping of adrenaline into her system.

'Go on. I'll certainly help if I can!'

God, she is smiling, her features resembling those of an excited child. I don't know whether to pity her or be repulsed by the curious nature she has that draws her to the murky and the macabre.

'A young guy came to us – Andrei, he was called. He was Romanian and spoke about his sister who worked at the house. Does that ring any bells?' I'm not prepared to tell her about the police and my discovery. She'll find out soon enough. She always does.

She narrows her eyes and smiles, her stubby fingers splayed out on the desk. 'You mean Cristina's brother? He's been in the pub asking about your family. Caused quite a ruckus over the past week or so.'

I ignore her last remark and turn away from the sardonic smile that's playing at the corners of her mouth. 'Yes, that's him. I don't suppose you know where he's staying?' I take a deep breath, trying to control the pulse that is throbbing in my neck.

'The last I heard, he was staying at the Premier Inn opposite the hospital.'

A small flame ignites inside my chest. It's not so far. If I can fight my way through the traffic, I can be there in under half an hour. 'Right, thanks for the information.' I'm trying to sound cool and unruffled even though my heart is pounding and my mouth is suddenly horribly dry. I turn and make to leave, Amanda's voice rattling in my head as she calls after me.

'Aren't you forgetting something? What about your council tax queries?'

I have only a couple of seconds to decide what to do. She has plainly seen through my ruse so it's pointless spending more time here than I need to. This whole thing with Cristina and Andrei will come out in the wash anyway and Amanda and her cronies can have a feeding frenzy, tearing apart our lives for their own titillation, so I continue out of the entrance, shouting behind me that I can come back another time and that I have other things to be getting on with that are more important than council tax.

I hear a small snigger from her and am relieved when I step outside, where the breeze laps around my face and hands, cooling my burning flesh and soothing my frazzled nerves. I hope Amanda is happy with her sad little life. As mean as it sounds, I also hope she spends her days pining after friendships and close relationships that will never materialise. Maybe then she will realise that spitefulness and malice don't get you anywhere in life except being very much alone.

The park bench outside the council offices offers some respite from my shaking legs and wobbly gait. It's situated far enough away from the main doors so as to allow me some privacy from Amanda and her prying eyes and clicking tongue. I imagine she's already on her phone, uploading gossip and supposition to keep the trolls fed. I take a few moments to gather my strength and am up and walking again, my confidence and energy restored.

The car seems to know its own way to my next port of call. I should call DI Harvey and tell her what I've just discovered about Andrei's whereabouts, I *know* that, but something in my brain is screaming at me to conduct this part of the journey alone, to speak to Andrei before the police find him. Once he is in their clutches, I'll not have any input. I just want to apologise for not taking him seriously. I was dealing with my own grief and trying to process everything, and didn't react as I should have when he called at Armett House.

There are only a handful of spaces left in the car park as I swing the car round after an arduous, three-mile journey that took way longer than it should have, due to heavy traffic and numerous ambulances trying to weave their way between the cars and into the hospital.

A blare of sirens pierces the air as I climb out of the driver's seat and head towards the reception area of the hotel. I don't have any strategies in mind, no well-thought-out phrases that will allow me access to Andrei. Any receptionist worth their salt will refuse to give out his room number, so I'm going to simply sit and wait, hoping he will pass through the double doors on his way to hunt for his missing sister.

Turns out I don't have to wait too long at all. For once, luck is on my side. It's as I'm making my way towards the desk on the pretence of enquiring after a room that I see him out of the corner of my eye. Without drawing attention to my movements, I stop and pretend to glance down at my phone, all the while edging closer to where he is standing. By his side is a small piece of luggage. He looks as if he is ready to check out or has possibly even already done so. I need to catch him before he heads back to Romania. It's imperative I speak with him. With no other knowledge of who he is or where he lives, this could be my last chance. I visualise poor Cristina's body, or what is left of it, wedged down that dark, damp well. I think of how frightened she must have been in her final moments, the terror of it all, and begin to walk towards where Andrei is standing.

'Well, hello! Fancy seeing you here.' A face appears in front of me.

I blink and widen my eyes. It takes me a second or two to speak, for the slightly distorted features to morph into somebody I recognise. Francis, an old colleague from university is standing in front of me, her teeth a bright gleam, her puffy lips spread into a beaming smile. She's changed almost beyond recognition. I manage a quick nod and a strained hello. We were never really that close yet she is acting as if we are long-lost friends. And now Andrei is leaving. I mumble something about it being good to see her again after all these years and that I need to leave to get to a really important appointment.

'But you've only just arrived?' Her voice is an eerie echo as I bolt past her in pursuit of Andrei, who I can see is sliding into a waiting taxi cab.

He cannot leave. Not like this. I have cleared too many hurdles to fall at the final one. I give Francis a cursory wave over my shoulder and am running towards my car, my eyes fixed onto the moving taxi that is weaving its way out of the loading bay and onto the main road.

Christ almighty. I can't lose him. It's my guess that he's heading to Middlesbrough train station but I don't know that for sure. He could be going to Darlington or any number of the other smaller stations dotted around Teesside.

The taxi is three or four vehicles ahead of me. I follow it as it makes a right turn out of the hotel and straight down Marton Road. He isn't going to Middlesbrough station. This is the wrong way. Darlington, perhaps? Or maybe he's going back to Armett House? My heart leaps around my chest. I don't want him going there. He'll spot the crime-scene tape. I want to speak with him first.

I bang my fists on the steering wheel as everything grinds to a halt, the sheer depth of traffic making any progress impossible. I bob up and down and side to side in my seat, trying to catch sight of the taxi. Frustration builds in my gut. I'm going to lose sight of him. After all this effort, I'm actually going to lose him.

And then we're moving again. It's slow but as we hit a slight bend in the road, I catch sight of him. We reach the crossroads and rather than take a left to Armett House, the taxi keeps straight on. I don't have time to feel confused as to where he is heading because the traffic clears and his vehicle speeds through the amber light and I'm caught on red. I let out a shriek of impatience and do something I have never ever done before. I swerve around the cars ahead of me, rev the engine and hurtle through a set of red lights in pursuit of Andrei's vehicle. An oncoming car brakes and another winds down his window and hurls a stream of obscenities my way. I continue, leaving the blaring of horns and startled expressions behind me. No time for guilt or apologies.

We pass the Rudds Arms pub and catch the lights on red again next to the Parkway. I'm low on fuel and not sure how long I can continue following him like this. If he travels straight on, past the next set of lights, we could be on the road to Guisborough or Whitby and then I'll lose him for sure. Fewer sets of lights and longer stretches of road to give him a head start. So without thinking it through, I hop out of my car, leaving the door wide open, and run to the taxi, hammering on the window and peering through the glass like a demented stalker.

More blaring of horns behind me. More shouting. It doesn't matter though. None of it matters because Andrei has seen me. He recognises me and before the lights change again, he opens the door and jumps out onto the road, his face collapsing with surprise and relief.

'You find her?' he shouts, his body trembling, his voice cracking with undisguised emotion. He takes both of my hands and clasps them tightly, his strength knocking all the air out of me. Tears prick at my eyes. I swallow down my guilt and feel my knees buckle as he speaks again, a huge smile lighting up his face. 'You find my Cristina, yes? Thank you, thank you, thank you!'

41

LYDIA

Something is wrong. She doesn't know how she knows that, but things have shifted. Damien is asleep beside her, his slumbering shape and gentle breathing a reassuring sound in the darkness.

Outside everything is silent. Soon the restaurants will open, the sound of awnings being wound out and the scraping of chairs, a noise she has become accustomed to in the past month or so, will start up. The city will slowly wake, people going to work, tourists wandering hand in hand, soaking up the atmosphere of the ancient surroundings. Will they come for her then? Or will it be later in the week? Because they will come. She knows it for sure. She has done a terrible thing and yet it felt like the only thing she could do at the time. There was no other way out. She was trapped. There was no way at the time of coming clean, and then once it was over, she didn't know what else to do. She just needed a few days on her own to think things through. The few days turned into weeks and now here she is, over 2000 miles away, lying next to the love of her life, waiting for that knock on the door. The knock that will tell her that it's all over. The deceit will come to an end and she doesn't know whether she will be filled with terror or overwhelmed with relief when it happens.

The children. The thought of seeing them again keeps her going. And Damien. She will always have him. They will always have each other. He'll stick by her no matter what, unlike Jackson, who bullied and cowed her time and time again, taking her hostage with his intimidatory behaviour and repeated threats. She couldn't allow him to go through with them so capitulated instead to his demands that they make that ridiculous jump. He first suggested it after an evening on the whisky. His drinking had worsened in recent months, gathering momentum like a tsunami, ready to wipe out everyone in the nearby area. Then every few days, he would speak of it, that joint suicide bid, talking as if it was just something they had to do: a *fait accompli*.

'I'll tell everyone what happened if we don't; you do know that, don't you?'

She heard that line over and over. And he would have told them too. Compassion, love, solidarity. Those things meant nothing to her husband. Jackson Hemsworth sailed a solitary path, navigating his own way through life, making his own rules, and nudging aside the morals that other people abided by. He saw himself as superior. A maverick. In truth, he was an amoral narcissist. A man who would crush others to get whatever he wanted. And yet in the end, his big ideas crushed him. He wasn't clever or strong enough to see it through to the bitter end. He would have killed her and crawled out of that river without missing a beat. But she got there before him. For the first time in her married life, she outwitted him. But it came at a price.

Now she waits. She watches and waits for the police to arrive, and while she waits, she formulates her story, the one she has had in her head since the day it happened. The one that will protect her family, because although she believes in goodness and kindness and being truthful, sometimes, just sometimes, the truth is too painful to bear, leaving unsightly scars that will never ever heal.

42

FLO

It all happens so quickly, Jess catapulting into the house at breakneck speed, phone in hand, her talk like rapid gunfire. She is babbling something about Andrei and Cristina to whoever is on the other end of the line. I wait, transfixed and also a little uneasy, trepidation jumping about in my stomach, until she hangs up and walks in the room, lips thin and tight. She opens her mouth to speak but then stops, placing her fingers on her temple and massaging it with a feverish action.

'What is it, Jess? What?'

'I found Andrei and have told him about the police at Armett House. I spoke to DI Harvey who immediately sent a car to collect him.'

'Collect him from where? How on earth did you find him?'

She grimaces as if in pain, then sits down next to me, her knees pulled together. 'Long story, but I went to see Amanda MacDonald. You remember her? She told me where Andrei was staying. I got there just in time. He was about to check out and was his way to see an elderly, infirm aunt who's in a care home in Nunthorpe before taking a flight back to Romania. I almost missed him. God, that thought makes me want to weep. But I didn't.'

'Please tell me, you didn't say anything about the fire or what they found in the well?'

Jess's brow crinkles like crepe, annoyance creasing her features. 'God, no! I'm not that stupid or thoughtless. I just said that the police are trying to track down everyone who worked at Armett House.'

'Didn't he ask why?'

'To be honest, I think he was just overcome with relief that somebody was finally doing something that it didn't cross his mind. He did say that he had called in at Middlesbrough Police Station to speak about Cristina last week but nothing came of it.'

I nod, suddenly proud of my little sister. While I was sitting here feeling sorry for myself and nursing my injuries, she was out there, putting together the important pieces of this weird and painful jigsaw, making sure its sharp edges all slot together to minimise any further hurt.

'So, what do we do now?'

Jess shrugs and sighs. She looks lighter somehow, as if the weight of the world has been lifted from her shoulders. It's not over for us just yet but we're edging ever closer to that elusive finishing line. 'I guess we sit and wait, see what happens next. See if DI Harvey and her team come up with any answers.'

'See if they find our mother?'

She nods and manages a brief smile. 'There is that possibility, yes.'

I watch her face, wishing I could see inside her head, observe those cogs whirring. She is pondering something, that much I do know. It's better to not ask so I sit and wait, counting down in my head until at last, she speaks, her voice firm and confident.

'I'm going to ring Father's phone. We should have done it before now.'

'She won't answer,' I say breathlessly, uncertain of what we should and shouldn't be doing given that this is now an active police investigation.

'Then I'll send a text. A heartfelt one asking her to contact us.'

I don't know how to reply, what to say to her to help this situation along, so I remain silent. Sometimes staying quiet is preferable to speaking up and saying the wrong thing.

The pain in my foot is a throbbing ache. I elevate it and ask Jess for more painkillers.

'Of course. I'll go and get them. I'll make us a cup of tea as well while I'm there.'

She arrives back looking happier than when she left, carrying a tray with all the necessary items on it. I know at that point, that she has done it.

'What did you say to her?'

She blinks repeatedly, accompanied by a deep sigh, and places the tray down next to me before handing me her phone.

It's a simple message but an effective one – that is, if our mother ever receives it. We don't know it was her that rang us on Father's phone. Even if it was her, she may have since discarded it, aware her location could be traced via its use. I read it again, this time taking longer, trying to digest each word and memorise them.

Hi Mother, if this is you using Father's phone, please get in touch. We love and miss you. There are important things you need to know. Whatever happened between you and Father is over. It's time for you and Coops to come home.
Love Jessica and Flo xx

A thought buzzes around my head. 'Won't she wonder why Ezra's name isn't on there?'

Jess shrugs. 'Perhaps. Maybe it will give her an extra reason to contact us.'

'If it was her using the phone, that is.'

'Yes. If it was her.'

I pop a couple of tablets out of the blister pack and swallow them down with a swig of tea, resting my head back on the cushion that is lodged behind my neck.

'I guess we now have to sit and wait, see what happens next,' I murmur. The pain in my foot nags at me.

'Yep. I guess we do.'

The silence feels interminable. Jess's phone remains quiet. No replies. Nothing at all.

It becomes too much and after a few minutes, I ask the thing that we should have asked as soon as Jess made the grim discovery in the garden. 'Do you think both Mother and Father were involved and that's why she fled?'

The last thing I want is for it to be true but it's a possible scenario we have to consider, if only to prepare ourselves for the inevitable grisly aftermath.

Jess shakes her head and brings her hands up to her eyes, pressing them into her sockets and rubbing back and forth furiously as if trying to erase everything that's happened, from her brain. 'I don't know. I honestly don't know. I mean, why disappear like this? Why didn't they just get a divorce?'

I look around at the room of my own average-sized property and think of the stately home we grew up in, with its grand rooms and antique furniture. 'Because of Armett House? Who would get it? Or perhaps it's because they were in on it together. Whatever it turns out to be.'

I don't expect a reply. What is there to say about this awful, unholy mess? I can't begin to think about unpicking the intricately bound tangles of this situation and am quite happy to leave the police to do it for us.

Jess stands. She appears to have shrunk a few inches in the last few days, her spine curved, her shoulders drooping. It's as she is leaving the room that I hear it – her phone. She stops, then turns and stares at me, her eyes wide, teeth bared in alarm, giving her a slightly demonic look.

She holds it in her palm, staring down at it before holding it to her ear and saying a tentative *hello*.

43

JESSICA

I wanted it to be her. Oh God, I wanted it to be her with every fibre of my being. What I wouldn't give to hear my mother's voice at the other end of the line. DI Harvey's call was ill-timed and my retort to her frosty remarks, colder than ice. I was expecting warmth and concern but instead was on the receiving end of a piece of news that chilled me, forcing me to perch myself on the arm of the sofa.

Andrei had identified his sister's ring, even producing a photo on his phone showing Cristina wearing it at a family gathering. A thousand creatures crept over my skin, swarms of insects biting at my flesh. It was her. Cristina is dead. And one or possibly both of my parents had killed her and tried to cover it up. That was why they jumped. And that was why our mother fled the country after surviving the fall. Christ almighty, it doesn't get worse than this. This must be the lowest point in our lives, Flo and I. We're currently scrambling around in the dirt, trying to survive.

DI Harvey doesn't say anything about our parents' involvement. She doesn't have to. Her silence says more than any words or accusations ever could. She finishes the call by telling me that she will be round in the morning for further statements and that we mustn't speak to anybody outside of the police force, especially the press. As if we would anyway. Flo and I are private people. We do, however, still have a funeral to arrange and attend.

'You've probably already gathered who it was,' I say, unable to disguise my disappointment. I sit for a few seconds, clutching the phone in my hand.

I hear Flo exhale, can even hear my own heartbeat as it pounds against my ribcage and whooshes in my ears. And then I hear something else. A buzzing that cuts through the subtle, hidden noises. In my hand, I can feel the vibration as a message comes through. Has Flo picked up on it too? Or am I imagining it; hoping and wishing for something to magically appear on the screen? Each passing second feels long and laboured while I sit, trying to pluck up the courage to turn over the phone and read what has been sent. It might be something trivial but I won't know until I read it. It could be something crucial: the message we've been waiting for, for what feels like an age. The last few weeks have had such a deep impact on us and now it could all be finally coming to an end, the answers we crave now finally within our grasp.

My breath is concertinaed in my chest when I carefully flip over my phone and glance down. Perspiration sits on my skin, damp and cold. I wipe at my face with the back of my hand and read what's written there.

Hello my loves. I'm so sorry. I'll be in touch soon. Take care xxx

And that's it. I want to laugh and scream and dance around the room. I also feel like curling up into a foetal position until this is all over. I hold it up for Flo to read it. Her eyes scan the text. She leans back and briefly shuts her eyes, saying nothing.

Time ticks by, the silence a deafening sound that crashes in my head.

Then, 'You do realise we'll have to let DI Harvey know, don't you?'

I sigh and nod. 'I know. But not just yet.' I want to have these few minutes alone with our thoughts. Alone with our mother. It's the closest we've been to her for weeks and weeks.

Flo smiles, her thoughts aligned with mine. I read the message again, then make the call to DI Harvey and prepare myself for her whirlwind arrival and brusque, formidable ways.

'At least she let you keep your phone,' Flo murmurs, trying to inject a note of cheeriness into her tone.

'Small mercies, eh?' I smile and roll my eyes.

After showing Harvey out and breathing a sigh of relief at her exit, I spend the remainder of the day on the phone to the undertakers. The police had contacted me shortly after Harvey left to say Ezra's body had been released and that we were free to go ahead with our arrangements. The thought that Mother wouldn't be here to attend made me weep with despair but there wasn't anything else I could do. DI Harvey had given us strict instructions not to make any further contact with her. They were close to finding out her location so we had to sit tight and simply wait. It will kill me, knowing she is out there somewhere. So close and yet still so far.

44

LYDIA

They are both sleeping when the police arrive, banging on the door with enough force to wake the entire neighbourhood and entering the small villa with a flourish, their faces reddened by the exertion of their movements in the early-morning humidity.

Lydia slips on a thin dress and scrapes back her hair into a ponytail while Damien dresses in shorts and a T-shirt, his own hair ruffled by a night of restless sleep after reading the message from her children. She should have gone home before now, she knows that. She just wanted some time with her love before the authorities intervened and dragged them apart, taking them in separately for questioning. She isn't an idiot. She knows what comes next, how difficult it's going to be. How suspicious her disappearance looks.

She wonders, as she slips on her sandals, if they have made any discoveries yet, if that is what has triggered this detection of their whereabouts. The number of police officers suggest they have. This is more than somebody faking their own death. There is a ring of urgency to their commands. A hardness to their features. It doesn't matter. She has her story sorted already, has gone over it a thousand times or more in her head.

She musters up a smile and turns to look at Damien one last time as they are led out to the waiting vehicle.

Neighbours, alerted by the noise, stand on their doorsteps, arms folded, lips pursed in disapproval. Shopkeepers stop going about their daily routine to watch this unseemly performance. If they knew, they would pity her. If they knew the truth – the real truth, that is. But they don't. There are only two living souls who know her actual story, the reason she is here, and as long as there is breath in her body, it will remain that way.

The interior of the car is thankfully cool as she slides in and rests her head back. She closes her eyes and takes a long, juddering breath, steeling herself for what lies ahead and waiting for the rest of her life to begin.

45

FLO

The last month has been difficult. After a small and thankfully expedient funeral for Ezra last week, we were told about our mother's arrival back in the UK from Malta. I had been right. Amidst all this horror and fear and uncertainty, I had been right about one thing. That gave me some ease, knowing she had at least managed to get back to her dream location after having it denied to her for so many years. I hope when this is all over, she will be able to go back there again. I find myself hoping for lots of things lately, most of my wishes involving our family being able to shed itself of its fragility. We're held together by the flimsiest of threads. One tug and our connection will sever, the force of it sending us hurtling back into the shadows. None of us want that. Living in the darkness is a grim place to be.

Mother continues to be questioned by the police. She was allowed to see us when she first arrived back here. It was a clinical reunion and brief, surrounded by serious-looking officers, but it didn't matter. Just being able to catch a glimpse of her again was enough. It gave both me and Jess a foretaste of what was to come.

Our future. A tiny sliver of happiness. It's a long way off, our grief still raw and unabating, but we'll take it one day at a time.

Telling her about Ezra was the hardest part. Worse than the continual police interventions and questioning. We made sure we were together, Jess and I, when we told her. She took it badly. Of course she did. He was her boy. Her only son. Her weeping and the rocking of her body as she listened to what we had to say is a memory I would rather forget. She will never get over it. None of us will. We're taking each day as it comes.

Armett House will remain with our family. In a way. Although difficult and costly to maintain, Mother doesn't want to part with it. She is determined to erase the bad memories and replace them with good ones. New, untainted memories. So since getting back to England, she has been in talks with the National Trust. Part of the house will be open to the public and she and Coops will live in the other part, paying a small amount of rent for their wing of the house. It's a way of making sure there is enough money for Armett House's upkeep. With the money from the sale of Coops' cottage and the money from the part sale, she will be able to live comfortably for the rest of her days with some spare. She already has plans for that cash, talking about purchasing a villa in Valletta, the place of her dreams. It won't be cheap. Land is at a premium in Malta, its tiny size dictating the price of properties which are often sky high. She wants it to be a family holiday home, somewhere we can all use whenever we need a break from the drudgery of our everyday lives.

Jess and I return to work next week. My foot and arm are healing nicely and we both need some normality back in our lives. I, for one, need my routine back. Despite the heavy workload, I miss my job and I miss the pupils. Immersing myself in my teaching duties will help to alleviate the stress and hopefully erase some of the awfulness of what we have been through. I will use the good times to counteract and cancel out the bad ones. I make it all sound so easy. It isn't. Like Jess, I have good days and bad days but I'm not going to sit around the house wallowing in my own misery. There is a life going on outside these four walls and I want to be a part of it.

46

JESSICA

In the words of Charles Dickens, it's been the best of times and it's been the worst of times. We've got our mother back but we don't have Ezra. I feel his loss every single day. Flo seems to be handling it better than I am but that's not to say I'm about to give up. Mother is still grieving. She has had less time to come to terms with the news of his death. Ezra would despair at me if I sat around day after day, gnashing my teeth and wringing my hands, grieving his absence, and putting little or no effort into living my best life. He always put so much effort into everything he did and that's what I'm going to try and do.

Yesterday, I met up with Diana in a coffee shop in a tiny village in North Yorkshire, a place where we could speak without being overheard by locals. We decided it would be our first and last meeting and that our secret would remain just that. There is nothing to be gained from Flo knowing who her real mother is. Diana told me about a card she sent to Armett House after Flo was taken from her, asking our mother to love Flo as she would. She asked me to hide it if I ever came across it, in case anybody stumbled upon it and began to question its provenance.

'I see her sometimes around town,' Diana said as we sipped our coffee and nibbled at a piece of shared cake. 'She's very beautiful.'

'That she is,' I replied. 'Inside and out.'

Andrei flew back to Romania a few days ago. Cristina's belongings and her remains will be flown back once the police have completed their investigation, which hopefully won't take too long. Mother told them how Father had forced her to jump from that bridge, telling her that if she didn't, he would tell everyone she had helped him to kill Cristina. She told them that she knew nothing about what had happened, believing the poor girl had returned to Romania but Father had beaten her and threatened her, saying he would expose her affair with Coops if she didn't relent. She had originally planned on waiting until he had jumped and then escaping but he dragged her with him. Panic took over after she survived and clambered out. She had returned to Armett House in the early hours, dumping her wet clothes in the bin and parking Father's car in the garage before collecting a few things, if only to give herself some time to think, but then hours passed and she knew then that she had to flee, worried Father had survived and was following her. She knew he would kill her if he ever caught up with her so she took her passport and went to the one place where she felt safe.

The evidence against Father was there and her story added up. Poor Cristina's remains were too charred to extract any DNA but some of her clothes were found and Father's prints and DNA were all over them. That was enough for the police to believe he had killed her. And if Mother's story is good enough for the police, then who am I to question their findings?

47

LYDIA

She looks around the room, drinking it all in, the starkness and austerity of it, thinking how fortunate she is that they believe her. Her husband wouldn't have coped in such a situation. Jackson wasn't used to being told what to do. It would rankle him, being made to sit here in this room and answer all these questions. Being held accountable to people in positions of authority. People who were younger than him. He was used to being the domineering, authoritative one, the man who called all the shots. But they believe her, all these police officers and detectives. She can see it in their eyes and their body language. The way they soften when speaking to her. The way they crack jokes in her presence, trying to creep their way gradually and surreptitiously into their questioning techniques without scaring her or forcing her to clam up. And they also know by now what a monster her husband was. What a bully he was. They know of his philandering ways, how he had an eye for young females. Underage girls. Girls who were barely out of puberty. Local people and neighbours, even her own daughters, have all offered their own versions to the police of the type of man that Jackson Hemsworth was and each description was less than flattering. Some thought of him as mildly amusing and amiable if you caught him on the right day, but most knew him for what he was: an untrustworthy individual with the morals of an alley-cat.

She has been told that the most she will have to face is possible community service for wasting police time but even that is looking unlikely given Jackson's domineering and abusive behaviour. She panicked after clambering out of the river that night. That's what she told them and part of that is true. She had been filled with euphoria knowing he was dead but she also had a plan, a need to escape just for a short while. Things had been left undone at Armett House; she knew that. She had to put some distance between herself and that place to escape the horror of what occurred there. But then hours turned into days and days turned into weeks and then without realising it, too much time had passed to return without looking guilty. She could have lied and claimed she had suffered a breakdown. That crossed her mind, but when the police heard about Jackson's behaviour, she didn't need to fabricate any illnesses to excuse her own part in the whole shabby affair. It was clear she was a victim of his manipulative and devious ways. Damien is going to be charged, but again, his part in any purported crime is minimal. He was a man who was simply helping out a frightened and abused woman.

Relief floods through her veins: a sense of liberation that it is nearly all over, that she can put this episode of her life behind her and look forward to a happy future. A future without Jackson in it. A future where her husband who slept with a young girl will also be blamed for her death. And that is as it should be because she has earned this bit of freedom. For so many years, she had to put up with his lurid behaviour, his wicked, wicked ways. She even went along with his suicide plan. But that was because he left her no choice. If she hadn't agreed to it, he would have gone to the police and told them what actually happened that night, how that young girl really met her untimely demise, and she couldn't let that happen. It *was* an accident. A horrible, dreadful accident. Poor Cristina wasn't supposed to get caught up in the maelstrom of their fractured marriage. Catching them together was almost the undoing of Lydia and she had wanted to pick up the nearest heavy object and smash it over Jackson's head. Something snapped inside her. Something taut that had been at breaking point for so many years, shattered and turned her into a different person. A woman on the edge.

He helped her hide the body and at that moment, they were in it together. Locked side by side in a troubled cesspit of their own making. Their threats flew back and forth. She would tell of his philandering, paedophilic ways and he would tell of her dirty secret. The secret murder that she had helped cover up. They reached a stalemate, neither able to navigate a way out of the mess he had created with his sexual, deviant ways and continual bullying.

Until that evening, that is. The evening when they drove to the bridge, ready to end it all. Except she wasn't prepared to go down without a fight. She shed the stones from her pockets on the journey there, had a spare set of keys tucked inside her underwear and she had learned how to swim without him ever knowing, which helped her to survive in the icy depths of the river. She could have died with him. It was a risk but it was one she was willing to take.

Nobody will ever know the truth of Cristina's death. She feels devastated for that poor young woman's family and has asked for her condolences and apologies to be passed on to Andrei and his parents. A small act but it's the only thing she can do. Perhaps once this episode of her life is over, she will visit them, let them know how deeply sorry she is. And she is. There is no pain in the world that is worse than losing a child. And she should know. Finding out about Ezra's death cut her in half. Her beautiful, beautiful boy, gone. She had steered clear of using the internet while she was in hiding and was told the devastating news shortly after she landed back at Newcastle Airport.

She shivers and pulls up her collar to shield herself from the cold. It's a heavy load to carry around – knowing the secret of another person's death. Eating has been difficult. Her weight has plummeted. Every whisper of wind has cut through her, chilling her to the bone. She plans on visiting Malta again very soon to soak up some of the sun's rays, relax and savour the local food and wine and enjoy the rich culture. She will take her daughters with her.

Her daughters.

No Ezra. Her throat tightens. She swallows and fights back tears. So many secrets in the Hemsworth family. She had always had reservations about his relationship with Amber but how could she have ever broached the subject and tried to talk him out of being with her without revealing the deeply dishonest thing that she and Jackson had done? At the time, she did it out of a sense of loyalty to her husband, taking on somebody else's baby. She was young and loved him, thinking it was a one-off, his affair, something that would never happen again, not realising that it was an intrinsic part of his nature, a trait he was unable to, or refused to, shed. Being unfaithful and coaxing young girls into bed was a part of his DNA. But as for Flo – as far as Lydia was concerned, Flo was her daughter. And a wonderful one she was too. Always loving and kind. So unlike her father. There were times – and she is horrified to remember it – when she wanted to take her anger at Jackson out on his only daughter. But she didn't. She kept it within, scribbling in diaries and venting her spleen in places where nobody else could see.

His only daughter.

That's another family secret that very few know about. Jackson always suspected that Jessica and Ezra weren't his but couldn't prove it. He treated them with utter contempt and she knows that she should have done something about it but that would have meant moving out of Armett House with her children. Jackson wouldn't have let her take Flo. He would have done everything in his power to stop her. And so she stayed put. She only hopes that the compassion and tenderness shown to them from their real father made up for his callousness and cruelty. Damien has stuck by her through everything. He has stuck by his children through everything. She wouldn't have made it this far without him. He is her rock. Her saviour. They will face the future together. Whatever it brings.

48

BEFORE

She could hear them. He didn't even make any attempts to hide it anymore. Since she and her husband had started sleeping in separate rooms, his exploits were patently obvious. It sickened her, and yet at the same time, there was still a small part of her that felt jealous. No, not jealous. That was the wrong word. Defeated. Humiliated. Two words. Two out of many that summed up her feelings towards the man she once loved. Striking up a relationship with Damien decades before had saved her from a pit of despair. Had she been alone all these years having to suffer the indignity of Jackson's philandering ways with naïve, nubile females, she would surely have gone mad or done something dreadful to herself. Something horribly final.

Her feet shuffled along the landing, stopping outside his bedroom door. Slowly, her palms damp with perspiration, she turned the handle, moving into the darkness of the room with stealth-like precision. Behind her, she heard another noise. She stopped and listened but could hear nothing else except for the thrumming of her heart, and those ghastly moaning sounds emanating from under the bedsheets. And his whispers; those words of encouragement that he was murmuring to try and quell the nerves of a frightened young girl. Was she a willing participant or had he brought her here under duress? The thrumming in Lydia's neck sped up, pounding in her ears and making her feel faint. She clung onto the doorframe, then with fingers moving in a spider-like motion along the wall, she flicked on the light.

A scream and a guttural, furious hollering from the bed. And another roar from behind her. She snapped shut her open mouth, fearful the ominous sound had come from her, then spun around to see Ezra standing behind her, his eyes wide with horror. She watched him stagger into the room and could smell the fumes that trailed in his wake. He'd been drinking. All these months and months without and he had lapsed.

'What the fuck, Father?'

'Ezra, please don't.' Lydia's voice was a plea, a screeching whisper to a drunken young man who carried so much hurt and anger inside him that it was tearing him apart. 'You need to leave, Ezra. Come on,' she said softly, 'let's go downstairs and I'll explain.'

But she didn't get time. She watched in horror as her son lurched towards Jackson and his latest conquest, a young girl called Cristina who worked and boarded at the house; a poor frightened young female who looked utterly terrified at this latest turn of events. He stood over them, Jackson's older frame looking decidedly puny next to Ezra's stronger, youthful build.

'You need to get out of here!' Ezra roared at the girl.

'Cristina,' Lydia said as softly as she could, passing her a dressing gown off the edge of the bed. 'Just do as he says and nobody will find out what happened here.' She took a breath and stopped. 'Not unless you want us to, that is. If he hurt you in any way or forced you—'

'Forced her?' As always, her husband's voice filled the room, obliterating everything else. 'Fucking forced her? What do you think I am – some sort of monster?'

No replies were needed. Everyone present knew Jackson for who he was. What he was. A philandering fool. A cruel tyrant. He was the worst kind of monster, the type that masqueraded as a normal individual. Somebody important that people looked up to. Somebody whose commands they were too afraid to refuse.

Cristina put on the gown, wrapping it around her tiny body, and attempted to get out of the bed.

'Stay!'

He pulled her back, his strong hands digging into her bony shoulders, his fingers pressed against her neck. Tears welled up in her eyes.

'Let her go, Jackson.'

'Yes, Father. Let her go.' Ezra's voice had a mocking, sing-song quality to it.

Lydia tensed. Jackson hated being ridiculed; his ego was too big to allow any scorn pass unnoticed and unchallenged. She watched, fear building in her gut, as Ezra and Jackson locked gazes, both sets of eyes burning with rage.

And then it happened. It all took place too quickly for her to intervene. Ezra leaning over his father, Cristina trying to duck under his arm. Jackson throwing the first punch and knocking Ezra backwards. Lydia looking at the bedside lamp, wondering if she could use it to protect her son. Jackson would have no qualms about belting Ezra until he was unconscious. She couldn't let that happen. Not again. Too many times over the years, he had punched and hit the lad and she wasn't about to let him down again by being a passive bystander. This time, she would intervene.

She watched as Ezra fell to the floor and on instinct, she picked up the heavy lamp, its marble base a deadweight in her small hands. She would use it if she had to, fear or no fear. Danger or no danger.

She heard Cristina scream as Jackson leapt out of bed and dragged Ezra up off the floor, raising his fist over the lad's face, ready to pummel it to a pulpy, bloody mess. He looked comical, standing there in his underwear, skin dangling from his reedy, ageing arms, a small pot belly hanging over the waistband of his boxer shorts. She almost laughed. Almost, but not quite, letting out a snort of derision instead.

He turned to look at her, his eyes narrow slivers of ice. 'What the hell are you doing here, anyway? Why don't you just fuck off?'

Anger flared in her belly, rising through her neck and exploding in her head like a thousand fireworks all going off at once. She took a step towards him. He moved towards her. The lamp was still clutched in her hand. And then it wasn't, the heft of it replaced by a sudden lightness as it was snatched out of her grasp.

'Come on, old man. How brave are you now then, eh? Squaring up to a defenceless woman?' She blinked and saw Ezra holding the lamp, brandishing it above Jackson's head. 'Come on!' he shouted. 'Not so courageous anymore, eh? Brave enough to bed every child in town and knock women about but not brave enough to fight anybody your own size?'

Ezra lunged at Jackson but the older man was still agile and managed to dodge out of his way just as Ezra brought the lamp crashing down.

It was the silence that made the situation feel unreal. They were stuck in a moment, everything falling away from them as Cristina's small frail body fell to the floor, hitting the floorboards with a crack. And the blood. So much blood. An immediate pool of sticky scarlet that gathered beneath the poor girl's body.

Nobody said anything. Lydia was the one to break the silence.

J. A. BAKER

'Leave, Ezra. Please, just go. We'll sort this. Go home and sober up. None of this ever happened, okay?'

She envisioned Jackson trying to stop him and was both relieved and surprised when he stood, mute and motionless, and let the boy leave. The rest was a blur – how the poor girl tried to slither away from them under the bed, how she was dead by the time they roused themselves and were able to do anything constructive or helpful. How Jackson carried her body down to the cellar, leaving it there for days and days, attracting all manner of vermin that he had to poison before finally wrapping her body up in sheets and burning it in the large bin outside, disposing of the parts that wouldn't burn and dropping them down the old, disused well. How for the longest time, he threatened to tell the police about what Ezra did. She couldn't let that happen. It was an accident. A terrible, dreadful accident. Her son wasn't a natural-born killer. He was a wounded soul and Jackson was the one who had wounded him, berating and beating the lad time and time again. So she threw her own threats back in his face, telling him how she would report him for having sex with underage girls. It was worth it to see the colour drain from his face as she spat the words at him. It wouldn't have been so difficult to talk to a few of the females in town and gather the evidence. He knew that, and so they became locked in a battle of wills until one day, he decided enough was enough. He had a plan.

'Hear me out,' he said as she made to protest. 'Just hear me out...'

ACKNOWLEDGEMENTS

First and foremost, my gratitude goes to my editor, Emily Ruston for her kind words about this book and helping to restore my flagging confidence. Six years and sixteen books later, the imposter syndrome is still very real. Emily, you are a gem! I would also like to extend my gratitude to Emily Reader, my copy editor who did a tremendous job with finetuning my story and grammar. Thank you, Emily, for all your help. Two Emilys are always better than one!

As always, my thanks go to my family and friends for their ongoing support with my writing endeavours.

The setting for this book was inspired by the local stately abode near my childhood home. It is thankfully still standing, unlike many in the surrounding areas that were unfortunately demolished decades ago during a period of huge post-war expansion on Teesside. As a child, my friends and I would play in the woods and visit the house, welcomed by the owner, Ruth Pennyman, who was a wonderful lady and a huge philanthropist. Thankfully, she bore none of the traits shown in any of my characters in this book and her name is revered throughout the area. With this in mind, I would like to give a posthumous thanks to Mrs Pennyman for her input into my life and providing me with the most wonderful setting any writer could ever want or need – a large, old house next to a dark lane and surrounded by a woodland area. Perfect.

A big thank you to all the staff at Boldwood Books for their continued support with editing, proofreading and marketing my books. You guys are ace.

I am lucky to have a gathering of people in my ARC group who read and review my books on a regular basis. This is a tricky one in case I miss anybody out, so if I do, apologies in advance. A massive thank you to Mark Fearn, Theresa Hetherington, Dee Groocock, Dawn Bennett, Lynda Checkley, Livia Sbarbaro, Donna Wilbor, Maggie Steel, Rebecca Charlesworth, Aileen Davis, Josephine Bilton, Colin Blackman, Ronnie Jacobs, Michelle Ryles, Donna Morfett, Mary Snaddon, Carol Flynn, Ellie Shepherd, Caron McKinlay, Kerry Foyle, Ruth Matheson, Philomena Callan and Susan Hunter. Please, please forgive me if I've missed you out. As always, by the time I finish writing and editing a book, my head feels like it's stuffed full of cotton wool and any omissions are a genuine oversight.

To my author friends, Anita Waller, Valerie Keogh and Diana Wilkinson, thank you for keeping me sane. If you know, you know!

I love to chat to readers on social media and can be found at:

Facebook.com/thewriterjude
Twitter.com/thewriterjude
Instagram.com/jabakerauthor

Bring coffee and cake ;)
Best wishes,
J A Baker

ABOUT THE AUTHOR

J. A. Baker is a successful writer of numerous psychological thrillers. Born and brought up in Middlesbrough, she still lives in the North East, which inspires the settings for her books.

Sign up to J. A. Baker's mailing list here for news, competitions and updates on future books.

Follow J. A. Baker on social media:

facebook.com/thewriterjude

x.com/thewriterjude

instagram.com/jabakerauthor

tiktok.com/@jabaker41

ALSO BY J. A. BAKER

Local Girl Missing

The Last Wife

The Woman at Number 19

The Other Mother

The Toxic Friend

The Retreat

The Woman in the Woods

The Stranger

The Intruder

The Quiet One

The Girl in the Water

The Perfect Parents

THE
Murder
LIST

THE MURDER LIST IS A NEWSLETTER DEDICATED TO ALL THINGS CRIME AND THRILLER FICTION!

SIGN UP TO MAKE SURE YOU'RE ON OUR HIT LIST FOR GRIPPING PAGE-TURNERS AND HEARTSTOPPING READS.

SIGN UP TO OUR NEWSLETTER

BIT.LY/THEMURDERLISTNEWS

Boldwood

Boldwood Books is an award-winning
fiction publishing company seeking
out the best stories from
around the world.

Find out more at
www.boldwoodbooks.com

Join our reader community
for brilliant books,
competitions and offers!

Follow us
#BoldBookClub

Made in the USA
Middletown, DE
31 July 2024